SECOND MOON

BOOK TWO OF THE WESTWOOD PACK

F.D. FAIR

Foundations Book Publishing
4209 Lakeland Drive, #398, Flowood, MS 39232
www.FoundationsBooks.net

Second Moon
Book 2
The Westwood Pack

ISBN: 978-1-64583-107-5

Published in the United States of America
Worldwide Electronic & Digital Rights
Worldwide English Language Print Rights

Chapter One

Lennox—12 years ago

I t's the first full moon since I turned eighteen, and I've never been more excited. I've spent my entire life watching my parents together, and seeing how happy they make each other has cemented in my soul that nothing less than a true mate bond will do for me. I'm not naive enough to think that I will find her at my first gathering, or even in this pack, but I know I won't stop searching until I find her.

"Damn, Lennox, you look great," Charleigh, my sister, says as she walks into my room.

"Thanks..." I reply as I roll up the sleeves on my dress shirt.

"Nervous?" She plops herself on my bed and patiently watches as I unroll the sleeve and begin again. Most teenage boys might think having two sisters would suck, but Charleigh, Felicia, and I are closer than any siblings I've ever met. Maybe it's because of how our parents raised us...or maybe it's genetics...I don't know. All I do know is that the two of them are my best friends, and I couldn't live without them.

"A little," I admit. "What if she doesn't want me?" I say, voicing my greatest fear.

Charleigh stands up, storms over to me, and spins me to face her.

"Now you listen here," she stresses each word with a poke to my chest, "You are a catch. Any woman would be lucky to have you for a mate."

The fire in her eyes makes me stand up a little taller. I'm not self-conscious, but the girls in the Ironwood pack aren't always the nicest. Olivia, the lead mean girl, loves to make everyone else feel small. Sure, she's beautiful, smart, and funny—at least to people in her inner circle. If you aren't...well...she makes it a point to either pretend you don't exist or to make your life a living hell. Luckily, I'm in neither category. She has no idea I am alive.

"Even Olivia?" I ask Charleigh, voicing what I've been wondering. "She's so perfect and I'm..." I look down at myself. I'm physically fit like most shifters, and I've been told that I'm easy on the eyes. My personality is vastly different from others my age. I am quieter and like to stay at home with my family. I am the type of guy to order a pizza, put on some Netflix, and chill instead of going out to parties. Girls like Olivia like to be at the center of everything, followed by a posse of others. I don't think Olivia has ever "Netflix and Chilled" in her life.

"Olivia," Charleigh says her name as if it leaves a bad taste in her mouth, "doesn't deserve you. I will never understand your obsession with her."

"I'm not obsessed..." I counter. Am I? I think about it for a minute before it dawns on me..." Shit."

"You've been obsessed with that bitch since grade school." Charleigh nods patiently, happy I've finally caught up. "Following her around like a lost puppy. You're lucky that Matteo doesn't find you much of a threat or your high school experience would have been much different."

"Yeah. I guess. I honestly don't know what it is about her that I'm so drawn to..."

Charleigh snorts. "I wonder if it has anything to do with her massive boobs and long, blonde hair." She flips her own blonde ponytail back and forth and pushes out her chest. "Oh my god. Like my blonde hair is totally real and not box dyed."

I try to hold in my laugh at Charleigh's impression but can't. She's spot on. After a moment, Charleigh joins in on my laugh, and we both flop back on my bed.

"Seriously, though. What if my mate rejects me?" I whisper, feeling vulnerable.

"Then I'll kill her," Charleigh deadpans, rolling over toward me.

"I'm being serious, Char..."

"So am I. If your mate is stupid enough to reject you, I will have absolutely no problem ripping her throat out right then and there."

"You can't do that. You would be punished, and we can't lose you." My throat tightens at the thought of what would happen if she actually were to retaliate. "I can't lose you. If I get rejected, I'm going to need you more than ever. Promise me you won't," I plead.

She looks into my eyes for a couple of breaths before she nods.

"Fine. But if there is a way for me to do it without getting caught, I'm going for it."

The corners of my lips tip up into a smile.

"Deal."

"Okay, Len," she claps her hands together and moves to get up, "no offense, but you reek of anxious teen boy. Go try to wash it off before we need to leave."

I sigh, but I know she's right. One bad thing about being a shifter is that you can't hide anything from your sisters if they have a keen nose.

Charleigh makes a parting shot and laughs as she closes my door behind her.

3

"We don't want your mate to smell you coming from a mile away."

I make my way over to my bathroom, slipping out of my clothes and hopping into the warm shower. I stay under long after I'm done cleaning myself, and only get out finally when the water starts to cool. I don't know what it is about going to this gathering that has me so anxious. Maybe I'm more concerned about being rejected than I thought.

Once I'm ready, I slip down the stairs to meet with my gathered family. Luckily, this get-together isn't just for finding mates. This is the pack run, so my family gets to be with me. Otherwise, I'm not sure if I'd get up the courage to go myself.

All my friends have no desire to find their mate yet and are purposely avoiding going to any gatherings where there's a chance. We all graduated high school in the spring, so the chances of running into female wolves outside of regular gatherings are slim, especially when most are traveling for the summer before starting college.

I, on the other hand, decided to go straight into an apprenticeship and become a tool and die maker like my dad. It will be hard work for little compensation in the beginning but will pay off in the end. The urge to hide away like my friends is strong. I'm not sure why this fear of rejection has taken hold, but this is the first pack run since I turned eighteen last week and attendance is mandatory unless they have prior permission from Alpha Christian, which I don't have. I guess if I am lucky enough to meet my mate and she is already planning on moving away for college, I may have to rethink my plan, but that's the joy of doing an apprenticeship. I can find a job anywhere.

I am getting ahead of myself again, and I try to pull myself back into the moment. My mate may not even be at this gathering; she may not even be in this country; it may be years before I meet her.

The walk to the clearing is short but peaceful. I take in the scenery. The same trees line my path that I've seen a million times, but for some reason I'm looking at them a little differently today. I can't put my finger on exactly what is different about them, or maybe it's me. Even my normally boisterous sisters are quiet, leaving us to hear the small howl of the wind, the chirping of the birds, and the chatting voices of the pack as we get closer.

As I step into the clearing, my body begins to buzz with excitement. My wolf perks up, scanning the area as if he knows something I don't.

Is our mate here? I ask him.

He doesn't respond, just continues his scanning, laser focused, searching for something. Searching for her...

"I'm going to take a walk," I tell my family, not turning my head to look at them as I am already stepping away.

"I'll come with you," Charleigh says, linking her arm through mine.

"Me too," Felicia adds, and the three of us begin walking.

"Thanks." I try to say more, but my wolf is pulling me deeper into the crowd, pushing at my skin and urging me to walk faster.

"Whoa, slow down, Lennox," Charleigh says, trying to keep up with my long strides.

"Can't," I grind out, continuing my fast-paced walk. I feel the two of them drop back behind me, but I can't bring myself to wait for them.

That's when I see her and freeze. Our eyes lock across the crowd.

Mate, my wolf says, his eyes already flicking to the man she's hanging off of, with a growl.

Olivia...Olivia is my mate. My heart begins hammering in my chest, and I'm ready to rush across the divide between us.

I see her eyes go wide, stunned momentarily before leaning in to whisper something to Matteo, and his eyes instantly lock with mine. His wolf starts exerting his dominance, and it makes me cringe.

I'm not a weak wolf, and I could probably match him in dominance if I wanted to; however, in a pack like ours, even though I have a dominant wolf, I can never move up the ranks because of who my parents are. We aren't the lowest members of the pack, but we aren't at the top either. My mom is a teacher, and my dad is a tradesman.

My wolf pushes against me harder, wanting to challenge this man who dares to lay a hand on our mate. She's ours. But I know that if I were to challenge him in any way, it would be a death sentence for me, no matter the outcome. Winning the challenge would mean the Alpha would have me executed for overstepping my station, and losing the challenge would mean I'd already be dead. Either way would be game over for me, so I keep my wolf reined in.

Matteo comes stomping over to me with Olivia still hanging on his arm.

"She's mine," he says through clenched teeth.

All I can do is look over at my supposed mate for assistance. She knows as well as I do, we are fated to be together. Why isn't she saying so? My thoughts are confused and blurred by the absolute need of my wolf to claim and protect her, but even I do not expect what happens next.

Olivia tosses back her head of shining hair, bares her throat to the open air, and barks out a laugh.

"As if I would ever choose to be fated to a loser like you. I, Olivia Murphy, reject you..." She turns back to her friends, and one steps up to whisper in her ear. "Lennox, whatever your last name is, as my mate now and forevermore."

The rejection is quick and final, as if it was waiting on the tip of her tongue all this time. She didn't even know my name...

I drop to my knees. It feels like a white-hot poker is being jammed through my chest repeatedly. My breath hitches and halts around the pain, and I am sure my heart will stop beating. There's nothing I can do to stop it. I know it needs to run its course, but the pain is almost unbearable. I vaguely feel Felicia coming to kneel beside me, enveloping me in a hug while I hear Charleigh laying into Olivia.

She's always been fiercely protective of us. She is the one I can count on through thick and thin to fight at my side, whether I'm in the right or not, even though she is two years younger than me.

My wolf whines in my head, unable to understand what just happened, only feeling that part of his soul is being ripped away. I want to comfort him but can't. My heart feels like it's been snatched out of my chest.

When I am finally able to stand, I look over at my mate...my mate no longer...and watch her walk away laughing with her friends as if nothing happened. Doesn't she feel this? Doesn't she realize what she just did?

"It's going to be okay, Lennox," Charleigh coos to me, and I turn to her, raising my lip in a snarl.

"What about this is going to be okay?" I snap.

She steps back, tears welling in her eyes as her hand rises to rest on her own chest. Instantly, I regret speaking to her that way.

"I'm sorry," I plead, taking a step forward, but she shakes her head and walks away. My head drops down in shame having taken my pain out on her when she was only trying to soothe me.

Felicia wraps her arms around me.

"It's okay, Lennox. She'll understand."

I slip my arms around my baby sister, holding her tight as tears form in my eyes. "I..."

"Shh. You don't have to say anything. Let's just go home," she says, stepping back and guiding me to our house.

Unlike the walk here, I don't enjoy the calming scenery. I am unable to process anything around me beyond the pain I'm feeling. Luckily, our home is less than a fifteen-minute walk away.

As soon as I see the front porch, I walk up the two stairs and plop down, placing my head in one hand while the other rubs my chest. Why does this hurt so much? Mother Moon, this is embarrassing. What am I going to tell everyone? What is so wrong with me that she rejected me without even knowing me? Am I so ugly that she wouldn't even give me a chance?

I hear footsteps and glance up to see my parents walking toward me. My mom freezes, her hand going to her mouth and tears welling in her eyes. My dad stops next to her, seeing if she's all right before following her line of sight and finding me. His lips tip down into a frown, and his eyes soften.

Do I look that bad?

My mom rushes forward, wrapping her arms around me. She holds me close for a moment before pulling away to look into my eyes for her pronouncement.

"I don't care who she is. She doesn't deserve you."

The barrier I had erected to keep the tears away comes smashing down with those words. I didn't dare cry in front of the pack, but here, safe in the arms of my mom, I let them fall.

I sag into my mom's arms and let out all the pain that I'm feeling, the grief for my lost future, the injustice of my worst fear coming to life.

"Rose," my dad says, stepping up, and I lift my head to look at him. His face flashes with pity upon meeting my gaze, but he schools his features quickly. "Why don't you go inside and make us some tea while Lennox and I have a talk?"

She squeezes me tight one last time before standing up and walking into the house as I wipe the dampness off my face.

"Son. I know it hurts," he begins as he takes a seat on the porch next to me. "My best friend Kevin was rejected by his mate, and I had to watch him struggle."

My mouth drops open. I have never met someone who was rejected before.

"Who's Kevin?" I've never heard him mention anyone named Kevin before.

My dad takes a deep breath and levels his blue eyes at the horizon.

"He's gone now, Len. There are two types of rejected mates... There are those who wither away, letting their wolves take over until they are no longer able to shift back. Then there are those who fight. They push through the pain and come out stronger. Kevin was..." he glances thoughtfully at the surrounding trees. "Sometimes when I'm out for a run, I think I catch his scent and wonder if he's still out there, living his life out as a wolf. You can't do that," he says, looking directly into my eyes. "Your mom and I... we need you to fight, Lennox. Push through the pain. I can't lose you the way I lost him. We will do anything in our power to help you through this. I know it's hard now, but you have to feel this pain so that you can overcome it."

Although I knew adulthood was on the horizon, I cannot comprehend the feeling of having a problem not even my parents know how to solve. I am now facing a future full of problems neither of them truly understands.

I only know that rejections happen because of what we learned in our shifter classes through the pack. It's also where I learned that it is possible, although rare, for a shifter to find their second-chance mate, but I'm not sure I want that. If she rejected me too...My dad slips his arms around my shoulders, and I fight back the tears.

"It's okay to cry, Lennox. Only a strong man isn't afraid to shed a few tears." With his permission, the tears flow once again, my shoulders shaking with sobs.

"She didn't even know my name, Dad," I whisper. The admission of this fact feels particularly painful.

"It doesn't matter why. Your mom was right. Whoever she was, she doesn't deserve you if she didn't even give the bond a chance."

"It was Olivia," I tell him. He sucks in a breath that he releases as a small growl.

"Wolves like her only care about status. If I were you, I'd take this as a blessing."

I nod my head, knowing that he's right but not able to say anything. It's still too raw, too new. Knowing that I would never have been able to make her happy doesn't lessen the pain at all.

Once again, I hear footsteps on the driveway and raise my head to see Charleigh, streaks of tears still on her face. I stand up and run toward her, wrapping my arms around her.

"I'm so sorry, Char."

She returns my embrace with a sigh.

"I know, Len. You've just never talked to me like that before, and it caught me off guard."

"It doesn't make it right. I was in a lot of pain, but I should never have taken my pain out on you."

"I understand why you did," she says, stepping back out of my embrace and wiping her face. "Can I kill her now?" she asks with a smile which I return. For the first time since Olivia rejected me, my heart feels a little lighter.

"We talked about this already," I chuckle.

She lets out a disappointed sigh.

"So, if I can find a way to get away with it..."

The two of us walk into the house chuckling. Felicia, Mom, and Dad all sit around the kitchen table with mugs of steaming tea. All my favorite snacks, salty and sweet, have been pulled from the cabinets and drawers and recklessly piled between them.

I look at each of them, and my heart expands. There is a throb of pain on the other side of that stretch, but it is dulled by the love I feel emanating from my family.

Who needs a mate when I have this?

10

Chapter Two

Skarlyt—Just Over Eight Months Ago

As soon as I hang up the phone, I begin to jump up and down while spinning in a circle, screaming in excitement. My best friend finally found his mate. Sure, she's from a little town hours away. Sure, he said it was complicated. But it's still the best news I've heard in forever. Now Alaric can stop complaining about not having a mate and having to spend so much time away from home. I empathize with his loneliness—I truly do—but I trust in the goddess that we will all meet our mates precisely when we are meant to and not a moment sooner. I learned when I was younger to stop trying to rush my future.

There were some that thought Alaric and I would end up as mates. After all, we are usually always together, but that would be gross. He's my brother from another mother. The yin to my yang. The laces to my sneakers. But not romantically—never romantically.

"Come on, Skarlyt," I say to myself, lifting my hands and calling on my air magic to float around me, drying my wet hair. That's one of the best things about being a witch—never needing to spend hours under a blow dryer. A wave of my hands paired with a little focus and, poof, perfectly dry hair with none of that pesky heat damage.

Most witches need to recite a spell in order to do something as simple as call upon the air but not in my coven. Everyone in the Coven of the Moon can perform spells the way other covens do, but we also have access to some elemental powers without needing to chant or complete a ritual. It is a sign of strength and proof that Mother Moon trusts us with her gifts.

Some of us, like those in my immediate family, have access to more than one element at once. I am the first in my family line to have access to all four elements. Even though my earth element is dominant, I still have access to water, fire, and air as well. Air is the toughest for me, but I still have no trouble doing things like drying my hair. My brother, Sebastyn, is the second born in our family line to have all four, but his dominant element is water while fire is the hardest for him to wrangle.

We all have our strengths and weaknesses.

I shake the thoughts from my head and walk out of the en suite bathroom into my bedroom. My little cottage isn't much, but it's perfect for me. Like the rest of the homes in this area, it was built into the forest in the least intrusive way. It looks like it is meant to be here. Of course, I used my earth magic to help camouflage it a little and encouraged the vines and branches to grow around my little home.

Just inside the front door, I have my small living room, dining room, and kitchen combo with a wood-burning fireplace. It's a pain in the ass to ensure I have enough wood to last throughout the winter, but the smell is nice. Further back into my little cottage, there are two bedrooms on either side of the hallway with bathrooms connected to each. At the back is my favorite spot in the entire world: my work room. I have it set up exactly how I want it: not a thing out of place. All my herbs are growing nicely in my tiered shelves by the window, a long island in the middle is filled with my burners, pots, vials, and mortar and pestle. On the other two walls are shelves filled with spell books, herbology books, naturopathic medicine books, and even my romance novels. Like I said, perfect.

And being on pack land and outside my mother's constant insistence that I step up as coven high priestess? Well, that's just a bonus. I'll step up when I'm good and ready and not a moment sooner. It's like she doesn't even know me.

But today is not the time to think about that...It's time to celebrate Alaric meeting his mate. Usually, I would celebrate with him. Since I can't, I have to do something to distract myself. If not, I will hop in my car and drive down to no-man's-land in Morpeth to meet his mysterious woman myself. I can't wait.

As much as I love Alaric—and I do—I desperately need a friend of the female variety. I've never really gotten along with many women...I guess they think I'm weird. At least, that's what the girls in school always said, and maybe I am. But being weird isn't something to be ashamed of, it's something to be celebrated...

I think of myself as an "acquired taste."

Still clutching my towel to my chest, I step in front of my closet to survey my options. I want to go out dancing, and I don't care that I'm going alone. It's not like I've ever cared before. Maybe I'll even find myself a hunky man to spend the night with. One can only hope. It's the added bonus of Alaric being gone...he won't be there to growl at men when they get too close to me. Even though we aren't romantically involved, my past choices in men are questionable to say the least, so now he's taken up the role of protector. The problem is that apparently no one is good enough for me, which puts a real damper on my sex life.

It's also difficult to explain to any handsome suitors that the alpha staring them down from the corner is nothing to worry about.

I decide on my little black dress—every girl needs one. It looks classy, but I can still slut it up a little to ensnare my prey for the night. It has a halter top with a deep, plunging neckline that shows off my large, perky tits and flat, toned stomach. It says, "I'm a lady, but I'm down to fuck." Exactly what I'm looking for.

I curl my long, black hair loosely, so it's hanging in loose waves down my back all the way to my ass. I throw on a light touch of makeup: a dusting of bronzer to smooth out my sun-kissed skin, a sharp wing of black eyeliner, a swipe of mascara to highlight my bright blue eyes, and a thin coat of pink lip gloss to finish off the look. I slip on my ballet flats that don't necessarily go with this outfit, but I really don't give a shit. I'd rather be comfortable when I'm dancing. I look at myself in the mirror one last time. Yes. That's it. I look fucking hot.

I get a ping on my phone and check it. Sweet, my SuperUber is here. Time to go get fucked up. We only have two SuperUber drivers—supernatural Uber drivers—operating within Parry Sound, so sometimes the wait can be extreme. It is worth it, though, when you're all hopped up on Faerie wine and unable to control your magic or shift to make it home safely at the end of the night.

I head out the door of my little cottage and jump into the back seat of the SUV in my driveway.

"To Supernatural, please," I tell the driver.

Supernatural is the name of a bar in Parry Sound that caters to all types of supernatural creatures, including shifters, witches, vampires, and anything else that decides they want to have some fun. Although supernatural beings of any type are welcome, it is exclusively open for supes. There's a charm on it that deters any humans from wanting to enter, so it's sort of a safe haven for us. Even the human portion of Parry Sound is a nice, pleasant place to live, but Supernatural is the one public place where we can be ourselves and let our hair down, so to speak.

As the driver pulls up to the front of the bar, I watch a couple of vampires and Fae walk in. Oh, the vampire is pretty damn sexy. He is what you'd expect a vampire to look like: tall, muscular but not bulky like most shifters, with his long, brown hair pulled back into a bun. Rather than being pale, though, he has an olive complexion that I'm really digging. Maybe he'll let me climb his mountain later and get answers to some long-time questions of mine at the same time. A giggle escapes me at that thought...What I wouldn't give to have "insider" information to all my vampiric curiosities.

I pull out my phone and transfer the driver the payment with a generous tip because I'm in a great fucking mood and feeling generous.

"Thanks," I say as I slide out of the car and walk up to the door.

"Greetings, boys," I nod at the bouncers as I walk past them into the bar. I've been coming here for so long that they know me by name and never stop me to ask for ID.

I can hear and feel the bass vibrating as I step through the doors. Every time I come here, I feel like I've stepped into Faerie. My earth magic begins vibrating just beneath the surface, comforted and encouraged by the green everywhere. Vines grow up the walls, flowers hang from the ceiling, and a giant elderberry tree grows out of a large dirt patch in the center. Although the music pumps loud and raucous, there's a calmness around that tree and in the flowering vines that makes it feel like home.

Faerie wine is made from elderberries infused with magic, and this beautiful, well-tended tree ensures that Supernatural has a never-ending supply of the stuff. It tastes different for everyone. That's the magic of it, and that's why it's so addicting. If a drink tastes like just what you need, you never want to stop drinking. It's also the easiest way for any supe to get drunk. A shifter would have to drink two cases of beer to feel the slight buzz they can get off one glass of Faerie wine. The prices are understandably high.

I walk up to the bar and greet my friend and the owner, Trevan. He's a Fae working as a bartender. He looks almost human. Well, except for his ocean-blue eyes and matching hair, which is just long enough to hide his pointy ears. I've always loved his hair color. No matter how much I've tried, I just can't seem to replicate it. It bugged me for years before I finally gave up. I've learned to love my pitch-black hair, but I would still take that cerulean hue in a second if I could.

"Hey, Skarlyt, haven't seen you here in a while." Trevan's voice is deep but musical.

"Hey, Trev. Nope, I've been busy. Can I get a Mystic Eight?"

"Comin' right up," he says as he begins making my drink. "What brings you out tonight if you've been so busy?"

"I am celebrating," I say, already studying those standing at the bar to determine if they are suited to celebrate with me.

I give up on those in my immediate vicinity and decide to scan the room for the vamp I caught sight of outside. Even if it isn't him, my conquest for the night is likely on the dance floor.

"You got some good news?" Trevan asks casually as he tips a few ounces of something fruity into my drink.

Before I can answer, I freeze. My eyes are drawn to the dance floor and catch on a sight that hits me like a punch to my stomach. My hand flies to my mouth. There, out on the dance floor grinding on some blonde bimbo who is wearing far too little and probably just graduated high school, is the one man I wished to never see again.

"What the fuck is he doing here?" I snarl under my breath.

Years ago, I vowed that if I ever saw him again, I'd curse his dick to fall off. Some said that was excessive, but not me. He's the worst kind of person there is...the kind that will do anything to get what they want, leaving destruction in their wake.

It's been twelve years since I've seen him, but it feels just like yesterday...

I'm sixteen and desperately in love with my boyfriend and child-hood sweetheart, Kirnon. For weeks, I've been going back and forth, debating if it is finally time to lose my virginity to him. While getting ready for the dance, I decide I am sure.

He has been putting a little pressure on me lately. I always envisioned waiting for my mate, but Kirnon warns me that it may be years before we find our true mates—if we ever do. Besides, don't I think it will be him anyway?

When he assures me that we can take each other as chosen mates, it doesn't take much convincing. True mates may be a gamble against time, but the second he said we could choose each other, my heart thumped wildly in my chest. That's all I've ever wanted. Him and me forever.

We get all dolled up, ready to go to the semi-formal dance. I am in my ombre black-to-sky-blue mermaid style dress, and Kirnon is in his black suit and sky-blue shirt to match. I told my parents that Alaric and I are staying at a hotel in town with a group of people, which is partly true. Alaric and I are staying at a hotel. I know they assume we're sharing a room, and I don't correct them. The truth is that I got a room with Kirnon, and Alaric got a room for him and his date for the night—a human named Catriona.

We have so much fun dancing the night away, and it seems like the party ends way too soon. Without knowing how we get there, Kirnon and I are standing at the door to our room, hands and mouths all over each other, fumbling in impatience. We finally break apart to open the door, and I freeze.

Sometime before the dance, he must've come to the room in secret. I look around, seeing candles spread around the room and rose petals scattered over the bed. It is the most romantic thing I've ever seen, and tears of happiness spring to my eyes. If I had any doubts that I loved him before, they vanish. He cares enough about it being my first time to set all this up in order to make it special for me. I squeal in delight and jump on him, wrapping my legs around his waist.

I kiss him with passion, running my fingers through his hair and pulling him closer to me. I move my lips down to his earlobe and begin sucking on it before making my way to his neck, all while he is walking us closer to the bed. He places me on the bed and begins undressing me, so I begin to do the same. Within seconds, we are both naked, and he is joining me on the bed, fusing his mouth with mine.

What happens next isn't like what I'd seen in the movies at all, but it doesn't deter us. We make love dozens of times over the course of the night, with each time getting better and less painful, until we eventually fall asleep in each other's arms.

Waking up the next morning to Kirnon's arm around me and our legs tangled together is amazing. I've never felt happier.

Kirnon was right. It is better that we didn't wait for our mates. We don't have to wait to be happy together as each other's chosen. A smile graces my lips at my thoughts. I've just claimed my mate. Unofficially, of course, since we're not eighteen yet, but damn it feels good.

Kirnon must sense me staring at him in his sleep, because he chooses that moment to wake up.

"Morning," he says, getting up out of the bed and heading to the bathroom.

"Morning," I reply, even though he is already closing the bathroom door. Huh, that was weird. Why do I get the feeling that something is wrong? We had an amazing night together. Didn't we? I've never slept and woken up with anyone before, but I can't help but feel like something is wrong.

I get up myself and begin getting dressed. At least admitting to my parents that we were sleeping here gave me an excuse to pack a bag and drop it off the day before.

Once Kirnon comes out of the bathroom, I walk over to him, ready to give him a hug and kiss and maybe pick up where we left off last night. I stop mid-stride, noticing the pinching of his dark eyebrows.

I know Kirnon well enough to instantly tell there is definitely something wrong.

"What's going on?" I ask him. "Are you okay?"

"I'm moving tomorrow," he replies, his tone is nonchalant though he looks ready to vomit. He doesn't stop to look at me. He just bends to pull on his shoes as if he's rushing out the door, as if he's not crushing my entire future with those words.

"No, you aren't." I can't understand what he's saying. "Where are you moving?"

"We're moving to another pack tomorrow and won't be coming back," he tells me.

"How will—how far—" Still baffled, I wonder what that means for us? Finding it impossible to process what he's saying, I sit on the bed and begin to cry.

He simply shoulders his bag and says, "I had fun last night, and I hope you have a good life, Skar," before he walks out the door.

That's the last time I saw him. He tricked me. He knew he was leaving but chose to take my virginity and walk away. So, yeah. I vowed that the next time I saw him, I would curse his dick to fall off. In my opinion, it would be justified.

Though, looking at him now, I have to admit that he looks really fucking good. Like really good. He still has his signature undercut, with the back and sides shaved and his black hair still long on the top. His blue eyes still sparkle like diamonds when the light hits them the right way and his body...Oh, Mother, I thought he was fit when we were younger. He's filled out since then, and his muscles look even more defined. Maybe one last ride before his dick falls off. It can't hurt, right?

"Are you all right, Skar?" Trevan hands me my drink and must be able to read some part of my expression. "First one's on me."

"Many thanks, Trev," I say, raising my glass to him and taking a drink. A tingle begins climbing up my spine, alerting me that someone is behind me. I know who it is already, even though I haven't felt those tingles in a long time.

"Rum and Coke please, Trev," a familiar voice says, making my spine snap straight before turning around.

"Hey, Kirnon. Long time, no see," I say before downing the rest of my drink, needing some liquid courage. For some reason, even after twelve years apart, my body still reacts to him and tries to inch closer.

"Mine," I think I hear him say with a growl, but that can't be right.

"What was that?" I ask him.

"Nothing," he says, shaking his head. "I've been good. How about you?"

Oh, so we're going to do small talk, are we? Well, in that case.

"Can I get another drink, please, Trev?" I say, turning toward Trevan, realizing he's already got one ready for me. "Thanks."

He gives me a wink and nod in response, seemingly sympathetic to my situation. We were already good friends when Kirnon left, after all, so Trev knows it all. I turn back around, re-focusing on Kirnon. "Oh, you know, I haven't been abandoned by any lovers recently, so that's new." I tell him while shrugging my shoulders and taking a sip of my new drink.

I don't get a chance to say anything else because the next thing I know, Kirnon has grabbed my hand and is pulling me toward the back of the bar.

"What are you doing? Where are you taking me?"

"Need to," is all he says while pulling me along with him into the bathroom and locking the door.

"You need to do what?"

"I need to taste you," he replies while lifting me onto the counter and dropping to his knees. Not exactly how I envisioned my night going, but I did say I wanted one last ride before I curse his dick to fall off. Pushing my skirt up and panties over, he dives into me like a man starving. Well, more like a very sloppy starving man. I'm not sure what kind of woman he's been with since we were last together, but the sloppiness of his movements isn't doing it for me.

I'm no longer that sixteen-year-old girl who doesn't know what she wants or likes. I am now a confident woman who knows exactly what she requires in her partners.

"Stop moving," I tell him as I grab his head to keep it in place while grinding my pussy on his tongue, so that it's moving on my clit with perfection. "Just like that," I encourage him as he begins to move again. Ugh, do I have to do everything? "Stop," I say, beginning to grind on his face once more, "Suck on... Yeah, just like that... Now flick it with your tongue. Oh, yeah..." Maybe he just needs some coaching.

Although it seems at odds with his large frame and dominating presence, I can tell by his desperation that he wants to be taken to task. After everything he did to me, I am not afraid to use my words now.

"You're a fucking dog for running away," I say, starting to lose myself to the feeling of his tongue and fingers, "and now you're back begging for what you left. I'm going to cum all over your fucking face, and you're going to lap it all up, aren't you?"

He nods obediently through his flicking and sucking.

"Kirnon," I cry out as my orgasm rolls through me, and he laps up all my spilled juices.

Once he seems to be satisfied, he stands up and begins undoing his pants. I came out tonight hoping to have at least one big "O". Why not try and get some closure while I'm at it? If he's as bad at fucking as he is at eating pussy, I'll just have to take control. Then I'll know once and for all that him leaving was really for the best.

He slides his cock inside me in one quick thrust. Mmm, this feels so good. No one has ever filled me quite the way Kirnon has. I can't tell you how many times I've had this scenario play out in my head. Most of the time, it was in a bed or a car in the forest. Sometimes with a partner and sometimes alone. I'm ashamed after each time, though, because I shouldn't have been having delicious daydreams about the man who betrayed me.

Oh goddess, this feels so amazing.

"You feel so good," he says to me as he picks up his pace, slamming in and out of me with enthusiasm.

At one point, I think I see his canines drop in his mouth, but he quickly pulls me forward into an embrace. We don't kiss, not once, which is fine by me. Still, I can't help but feel like something big is happening here.

"Oh, yes, just like that," I yell out as I start to feel my release building.

My magic, having a mind of its own, starts to flare in my palm and flows into Kirnon's chest just as we both find our release.

"What the fuck did you just do?" he spits at me, pushing me away from him with the same heat that he had just pulled me close.

"Oh Mother." Oh Mother... Oh Mother... He's my mate.

I should be happy instead of panicking. Shouldn't I? We should both be excited. So, why do I feel like the other shoe is about to drop? I look from my hand back up to his face, shock still covering my features when I notice his snarl.

There's no real change, but I suddenly know what I didn't moments before. My mate is standing in front of me. Although we were just panting in each other's arms, the magic of the moment is shattered by that knowledge.

"No mate of mine will be a witch," he says while removing himself from me and pulling his pants up. What? Is he serious?

"Are you serious right now? A witch is good enough to put your dick into but not good enough to be your mate?" He doesn't say anything, he doesn't need to. "You know what Kirnon. Fuck you." I spit, readying myself to jump off the counter but freeze as he begins to speak.

"I, Kirnon Knight, reject you, Skarlyt Moon, as my mate now and forevermore."

Wait...what? Before I can even get my words out, I am nearly knocked sideways by the pain in my chest. The pain dragging through my heart is so great that I can't say anything. All I can do is watch as he unlocks the door and walks away from me for a second time.

I pull my knees up to my chest, still atop the counter in the women's bathroom, and just cry. Why would the goddess pair me with the one man who broke me? How could she be so cruel to let him break me again?

It's painful to think about, but I know these three things are true:

Kirnon is my mate...

My mate rejected me...

And I'm going to make him pay one way or another.

Chapter Three

Lennox—Eight Months Ago

T he last twelve years have been the same thing over and over. Each day I get better, and the pain of rejection stings a little less. I moved away to Alberta a year after Olivia's rejection, unable to continue living in the same pack and watching her and Matteo go about their lives together as chosen mates.

The day of their mating ceremony was the final straw and the day I decided to leave. It's been hard to live so far away from my family—especially Charleigh and Felicia. I've seen them so little over the last ten years that I hardly feel like part of the family anymore. We call and talk, of course, and with today's technology, we have been Facetiming, but it's not the same.

I stop at the Hole in the Wall to grab steaks to surprise my parents with, ensuring that I grab a couple extra to feed Felicia and her mate. I was sad to have missed the mating ceremony last month, but I couldn't bring myself to come and chance seeing Olivia and Matteo. At least when I just come for a visit, I can avoid them. At a big pack event like that, it would've been impossible.

I grab a cart and walk through the doors, taking a deep breath.

No matter how many bad memories I have in this little town, it will always be my home. I walk over to the butcher counter.

"Hey, Bobby. Can I get eight New York strips, please?"

"Sure thing, Lennox. It's good to see you," he responds, reaching into the display and lifting out the biggest ones before wrapping them up and passing them to me. "You just home for a visit?"

"Yup. I missed Felicia's mating ceremony, so I figured a surprise steak dinner will make it up to her," I say as I place them in the cart.

"You're driving these up to Parry Sound?" he asks, and I turn to him in question.

"Why would I do that?"

"Oh, you don't know?" he says, and I tilt my head, even more confused than before.

"Don't know what?"

"Maybe it's not my place," he says and abruptly turns, leaving me standing there wondering what the fuck is going on. But Bobby only does things in his own time. I've learned better than to try and push him when he does that. He's never going to tell me.

After a few moments, I realize he's not coming back. I shake my head, moving toward the produce section to grab some big potatoes and corn on the cob. Just as I pick up the first potato, my spine snaps straight, and my wolf begins to whine. Shit.

"Lennox," Olivia exclaims, running over to me and wrapping her arms around my neck as if we're old friends. It's the same thing each time I see her now. She flirts with me and asks me for sexual favors, which I always refuse. I'm not stupid. I know it would just be a setup, and, although my wolf still mourns for his mate, I refuse to put us through the pain of rejection again. Not only that, but it would also be a death sentence to fornicate with the beta's chosen mate.

I'm sure it has something to do with them not having any children yet. I don't know if they have tried and can't, or if there's something else at work. I've heard that if you reject a mate, it can lead to infertility. They could be trying to get me to impregnate her unknowingly. As if I'm that stupid. I would never willingly father a child to be raised by those two.

"Olivia," I grind out as my wolf pushes to the surface, trying anything to get closer to his mate. Her always perfectly quaffed blonde hair is hanging over her shoulders, her bright blue eyes are highlighted by the dark eyeliner and fake lashes, making the blue really pop. My eyes dart down to her lips, her perfectly plump, ruby red lips. I shake my head, clearing the thoughts of wanting to feel how soft they are against my own.

She rejected us. She doesn't want us, I berate him. He's acting like a love-sick puppy, taking scraps of her affection.

She rubs her body up against mine before stepping back, sliding her hand down my arm, keeping contact wherever she can. I wonder if somewhere deep inside, her wolf is as miserable as mine.

"I've missed you," she purrs.

"You rejected me, or don't you remember that?"

She waves her hand in the air as if that's not a big deal.

"That was so long ago. Things change. I've changed."

I shake my head and take a step back. "Are you and Matteo still together?"

"Of course. But that doesn't..."

"Then nothing has changed. You're a mated wolf, Olivia. You need to start acting like it."

"Come on, Lennox," she coos, stepping back up to me, trailing her perfectly manicured fingers down my chest and stomach and over my cock, which twitches at her touch. "I can tell you still want me."

I close my eyes and pray to Mother Moon for strength. My wolf once again presses to the surface, whining for his mate.

I try to step back but feel a hard surface trapping me. "Olivia," I whisper. She takes that as agreement and she presses her lips to my throat, circling with her tongue the way I've dreamed she would around my dick.

I let out a small moan, blaming my wolf entirely for allowing this situation.

A throat clearing has my eyes snapping open, and I realize that we're in the middle of a grocery store filled with pack members. I take my hands from where they were resting at my sides and gently push her back. "Stop," I growl glancing down at the bite on her neck. Matteo's mating mark.

Seeing this, the fog from my wolf seems to clear as well. He adds his own anger to the growl. "You need to stop doing this. There is nothing between us. There never has been."

I turn around and begin to walk away when she calls out so softly that the humans in the store wouldn't hear, knowing that I definitely would.

"I'll pay you."

I spin. "What?"

She takes a small step toward me, her bravado from a moment ago vanished.

"I really want a baby, Lennox. Matteo and me..." she looks down at her feet, "we have tried, but we can't."

For a moment—just a moment—I feel sorry for them, but then I remember that this was her choice. She chose to reject me...chose Matteo over me.

"You should have thought about that before you rejected me, Olivia. You made your bed, now you have to lie in it."

"I was just a kid. I didn't know," she whispers so quietly that I wouldn't have heard it if I wasn't a shifter.

"You should have. I was a kid too, and I knew." With that, I grab the closest potatoes without looking at them and head to the check out.

As I hop into my rental car, I realize I forgot the corn.

"Dammit," I curse.

I hope my parents have something for a side because there is no way in hell I'm going back inside that store. Not with Olivia there. Knowing my luck, she'd assume I'd changed my mind when that couldn't be further from the truth. I would die a happy man if I never saw that woman again.

From the Hole in the Wall, the drive home is short. Before I realize it, I'm pulling up and parking in front of my childhood home. It hasn't changed a bit. The siding on the house is still as bright white as if it was just put on, the covered porch still has the two hammock chairs hanging from the ceiling, and my mother still keeps her gardens immaculate with bright orange, blue, and pink flowers. I can see where Dad has cut a new pathway through the wooded area that surrounds the property, but that's the only change I notice.

I open the car door and take a deep inhale. I can smell the last few days of the clearing's history. A light rain, a group of deer, and my parents running as wolves not long ago.

I walk around the car, reaching in the passenger side and grabbing out the grocery bag before walking up the stairs. I hear my parents laughing inside the house, and a sliver of jealousy works its way through me.

I should have that. If my fated mate wasn't such a bitch, I would have that.

I sigh, trying to release the complex emotions that spike through me at the thought. I don't want to feel jealous of my parents. I've always looked up to and admired their relationship.

"Mom? Dad?" I call out as I step through the door, immediately noticing the distinct changes inside. Boxes labeled and taped shut line the hallway. What the heck is going on here?

"Lennox?" My mom says as she walks out of the kitchen into my line of sight.

"What is going on? What are all these boxes for?"

My mom smiles and cheers my arrival as my dad comes up and wraps his arms around her.

"We're moving," he announces with pride.

My mouth opens in shock, and I almost drop the bag I was holding.

"What do you mean? Did something happen with the house? Do you need money?"

My dad growls low, obviously not liking me insinuating that he can't take care of his mate, and my mom slaps his chest.

"Stop that," she says before she turns back to me. "No, no. Nothing like that. Your sisters joined a new pack in Parry Sound, and we've been extended an invitation. Your dad has been talking about retiring soon anyway, so we decided we're going to sell the house and live out our retirement up there."

"Why am I the last to know everything?" I demand, still in shock.

"We didn't want to tell you until it was official. The girls just called yesterday to tell us they officially joined the pack. Alaric—that's their new alpha—is the one dealing with Christian, so we want to move as soon as possible before he has the chance to take the loss of five wolves out on us."

I walk toward them into the kitchen, placing my bags on the counter.

"So, they joined a new pack? How did that happen?"

"It's a long story," my dad says.

I raise my eyebrows at him and take a seat at the kitchen table. "I've got time."

"No sitting. If we're going to tell you the story, you have to pack at the same time," my mom berates me, and I quickly rise from my seat and follow her into the living room where she has empty boxes ready to be filled.

"You already know that Felicia met her mate, Josh, and he was from another pack." I nod my head to my dad as I begin placing books off the shelf into the box. "During their mating ceremony, Josh's alpha, Alaric, came down to attend," my dad says, and my mom cuts him off.

"Oh, Lennox. I can't wait for you to meet him. He is so different from Christian."

I whip my head toward my mother.

"Different how?"

"We only met him briefly at the mating ceremony and again before they went back to Parry Sound, but from what the girls told me, he runs his pack with compassion—not fear like Christian."

"As I was saying..." my dad begins again, and my mom abruptly cuts him off again.

"That's not even the best part..."

"Dammit, woman. Am I telling the story, or are you?" My dad growls playfully, throwing a crunched-up sheet of newspaper at her, and I try to hide my smirk. He's not really mad, after being together for so long he's definitely used to her cutting him off.

"You are, of course," my mom says with a soft smile to my father, motioning that she's locking up her lips and throwing away the key.

"As I was saying," he pauses, looking over at my mother pointedly. When she doesn't go to interject, he continues. "When Alaric came to the mating ceremony, it turns out that he met his mate." A smirk plays on his face.

After a couple breaths, I can't wait any longer. "And? Who was it?"

"Remember Phoebe? Charleigh's friend?"

"Of course, I remember Phoebe...but she's human." My brows furrow in confusion. It's not uncommon for a shifter to be mated to a human but for an alpha...That's different.

My dad shakes his head. "Nope. Apparently, she's not human. Not according to Charleigh anyway. She won't tell us what she is.

She said that we have to wait and see for ourselves. Something about us not believing her."

I pause my packing to raise an eyebrow at my dad. He can't be serious. Phoebe is as human as they come. We would've known if she was a supernatural with the amount of time she spent here. Plus, it would've made our lives a lot easier if she knew what we are. I had a hard time trying to stop my shift on multiple occasions when we were younger because she was here.

"Honey," my mom can't stop herself from urging him on, "honey tell him about the—you know—" and wiggles her fingers at him in a sign I cannot interpret.

My dad shrugs his shoulders. "That's not all. Apparently, Phoebe's husband, Tanner, was a mage with an entire coven living right under our noses."

"Impossible," I reply.

"It's true! Tanner is gone now. Alaric wants to believe that Christian didn't know about the mages, but we know better." He gestures between the three of us. "There is no way that Christian, being the monster that he is, didn't have some sort of deal going on with them."

I think about all the information my dad just gave me. Could Christian truly have known there were mages living in Morpeth? I want to say that no alpha would ever hand a pack member over to monsters like them, but this is Christian we're talking about. The same man who has called every pack I've tried to join since I left spewing stories about how I tried to take his beta's fated mate and was banished. Needless to say, I am still a member of the Ironwood pack—not from lack of trying though. I even tried to join smaller packs in Manitoba, British Columbia, and Saskatchewan hoping that his influence wouldn't reach there with no luck.

"We've had pack members disappearing for the last decade. You truly think that Christian has been handing them over to the mages?" I ask.

"Maybe not all of them. But I wouldn't put it past him to have given them a fair few if it helped him out." My dad replies, and I nod. It's not out of the realm of possibilities when thinking of what Christian would do for more power—even the illusion of having more power.

"I'm going to go get those steaks you brought on the grill," my dad says, interrupting my thoughts.

"There are potatoes too," I call out to him as he is already walking away. He waves his hand in the air, acknowledging me.

"Oh, Lennox, I'm so glad you're here," my mother says, walking up and wrapping her arms around me. "I feel like I haven't seen you in forever."

I hug her back just as fiercely. "I know, Mom. I wish I could come home more. It's just..."

"I know why, my love. You don't have to tell me. But I do hope you'll come around more after we move. Alaric even told us you were more than welcome to join as well."

"Really?" I say in disbelief, stepping back from my mom. He might say that now, but once he asks Christian about me, I know that's going to change. "Not if Christian has anything to say about it."

"Oh, honey, trust me. Alaric won't believe him without getting all the facts first. He's a very different alpha than what we're used to."

"I would love to believe that, Mom. But I don't have much faith. If it means that much to you, when I get my next leave in eight months, I'll come visit you and make a decision then."

"That's all I ask, honey," she says, patting my cheek. "Now let's get this place packed. It was going to take your dad and I a week to get everything ready to go, but with you here, we should be able to get it done a lot quicker."

I nod my head and go back to packing up my childhood home. After I finish with the books on the shelves, I grab a couple empty boxes and head to my old room. It's like stepping back in time. Nothing has changed at all. There are still Blink-182 posters up on the wall, and my desk still holds binders with all my baseball cards. I even see my POG set on the shelf. I wonder if they're worth anything. I grab a marker off the desk and write "Sell" on the box before placing my cards, POGs, and anything else I think might be worth some money inside.

By the time I'm done, I have two bags of clothes to donate, three boxes to sell, and half a dozen boxes filled with keepsakes. I've packed everything up except my bed since I'm going to use it for the next couple of days before heading back to Alberta. I thought I was going to have a relaxing time off, relaxing with my parents and sisters, but it turns out I'm going to be busier than ever.

I debate calling my sisters to ream them out for not telling me but decide against it. I want to see how long it takes them to call me. Maybe after talking to them, I'll feel better about this move, but, as it stands, my stomach is tied up in knots. What if my parents are trading one tyrant alpha for another? Better the devil you know, right?

Chapter Four

Skarlyt—Present day

Someone knocking on the door wakes me up. Ugh. Looking out of the window, I can see that the sky is still dark with a pink tint, telling me that the sun is just beginning to rise. I look at my watch...six forty-five in the morning. Who the fuck is waking me up at this ungodly hour? If someone isn't dying, I'm going to kill them myself.

"Skarlyt, I can hear you. I know that you're awake. Come open the door, please," Alaric yells out. Of course, he can hear that I'm awake. Damn wolf hearing.

"Hold your horses. I'm coming," I toss back to him while making my way to the door.

I look down at myself to make sure that I'm clothed, and I realize I haven't had the chance to hide my very obvious baby bump. Damn it. I can't believe I almost opened the door without hiding it. It's not that I'm ashamed. I'm just not ready to tell people the entire story.

I can tell that Alaric is suspicious. He's asked me multiple times if there was something wrong with my heart because it sounded like I had two different heart beats. Maybe he knows, and he's just waiting for me to admit it. Instead, I just keep telling him that I developed dysrhythmia, and I've been looking for a spell to fix it. He offered one of Phoebe's phoenix tears, but I turned it down, saying we shouldn't be using the tears for every little thing that happens. He looked skeptical, and I was worried that he was going to press the issue. Thankfully, he dropped it.

I rub small circles on my beautiful tummy and murmur the spell quietly to conceal it along with the scent before opening the door to Alaric.

"Somebody better be dead if you're waking me up this early," I growl out at him. I wasn't a morning person before I was pregnant. Now that I am, it's even worse.

"Ha ha," he says sarcastically. "Nobody's dying. The ceremony is today, so Phoebe kicked me out of bed saying it's bad luck for me to see her."

"Okay...that still doesn't explain why you're here waking me up at the crack of dawn," I reply to him while opening the door wider.

"I thought about going for a run but decided to come here instead. You can go back to sleep if you want. I'll just hang out and watch TV." He at least has the decency to look slightly ashamed for waking me up so early, but it doesn't make me feel any more awake.

"No, no. I'm up now," I say back with a little more snark than I probably should have. But seriously, who wakes someone up this early? If I had known of Phoebe's plan to kick him out this early, I would have just given him a key. Wait a minute; he has a key.

"Why didn't you use your key instead of waking me up?"

"I thought about it, but I thought it would scare you if you woke up to find me just chilling on the couch."

He has a point.

"I would have been scared but not sleepy. I mean, come on Alaric. The ceremony isn't until dusk. What are we going to do all day?" Although, thinking about it now, there's no way I would've had time to hide my baby bump if he had used his key...Probably better this way.

"I thought you would have an idea of what we should do," he replies. Goddess, help us. This is going to be the longest day ever.

As he settles on the couch, I run back to my room, grab my comfy oversized hoodie, and throw it on. I see my phone flashing and pick it up, noting several missed calls and texts from my mom. I hover my finger over the screen before deciding to call her back later.

* * *

Surprisingly, the day actually flies by with Alaric and me playing video games and spending quality time together. It is nice. We haven't done anything like this since Phoebe came to live here. I obviously do not mind, but our gruesome twosome became the three amigos, and, as much as they tried, I can't help but feel like a third wheel at times.

It's really not their fault. They did their best to include me in everything they did. I get it. If my mate wouldn't have rejected me, I probably wouldn't want my best friend around twenty-four seven either. It also probably would've helped if I had confided in one of them, admitted why I was hanging around so much. Admitting the whole "my mate rejected me and knocked me up" thing is not as easy as it seems. As much as I wanted to—and I did—I don't think I really believed it myself at first. Then, when I finally accepted it, it seemed like a bad dream. I was hoping to wake up.

It took months for me to come to terms with my predicament. Not that I would ever consider anything but raising the pup or witch growing inside me, but it was still a hard pill to swallow. Now that I know it's real and am ready for the next steps, I know that I need to tell someone. I'm just not ready to see the hurt and disappointment on their faces when I tell them how long I've known.

The worst has been when I'm alone with my thoughts. They've been dark. I mean, really dark. Nothing suicidal. I'm not that far gone. I might have plotted Kirnon's murder multiple times —exercising my inner vampire, inventing new forms of torture— but I'd never try to harm myself. Not that he knows about the baby, but who rejects their mate strictly because of what type of supe they are? I'm going to enjoy the day karma hits him. I want a front-row seat.

Alaric snaps me out of my inner darkness.

"Skar, we need to finish getting ready and go get the boys."

Oh yeah, the mating ceremony. That's right. I head to my room to get dressed, whispering the illusion spell on my stomach to extend to my new clothes. Once that's done, I finish buttoning up the linen shirt we chose to wear and braid my long black hair to the side.

Once we're both ready, we head down to the clearing to meet the boys.

As we stand in the center of the clearing by the lake at dusk, Alaric is fidgeting more than either of the boys standing next to us, and they fidget a lot. It seems like none of them can stand still. I wonder if my baby will end up being a boy, full of energy like them. Maybe it will be a girl, calm and quiet like Cybil. Either way, as long as he or she is healthy, that's all that matters.

It's almost dusk, and I now realize why Phoebe chose this time for the ceremony. The way the lake is reflecting the light of the slowly rising moon is gorgeous. The lake is smooth and calm right now; it almost looks like a solid piece of glass, making a perfect mirror for the moon.

I look around at the people gathered, noticing the confused looks we're getting. I know it's not typical to have a bridal party at a claiming ceremony, but Phoebe was raised human, and everyone wanted to have the boys involved. Because of that, we decided to make an exception. When we were planning, Alaric asked me to stand next to him in our matching linen pants and button downs as his best man—or woman. Charleigh agreed to walk into the clearing with Phoebe in their matching dresses as her matron of honor. We also made sure to get matching outfits for each of the boys, so they feel included.

"You need to go out and meet your mate soon, Skar, or we're going to break the tradition of our families having children close together," he tells me through his nervousness. If only he knew.

I did go out and meet my mate while he was at Josh's mating ceremony, meeting and falling for Phoebe. Our fairytale endings were perfectly aligned, but now I wish I never went into that bar. Still, Alaric will get his wish. By my calculations, Phoebe and I are due only a week or two apart.

I am saved from fumbling for a response by Phoebe making her appearance at the mouth of the path. Her eyes are practically glowing under the traditional flower crown that adorns her beautiful, dark curls. Her dress is moon-white where it covers her swollen breast, and it fades into a deep, ruby red where it flairs into a short train that brushes the path.

I'm not sure if the dress was intended to be that form-fitting or not, but it shows her swollen baby bump proudly. It makes me wish I could do the same. I know I won't be able to hide my pregnancy for much longer. If my due date is correct, I'll be giving birth in the next two weeks.

If I don't tell someone soon, I'll be doing it alone.

The ceremony is beautiful, and the night is filled with dancing and laughter. My cheeks hurt from smiling so much. I can't remember a time in the last eight months where I've had so much fun. Between my swollen ankles, lonely heart, and Braxton-Hicks contractions, I am not feeling quite like myself amidst the celebration. Far earlier than normal, I am ready to slip away to the quiet calm of my cabin. First, though, I track down Phoebe. She's hard to miss, sipping a glass of cold water and resting her own swollen feet in an Adirondack chair on the deck.

"Skarlyt, dear," my mother says, grabbing my attention and trying to pull me aside. "Skarlyt, I need to talk to you."

My mother, who has been trying to corner me all night, tries to intercept me, but I explain I have a gift to deliver.

"Skar," Phoebe complains as she overhears my excuse, "You know you aren't supposed to get us anything. It's not a wedding, so no wedding gifts."

I tease her for a moment, giving my mother time to politely step away. She doesn't take the opportunity, however, and simply waits nearby to hear the news I am here to deliver. I hand Phoebe the oversized envelope that contains her gift and begin to explain.

"I finally heard back from one of my contacts I reached out to when we were still trying to figure out what exactly you are. Well, it turns out you're not the last phoenix shifter like we thought. My contact found a birth certificate for you in London."

She tries to interrupt me, as always, but the building pressure in my stomach makes me impatient. I hold my hand up to slow her down. This news is exciting, but it is also sad. Her birth certificate lists two parents, but there are matching death certificates for both dated only a few days later.

"Do not get too excited because we don't know anything more than what I am going to tell you now."

Another ripple of pain through my abdomen makes my breath hitch. She must hear the shift in my voice because her eyes, now rimmed with tears, rip away from the copy of her birth certificate to meet mine.

"Skar?"

"The second paper is the really interesting one. Two minutes after you were born, another little girl was born in the same hospital with the same parents listed on her birth certificate. Her name is Sophia, and I am pretty sure she's your twin sister, Phoebe."

Just as I finish, the pain in my stomach gets so intense I double over, crying out as a gush of water escapes from my nether regions.

"What's wrong, Skar?" Phoebe asks, concern lining her voice. "What's that?" I can't reply as the pain increases, making it impossible for me to formulate anything other than a scream coming out of my mouth.

"We need to bring her inside and place her on the kitchen table," my mom responds. The next thing I know, I have Alaric's arms under my arms and legs, and I'm being carried into the house. When did he even come near us?

"What is going on?" he asks as he bursts through the door.

"She's going into labor," my mom responds. How the hell does she know that?

"*Labor?*" I hear both Phoebe and Alaric respond with almost-comical shock.

I'm in far too much pain to pay attention to the rest of the conversation and vaguely realize I've been placed on the kitchen table.

I hear my mom listing off random things: boiled water, towels, and sheets for Alaric to grab for me. I can't be going into labor yet. I still have two weeks.

I haven't bought anything. I haven't even painted the baby's room yet. It's too soon. Maybe I can stop it somehow, buy myself some more time. Just as I start to think of different spells I could use, a big contraction hits. The pain forces all rational thoughts from my brain.

"You're going to be okay, babe," Phoebe says as she comes to sit by my head and holds my hand.

"I think I'm dying," I say as I look into her eyes.

"You're not dying, silly," she responds. "We are going to have a long talk about the things we share with our best friends when this is over, though."

Oh, goody. Just what I wanted. Well, actually, I'd take the talk over this right now.

I scream out, "Mother fucker," as another contraction hits.

"Language," my mother berates me as she pulls off my pants and underwear, placing a sheet over the top of my legs to shield my lady bits from Alaric. "I can see the head," she says and begins ordering people around to gather the necessary items.

Maybe those weren't Braxton-Hicks... Could I have been in labor all day? Did the concealment spell do something to make it less painful?

"Here," Phoebe says, handing my mom a vial. "It's for after—to help speed the healing." As she turns to look at me, I can see the tears streaming down her face as it's pinched up in pain. I know that she always keeps a vial on her now. She doesn't cry nearly as often since she and Alaric have been together, but she keeps it just in case. The fact that she thought to give the vial to my mom is touching, and I give her hand a big squeeze.

"Okay, push," my mom tells me, snapping me out of my warm thoughts toward Phoebe. I scream, and Phoebe screams, although I'm not sure what she's screaming for. I push until I can't anymore, still feeling the urge, but I flop back.

"I can't," I cry.

"Yes, you can. One more time. Almost done," my mom orders, and I sit up once again. Alaric is at my back, rubbing soothing circles, and Phoebe is squeezing my hand tight. The urge to push rears its head, and I give a push with all my strength. Almost instantly, I feel relief and stop screaming, although Phoebe does not. Turning to look at her, I can see her hunched over, clasping at her stomach while I hear the most beautiful sound.

"It's a boy," my mother coos, holding her grandson in her hands for the first time. She looks from the baby to me with tears in her eyes as she places him on my chest.

I don't think my heart has ever felt this full. I love this tiny being more than my own life. How does this happen? I knew I loved him from the moment I found out I was pregnant, but now that I'm looking into his beautiful blue eyes and touching his soft skin, it feels like that love was just a tiny bit of what I feel now.

I'm distracted from staring at my beautiful baby boy as I am gently slid over on the kitchen table, and they place Phoebe beside me. What the fuck? That's about all I can think before I see Gran come in through the patio doors just in time to go in between Phoebe's legs, pulling down her underwear.

"Guess it's a two for one special tonight," she jokes.

I glance back at Alaric who looks like he wants to pass out, one hand resting on my shoulder and the other on Phoebe's back as if he can't decide who to help.

I reach up with my hand and pat his.

"Hold your mate, Alaric. I'm okay."

He looks down at me with wide eyes, but does as I say. He steps closer to Phoebe, supporting her from the back at the same time as she turns to face him.

"I hate you. You did this to me," she growls as a scream erupts from her mouth.

"I know, love. And you can spend the rest of our lives reminding me," he says, placing a soft kiss on her head.

"Okay, Granddaughter. It's time to push. Are you ready?" Gran asks her.

Phoebe shakes her head no.

"Well, that's too bad because this baby is coming whether you want it to or not," Gran says, and Phoebe sits up with a yell, her hand grabbing my leg and squeezing. I flinch from the pain. Damn, she's strong, but I don't complain.

Two pushes later, and Gran pulls out a baby with gorgeous red hair. "It's a girl," she gushes over her newest great-grandchild, wrapping her up in a towel before placing her on Phoebe's chest beside me.

What are the odds that we both give birth on the same day? It's almost like my labor kick-started her own—unless she's been having pains for the last couple of days as well. She just went through her own labor in silence while helping me through mine. Now, that's genuine friendship. Goddess, I love this woman, but what was she thinking?

Phoebe and I look at each other, then at our beautiful babies, before instantly breaking out in manic laughter. Only we would give birth minutes apart on the day of her mating ceremony.

"We have a few things to discuss, Skarlyt Leigh Moon," Alaric says, breaking me out of my laughter with a stern look before softening and cooing over the babies. Uh-oh I'm in trouble. He only uses my full name when he's really, really mad. I look up at him and then down at my son. I guess we do have some things to discuss, but not right now. Right now, I just want to relax and soak in the warmth of my baby boy.

"What are their names?" Gran asks. Phoebe and I look at each other, and I nod at her to go first.

"Aurora," she says softly, while placing a kiss on her head. She looks up at Alaric before turning to me.

"Kayne...Kayne Moon," I say, holding him closer to my chest.

Looking over at Phoebe and Alaric, I can't say that I'm not jealous of the support she has with him standing at the ready to help. Although we are crowded together in this strange scene, I can't help but feel like I have no one to share this moment with.

The peaceful moment doesn't last long, though, as both Alaric and my mother break into an argument about where I will sleep

44

for the immediate future. Alaric wins, as usual, with the stipulation that my mother can stay here and help me with everything.

Awesome.

No, not really.

I love my mother dearly, but I haven't lived with her for ten years for a reason.

Chapter Five

Skarlyt

Alaric gives me a whole thirty minutes to get cleaned up and dressed before barging into my room with Phoebe on his heels.

"Time to fess up," he demands.

Ugh, okay, I knew this was coming. I knew that one day I would have to explain. I just thought it wouldn't be for another couple of weeks. I'm not usually this much of a coward, but when it comes to Alaric...it's different. I'm not scared of him, but I'm terrified of disappointing him. I don't know if I'd survive if he were to write me out of his life. The one thing we've always promised each other is that we would never keep secrets. And I broke that promise for nine months.

"Okay, sit down, and I'll tell you. First, you have to promise you won't go out killing anyone just yet. Okay?" I tell him while looking right into his eyes.

I have to hold his stare for over a minute before he finally relents and nods his head in agreement. Phew, okay. That's done. As much as I want Kirnon to suffer—and I do in the worst way possible—I want to be the one to dish out the justice. It won't be the same if Alaric does it, and I know he will want to. If I'm honest though, now that Kayne's here in my arms and looks like a spitting image of his father with my eyes, it's hard to want him dead. Maybe I will just curse his dick to fall off after all.

I adjust my hold on Kayne while Alaric gets Phoebe situated in the chair in the corner, Aurora already suckling at her breast. Once everyone is settled, I begin telling them my tale.

"Kirnon is Kayne's father," I begin, and Alaric growls loudly enough to make the floor shake.

"Who's Kirnon?" Phoebe asks, looking between us in confusion.

And that's how I end up retelling the entire story, from my teenage years until today. By the end of my story, Phoebe is in tears while Alaric is so mad he just strides out the door. I already know he's going to shift. He's never liked Kirnon, especially after what he did to me when we were younger. He clearly has a good reason, though.

Alaric was the one who picked up the pieces the next day, after Kirnon left me. He was the one whose shoulder I cried on for countless nights. He's the one who put me back together and showed me that I'm worthy of love and deserved to have someone who cares about me. It took him more time than I want to admit to complete that last one, but he never gave up on me. He never told me I was stupid or that I should stop whining. He just held me when I cried and praised me when I didn't. That's why he's my best friend.

"Oh, Skar. I don't even know what to say. That was...I don't even have words..." Phoebe says, as tears flow freely from her eyes.

"You don't have to say anything, Pheebs. It happened, and there's nothing I can do about it. I wouldn't change it now though. I'm holding this beautiful little man in my arms, so why would I change anything? I feel like I could go through a thousand rejections just to be able to look into his little eyes, and feel his tiny fingers curl around mine," I tell her, and I can say with complete honesty that it's the truth.

"All the hurt, all the late nights crying myself to sleep, all the fits of rage trashing my cottage, every last tear; I'd do it again just to hold Kayne. My life is his. My heart is his. I can live forever without a mate as long as I have him."

"I know what you mean. I felt that way and still feel that way about the boys. I could go through every last thing that Tanner put me through all over again as long as the end result is that I have them in my life."

At that moment, the boys choose to make an appearance with Alaric following closely behind. Hopefully, he has calmed down enough to rejoin our little party. The boys always seem to have a calming effect on him, so my fingers are crossed.

"Here's your little sister, Aurora, and your new baby cousin, Kayne, is right over there," Phoebe says, holding out Aurora and then pointing to Kayne.

The boys are obviously excited, their eyes bouncing between both before deciding to greet Aurora first by placing soft kisses on her head and whispering sweet nothings into her ear. They tell her how much they already love her and will protect her for the rest of their lives. Since she's a girl and most likely a phoenix shifter, chances are that she will be the one protecting them, but I don't say anything. I don't want to ruin the mood.

They both turn as one, and they walk over to where Kayne and I sit.

"Hi, baby Kayne," Ryker whispers and places a soft kiss on his head as well.

Riley just looks up in my eyes and says, "Aunt Skar, when you're feeling better, we need to learn more magic to protect our new babies."

Oh, my mother, that is the cutest fucking thing I've ever heard.

I go to respond, but it's my mother who replies, choosing that moment to walk in.

"I will train you for the time being, boys. We need to give Skarlyt and Kayne time to settle into their new lives."

A quick look of disappointment flashes on their faces before they smile and nod at her. I know they love my mother, but the few times she's helped with their training, it's gotten a little out of control. She needs to remember that they are only half witches and have only been training for the past eight months, unlike most their age who start training as soon as they can, usually around four years old. Sure, they are also half phoenix, but boys normally don't inherit the phoenix genes. She tries to train them the same way she trained Sebastyn and I, which, I'll admit, worked. We both now have impressive control over our magic, but we detested our mother for a few years because of her rigorous training schedule and high expectations.

I think she is just a little impatient, wanting results faster than they're capable of delivering. I feel for them and understand what they're going through, so I decide to pump up their spirits a little.

"It won't take us long, boys. We'll be back to doing our lessons in no time."

This seems to satisfy them, and everyone looks around at each other, aware of the tension between my mother and me.

"I think it's time for my daughter and I to have a little talk. Would you all excuse us?" she says to the room, before coming up and putting her arms out for her grandson and helping me to my feet.

Man, Phoebe's tears really did the trick. I don't feel any pain at all in my nether regions. I've heard and seen horror stories as I did research for my own impending labor. In the videos I've watched and the books I've read about childbirth, after-care for the mother is explained in painfully great detail. They said that the bleeding and pain can last for up to six weeks—depending on how rough the birth was—and I was not looking forward to that.

My mother leads me to the couch in the sitting room just off my bedroom in Alaric's basement. I sit down, relishing the feel of how this couch sucks me right in, like a blanket wrapping itself around me. She takes a seat in the matching chair across from me, and we look at each other for a few minutes in an awkward silence.

"Mom, I can ex—" I start at the same time as my mom says, "What were you think..." I know this is going to be an argument, and I really don't have the energy for it right now. I raise my hand hoping that she'll let me go first, and she nods.

"Mom, I don't have the energy to have the argument that we are clearly going to have tonight, so I'm going to say my piece and go to bed. You can think of all the things you want to say to me overnight and tell me in the morning. Okay?"

At her nod, I continue.

"First of all, I wasn't deliberately trying to keep this from you. I was ashamed and embarrassed. I ran into Kirnon at Supernatural while Alaric was down at Josh's mating ceremony, and we had what I thought was one last night together. I didn't know until after it was done, he was my mate, and I most certainly didn't expect him to reject me on the same night. I was hurt, and I didn't want to be a burden to you or Alaric again like last time." I dip my head in shame momentarily before continuing. "And if I'm honest, I didn't want to hear the 'I told you so' comments that I'm sure are still going to happen.

"I was sick for a couple months and missed a couple of periods, but I thought it was just the stress of the rejection. Maybe I was in denial, but it doesn't matter now. Once I found out I was pregnant, I was already five months along, and just didn't know how to tell any of you."

I let out a small sigh, letting my exhausted muscles relax. "Looking back now, I realize that it would have been better if I would've just come clean and told someone about all of this, especially you and Alaric. I can't go back in time and change that, though. I can only move forward with Kayne and begin my new life as a mom and rejected mate."

By the time I finish my spiel to my mom, the tears are trekking down my face. I know it's probably just the post-baby hormones since I'm not usually a crier.

Instead of remaining angry with me, her face softens. She looks down at Kayne before coming to stand in front of me, kneeling down while placing him in my arms and raising her own to hold my face.

"Oh, baby. You could never be a burden to me. Or Alaric, for that matter. We love you. We probably would have said 'what the hell were you thinking?', but we will always support you no matter what. Do I think you should have told us? Absolutely. Does it change how we view you or this gorgeous boy in your arms? Not a chance.

"Honey, I knew you were pregnant, or at least was pretty sure you were. The goddess came to me in a dream last night and told me to stay close to you this evening. She said that you would bring a most precious gift into the world. I just want to help you however I can and however you'll have me. You're going to be tired and need help, even if you won't ask for it, and I will be here."

My tears aren't just trekking down my face now. It's like Niagara Falls is flowing out of my eyes. I knew in my heart that my mom would be like this. She's always supported me. It was my own pride that was hurt when Kirnon rejected me, and it was my own embarrassment I didn't want to face.

"Oh, Mom," I say and throw my one available arm around her in an embrace, sandwiching Kayne in between us.

She wipes my tears off my cheeks and stands, doing the same on her own face.

"All right, let me go magic up the room really quick to make it suitable for the little prince, and I'll be right back," she tells me and heads toward my bedroom door.

Kayne starts fussing a little, and I adjust him so that he can latch onto my nipple, which he does easily. Oh, man. This is not how I expected tonight to go. I thought I'd have a couple more weeks to get prepared, but how prepared can you really be?

"Welcome to the world, my beautiful boy. I will love and protect you until my last breath. You are loved more than you know," I whisper to Kayne as he sucks, his eyes rolling closed.

I just sit there and watch him, my perfect baby boy. Ten fingers, ten toes, beautiful straight black hair, piercing blue eyes, and looking like the spitting image of his father. I'm going to raise him to respect the mother's choice in mate, however, unlike his father.

"It's all set for our little man," my mom says a few moments later, as she comes walking out of my bedroom with a giant grin on her face. Walking into my room, I'm blown away. Usually, I have a small workroom attached to my modest bedroom down here. Now, my workroom is almost double its normal size and so is my bedroom. My normal queen-size bed is now a double with another double bed off to the side. I'm assuming that's for my mom. I can see that she has already set up a rail on one side of my bed, knowing that Kayne will be sleeping with me. She didn't even bother to magic up a crib. In the corner, she has fitted the top of my dresser with a changing table.

Tears form in my eyes for the umpteenth time tonight with gratitude for this wonderful woman. I understand better now that I'm her baby just like Kayne is mine, and I should've shared my struggles with her in the same way I'll expect Kayne to share his with me. It's crazy how being a mom for a few hours can make you look at the rest of your life so differently. I can see now why my mom did certain things that I didn't exactly agree with. I hope I

F D Fair

can be half the mother to Kayne that my mom was, and still is, to me. I'm one lucky witch.

"Knock, knock," Phoebe calls from the doorway, and I turn to see her standing there with a box of diapers with some baby-blue onesies on top. "We didn't know what we were having, so we have a ton of boy clothes upstairs for you and figured you could use some diapers as well."

My mom rushes forward, taking the box from her.

"Thank you, Pheebs," I gush, tears still trailing down my damp cheeks.

"And I have some wipes and other stuff in here for you," Alaric adds, walking in behind Phoebe.

I look up into his eyes, expecting to see the lingering anger simmering there, but there's none. All that's left is...I'm not sure. I've never seen him look at me like that before. Phoebe pats his arm.

"Constance, could you come help me with something in the kitchen, please?" She doesn't even try to make a good excuse, giving me a quick squeeze and kissing Alaric on the cheek before she and my mother walk out the door.

"I'm sorry," both Alaric and I say at the same time, causing us both to chuckle.

"Can I hold my nephew?" he asks, and I smile, walking over and placing him in his arms.

"I'm sorry for how I reacted, Skar. I shouldn't have gotten so angry," he begins.

"Alaric. You had every right to be angry. I kept this huge secret from you for months and lied to you when you asked me about the heartbeats. I just didn't want to be a burden to you again...Not after all you did for me the first time Kirnon walked away."

"Skarlyt," he growls, walking closer to me. "You were never a burden. You've been there for me just as much as I've been there for you. You were the one who helped me after my parents' acci-

54

dent. You were the one who consoled me after Zeke ran away and Axel withdrew." He adjusts Kayne so that he's resting in the crook of his right arm and reaches up gently, wiping away my tears. "You are the strongest woman I know." I raise an eyebrow at him, and he chuckles. "You are *one* of the strongest women I know, but you shouldn't have to face everything on your own. You have me, Phoebe, your mom. Hell, I know for a fact that if Sebastyn knew what was going on, he'd be here in a second. No matter what you think, we will do anything for you and never feel like you are a burden."

I nod my head. "I know. It's just so embarrassing. I let him do this to me a second time. How could I have been so stupid?"

"You are not stupid. Naive? Sometimes. Curious? All the time. But never stupid."

"Thanks, Alaric." I gently slip my arms around his neck, holding him close without squishing Kayne. When I step back, I gently pick Kayne back up, settling him in my arms. "You should go be with your mate and new daughter." He nods, placing a kiss on the top of my head. "Oh, and tell Phoebe thank you."

He gives me a smile as he heads out the door, back up to his new family, and Kayne and I snuggle into our bed and quickly fall asleep. I hear my mom creep in a few moments later. She stops at the side of my bed, gently pushing a strand of hair off my face and running her fingers down my cheek before doing the same to Kayne. I keep my eyes closed, feigning sleep, and hear her whisper.

"You are the best thing that's ever happened to me, Skarlyt Moon. The goddess was right. You gave me the best gift I could ever ask for. I love you both so much." She leans down, gently placing a kiss on my head before she settles into her own bed.

I want to respond, but emotions clog my throat. Maybe tomorrow I won't be as emotional...

One can only hope.

Chapter Six

Lennox

Pulling up to the Westwood pack is like breathing the first breath of fresh air in twelve years. Having to live in the pack where your true mate rejected you so she could mate with the beta has been hell, and that's putting it mildly.

After finding out during my last trip home that my family decided to join another pack, I was skeptical, worried that they were trading one horrible alpha for another. Though my parents tried to reassure me that was not the case, my own experience interacting with other alphas proves differently, but when my sisters finally called and told me that they transferred to the Westwood pack in Parry Sound, I finished up my contract for the oil fields in Alberta and flew here to see for myself. If I have to, I'll continue to travel and work as a lone wolf before I would ever return to the Ironwood pack, especially now that I have no familial ties there. Not as long as I have breath in me—I'm not that self-destructive.

I look around my hopefully new home. It's gorgeous here, with so much wooded area to run in. Everyone looks so friendly too. Each new person I drive by sends a small wave my way. This is starting to look really promising and vastly different from the Iron-wood pack.

Coming to the end of the drive, I can see now why Charleigh described it as a mini-community. There are small wooden cabins set back into the woods all over the place. It looks like they just grew naturally into the forest. How fucking cool is that? I pass by a small building that looks like a general store and another that looks something like a doctor's office. It's smart. Because of our enhanced healing and abilities, it's almost impossible to find a doctor that understands how to properly treat a shifter. Having a doctor in the pack is a huge plus in my books. It definitely doesn't hurt that said doctor is my baby sister Felicia. Unlike in the Iron-wood pack, here she will have her own clinic and treat all super-naturals—at least that is what she told me.

I pull up in front of the biggest cabin where Charleigh told me to meet her. I take another glance around, realizing that for the first time, there is no anxiety pooling in my stomach. I can't remember a time where I didn't feel some sort of nervousness pulling into pack territory. It seems that Beta Matteo and Alpha Christian have called every pack in Canada and told them all kinds of untruths about me, saying that I'm a liar and a thief, and that I tried to steal his mate from him. He, of course, leaves out the fact that she is my true mate. Thus, my reception at every pack I visit has been negative. The last pack I met in Alberta all but banned me from even shifting. They would only allow my wolf to run one day a month so that their wolves wouldn't be tainted by mine. I couldn't even explain the truth. What is my word against that of a pack beta or alpha?

Feminine squealing causes me to snap my attention toward the door of the cottage where I see both of my sisters running toward me. Goddess, it's good to see them. I didn't realize that I missed them so much. Hopefully, I don't need to leave them again any time soon, especially with my new niece being here.

As I hop out of my car, I am immediately tackled by both of my sisters at once. "Lennox," they cry out, jumping up and down without letting me go. I let them have their moment. I know they missed me just as much as I missed them. Over the past twelve years, I haven't seen them as often as I should have because of Olivia, and I'm determined to make up for lost time as long as I am able.

"Okay, girls, I missed you too," I say, chuckling to them. They both step back.

"I'm so glad you're finally here. Would you like to meet your niece?" Charleigh asks, as if that is even a valid question. Of course, I want to meet her.

"Lead the way," I tell her, and she takes my hand, leading me up to the cottage where I can see Ashton walking onto the porch holding a beautiful baby girl. Oh, my gods, she is too adorable...

I can't help but be envious that my younger sister not only has a mate who loves her unconditionally as the goddess intended but also started a family before me. I'm all for it if the result is this gorgeous little girl, though.

Ashton hands me the tiny bundle without a word, and I reach out to meet him, pulling Cybil into my arms. She has the most beautiful white-blonde hair and almost gray-blue eyes. She bears a striking resemblance to Charleigh at this age.

I still remember the day my parents brought her home. I was turning three in two weeks and my mother sat me down on the couch, handing me this little baby wrapped in a pink blanket. When her eyes opened and she wrapped her little hand around my finger, my heart stopped beating for myself. Instead, it beat for her. I knew then that there wasn't anything in the world I wouldn't do for her.

"Cybil, meet your Uncle Lennox," Charleigh says, looking between me and her daughter in my arms.

I can't help the swell of my heart as it fills with love for her. I am making a vow to myself to cherish her for the rest of my life. I don't know if I will ever get the chance to have one of my own, so she will be my surrogate daughter. I'm going to drive Charleigh crazy with the amount that I spoil her, but it's my right as her only uncle.

I notice Phoebe and a large man walking out of the door just moments later, Phoebe holding a little bundle of her own.

"Hey, Pheebs. It's good to see you," I say to her before she passes her baby to her mate and rushes over to give me a hug, sandwiching Cybil in between us.

"Hey, Lennox. Long time, no see," she responds.

Goddess, it really has been a long time. When Charleigh and Phoebe were younger, they were inseparable. There wasn't a family trip that Phoebe didn't come on with us. Every time Phoebe's family went on a camping trip, it seemed there was an open invitation for Charleigh to go with them too. They were together so much that it felt like Phoebe was a third little sister to me. I take a deep inhale and scent her.

She smells like fire and air—that's the only way I can describe it. I don't know how I missed her scent when we were younger. Maybe because she hadn't shifted yet? My parents wouldn't tell me what she was, but Charleigh and Felicia? They had no problem talking a mile a minute about Phoebe and her new powers. Finding out that she is a phoenix shifter was unbelievable. How did we never notice some of her mannerisms? The protectiveness over the people she cared about, her emotional response to social interactions, and physical contact being almost like a drug to her. Looking back now, there were a lot of signs, but we just passed it off as her personality traits.

The enormous shifter walking out with Phoebe steps up as we separate, holding his hand out to me.

"I'm Alaric. Alpha of Westwood pack and Phoebe's mate. Not necessarily in that order," he says, causing everyone to laugh out loud. "You're welcome to stay as long as you want, and you're more than welcome to petition to join us here.

"Your sisters told me a little of your old pack and the issues there, so please know that you are welcome, especially since your parents moved here a few months ago. I planned to say that we should give it a trial period since you've been a lone wolf for so long, but I'm afraid Charleigh and Phoebe might murder me in my sleep, so the offer stands."

Now that is funny. I could totally see them both doing exactly that in order to get their way.

"We wouldn't murder you in your sleep," Phoebe says, looking to Charleigh.

Charleigh nods, looking proud and adds, "We'd just torture you for a few weeks until you gave in."

Now, everyone on the porch is laughing as if that was a joke. I'm sure everyone here knows that it wasn't, and that they can go to extreme lengths in order to get their way. When those two get together, they can do great things. Sometimes evil things, but still great.

"That is very much appreciated. I agree to a trial," I tell him. "You're right. I have been a lone wolf for a long time and don't know how well I'll fit in with a pack anymore. Even if this pack isn't a good fit, I won't be returning to Morpeth or to the Ironwood pack. I didn't think I'd ever get another option, so thank you," I say, looking Alaric in the eyes. "And who is this little angel?" I ask, gesturing to the bundle now back in Phoebe's arms.

"This is Aurora, and the other two little monkeys over there are Ryker and Riley," Phoebe beams with pride as she nods toward the two boys playing on the porch swing off to the side, who both shoot me a wave. I've met them before when I ran into Phoebe in town when I was home for the holidays, but they look so different now. They are taller, of course, but they look healthier and happier too. I give them a short wave back and a soft smile.

With introductions out of the way, Charleigh suggests we head over to their cabin to get settled in. I say a quick goodbye to Phoebe and Alaric and promise not to be a stranger.

What a strange alpha. Not a bad strange, just different. I've never had an alpha who seems so laid back.

"Is he always that cool?" I ask Charleigh and Ashton as we walk.

"Oh, yeah. He's different from Alpha Christian. You'll get used to it," Ashton says before opening the door to the quaint cottage.

"I got that impression. Mom and Dad tried to tell me that as well, but I've met a lot of alphas over the years on my travels, and despite everyone telling me those so-called alphas were different, they never were."

Charleigh spins around and looks at me. "Do you think Phoebe would be with someone who was like Alpha Christian?" Her nose wrinkles in disgust.

"To be fair, Char, I haven't seen Phoebe in years. The last time I saw her, she was married to Tanner. Chances are she is very different from the girl I used to know."

"That's true, but trust me, she's the same Phoebe, just older and sometimes wiser," Charleigh chuckles.

"Take it from me, Alaric is nothing like my father," Ashton growls when he says the word father. It's strange to hear him call Alpha Christian that, even though our family has known that secret since before his mating to Charleigh. I have never heard him call Christian "father" even once. My mouth pops open in shock.

"If you are sure, Ash, I trust your judgment. After all, no one knows the cruelness of Alpha Christian better than you."

I glance around the house as we walk further inside. It's a lot smaller than the house they had on Ironwood pack lands. For some reason though, it feels more lived in, more homey. It's got an open layout kitchen, living, and dining room. There are baby toys spread throughout.

"Let me give you a tour," Charleigh says, leading me toward the hallway at the back.

She points out two bedrooms, her and Ashton's on the left, and a guest bedroom for me on the right with my own en suite bathroom. Awesome. Not that I'm thrilled to be right across the hall from my little sister and her mate, but beggars can't be choosers.

After living in group housing for the last twelve years straight, having my own bathroom is a privilege I will never take for granted again. Besides, if I decide to join the pack, maybe I can build my own little cabin somewhere around here...preferably in a more secluded area. I know Charleigh picked to live as close to Phoebe as possible. Those two were joined at the hip when younger. After so much time apart, I would expect them to be the same—if not worse— as they try to make up for lost time.

Cybil's room is on the left, with an adjoining bathroom to Charleigh and Ashton's room. It has baby-pink walls with little wolves painted all over it. As I look closer, I realize that I recognize the wolves, a white one for Charleigh, a black one for Ashton, a gray one for Felicia, and a rust colored one for me. They're all close together, forming a small pack.

I don't know how the fur of the wolf is picked when we shift for the first time, but somehow all three of us got different colored wolves. Our dad is a gray wolf, and our mom is white with a black patch on her chest, so I have no clue where our colors came from. I also know that I'm one of the few rust-colored wolves I've heard of, and I've met quite a few wolves over the years.

"That's us, right?" I turn to ask her.

"Yup. We're going to add Mom, Dad, Alaric, Phoebe, the boys, and Josh in eventually, but we wanted to make sure that we got us in there first."

I nod as I turn away from her, hoping to hide the misting in my eyes. It's so nice to be with my family again. I've been alone for so long...I just want a home. Somewhere I can set down roots, maybe take a chosen mate and raise a few pups if Mother Moon deems me worthy.

A feeling of peace settles over me as I drop my bag in my room. I've only been here for a few minutes, but somehow this place feels right...like this is where I am supposed to be.

"I'm going to go see Mom and Dad. Can you point me in the direction of their house?" I call out to Charleigh as I step out of the room and walk toward the front door.

"I'll walk you. They only live a few houses down. I didn't tell them you were coming," she says with a smirk.

I smile in return. "I didn't either. I was hoping it would be a surprise."

"It will. You should see how happy they are here, Lennox. It's like night and day. Not that they ever showed us how unhappy they were, but it's like a weight I never realized was resting on their shoulders is gone. Mom is working for Felicia at the pack clinic as her receptionist, and Dad has been helping out with local maintenance at the pack buildings."

"I thought they were going to retire?"

"As if those two would ever retire," she scoffs. "You know what they're like. They love to be busy."

True to her word, we walk for only five minutes, passing a few small homes along the way before stopping in front of a modest sized cottage. It's built much the same as the rest, out of natural wood, but this one has a beautiful covered porch sporting the old porch swing and bistro set I remember from Morpeth. As we walk up the steps, I scent both of my parents. My wolf thumps his tail happily, knowing that we are with our family once more.

"Honey, I'm home, and I found someone on my way over," Charleigh yells as she opens the front door and walks in without knocking.

"Is it Cybil?" My mom yells, rushing toward us from a room toward the back of the house.

She stops when she sees me before rushing into my arms.

"Hi, Mom," I whisper, emotion clogging my throat. It's been over eight months since I've seen her. I didn't realize just how much I missed her hugs until I was being crushed by her embrace.

"Oh, Lennox. I'm so glad you're here finally."

"Lennox?" My dad calls, heading straight for me as well. He wraps both my mom and me up in his arms.

He pats me on the back as he steps back. "How long are you staying?"

I look at Charleigh and then back to my parents. I haven't told either of them that I put my notice in and will not be returning to my job in Alberta because I didn't want to get their hopes up. But after being here, even if only for a short while, I know I made the right decision.

"As long as I fit in well with the pack...indefinitely. But even if I don't, I'm sticking around this area and will find a job so I can stay close."

My mother's eyes tear up, and she wraps her arms back around me while my dad beams at me.

"I could use a second set of hands with all the new builds and maintenance around the pack," my dad offers, "or your sisters could use some help at their clinics."

"Clinics, as in plural?" I ask, spinning to look at Charleigh.

She smiles. "Yeah, I'm a social worker and was a school counselor back in Morpeth, so I opened my own clinic here right beside Felicia for all supernaturals. After the attacks, we realized it would be good for everyone to be able to talk to someone about it who understands. That's one of the best things about Alaric and this pack...I don't just treat shifters and pack members. I can accept any supernatural patient."

All supernaturals? I have never heard of a wolf pack socializing with other species. The shock must show on my face because my mom chuckles.

"We told you this pack and Alaric were different."

"You did," I nod. "I guess I just didn't realize how different."

My mom leads us into the living room, and we all settle in, talking and laughing. At some point, Ashton, Cybil, Felicia, and Josh show up, joining in on our family time.

For a few moments, I just sit there and glance around the room at everyone...at my family, and dammit if it doesn't feel just amazing.

Chapter Seven

Skarlyt

It's been a week since my beautiful boy was born. I'm utterly exhausted. Even with the help of my mom, it seems like the only time Kayne settles is when he's in my arms. Not that I mind. I love his snuggles. The way he looks up at me like I'm the only person in the world is like nothing I've ever experienced. Each night, before I fall asleep, I thank the gods that they gave me this perfect little boy and think there's no way I can possibly love this tiny human more than I do right now. But then I wake up the next morning, and it's like my heart grew ten sizes overnight to make room for me to love him more.

The morning after he was born, a churning began in my stomach at the thought of Kirnon finding out about him. I've tried with everything I have to push those negative feelings away but can't. I'm not normally one to ignore my gut feelings...but surely Kirnon would never hurt him...Right? He's Kayne's father.

I know that Charleigh and Felicia's brother arrived today, and I should be up there greeting him with them, but I just can't get the motivation to leave my safe haven. With my worries about Kirnon, I haven't left Alaric's basement since he was born, and I don't plan to anytime soon. I don't want to risk it. Why? I'm not sure. I just can't shake the feeling that it's important to keep Kayne away from his father...

I tried explaining my irrational feelings to my mom and friends...only they don't seem to think they're irrational. Both Alaric and my mom are clouded by the hate they hold for Kirnon and truly believe he could be a threat to my happily ever after. They have gone as far as telling me to wait to register the birth until we have a solid plan in place. Alaric's current plan is listing himself as the father. That way even if Kirnon were to find out about Kayne, he may just think he's Alaric's son. I thought for sure Phoebe would've had my back when I said no to that plan, but she surprised me by agreeing. Maybe I'm not the one who has gone crazy...maybe it's all of them. As if anyone who actually knows us would believe Alaric and I would...Nope. Can't even think about it.

Surprisingly, my mom has been really great about the whole "locking myself in the basement" thing. She hasn't been pushing me to do anything I don't want to do—like leave this room—and is helping in any way that she can. On top of helping me out with Kayne as much as possible—changing diaper and clothes—she's also taken over my lessons with the boys and selling my stockpile of creams, lotions and potions.

At least I had the forethought to make and store everything in bulk so my income wouldn't dwindle after Kayne was born. It's too bad I didn't think about buying the essentials for when he was born. I was sure I had more time. That's me...procrastinator extraordinaire. My mom, though, has been a godsend. She's even gone as far as bringing my meals down to make sure I'm eating. Even Phoebe and Alaric seem to understand. They've brought Aurora down to spend some time with us too.

I don't know why I'm feeling like this, but I have the overwhelming urge to protect Kayne. I want to wrap him in a protective barrier until he's old enough to understand the situation with his dad and protect himself. Wait, maybe that's possible.

I put a sleeping Kayne down on the bed alone for one of the first times since he was born and rush to my workroom to see if there is a spell I can use for protection. I run through what I need it to do......I need to make one that keeps him safe, specifically from his dad. I don't know how well it will work. I know there are spells to protect you from outside forces, like charms and talismans, a simple bracelet can be spelled to do just about anything. I don't know if a generic protection spell will work on him though. Since Kirnon's blood runs through his veins, the link between them could be too strong, but I have to try.

I'm scouring through grimoires, ripping them down from the shelf, thumbing through them before tossing them into the useless pile, when my mom walks in.

"What are you looking for?" she asks.

"I'm looking for a protection spell for Kayne to keep him safe from Kirnon. I don't know why, but I have this gut feeling that he needs it, Mom," I respond.

She nods. "You know my take on that situation. I would never want to keep a child away from his father, but it's different with Kirnon. After what he did when you were younger and then what he did now..." A pang slices through my heart, lingering pains from his rejection, and her voice softens when she sees my distress. "If you have the feeling in your gut, it's usually for a good reason. The goddess works in mysterious ways and wouldn't lead you astray."

Whew. I'm so glad she doesn't think my idea is crazy. I mean, I know I'm the normal kind of crazy. Fun crazy. I know I can be hard to talk to because I jump from topic to topic. I am also slightly obsessed with vampires. Other than that? Totally sane.

Like, really. Why do they prefer drinking from someone's neck? I get that there is a big vein there, but there are more discrete places with large veins on the body to drink from—like the inner thigh. Also, what is it about drinking blood that gets them all hot and bothered? Like I *love* food, but every vampire that I've asked—which has been a lot—has either told me they get extremely horny while feeding or have told me to fuck off. Okay, I'm getting distracted again.

Instead of saying anything else, my mom just places a sandwich in front of me and starts going through the grimoires as well. I'm surprised she hasn't brought up that I didn't go up and meet with Charleigh and Felicia's brother. She's the one who taught me it was bad manners not to greet a new guest, so I am expecting a lecture.

"You know...I saw Charleigh and Felicia's brother, he's quite handsome," she says, and I groan. I knew the silence was too good to be true.

Nonetheless, her comment makes me wonder if he is "handsome," as my mother called him, or "hot." I've heard his sisters and Phoebe talk about how laid back and cool he is. I am also finding myself curious if he has a mate already or if he's still waiting.

Wait, why am I thinking that? I'm swearing off men. After the number that Kirnon did to me—not once, but twice—how can I ever trust another man again? I can't. That's the simple answer. I can trust that little boy sleeping in the other room, Sebastyn, Darren, and Alaric, but that's it. Even Ashton, as nice as he seems, isn't on my "men to trust" list. I guess the boys can be added to that list too. Can't leave out my little munchkins, even though they technically aren't men yet.

Despite who and what their father was, Phoebe has done such an amazing job of raising them to be sweet and caring. I can only hope Kayne turns out half as good as those two.

Kayne starts crying and I turn to go to him, but my mom holds up a hand and heads off into the bedroom. She comes back a minute later with Kayne in her arms.

"I think he's hungry," she says, handing him to me. He probably is. *Typical man,* I chuckle to myself. He's always hungry. It's why I'm so exhausted. Who knew that a baby would eat this much? He wakes me up every two hours like clockwork. I can't wait until he sleeps through the night. Although my mom keeps reminding me that this time will go by too fast and that I'm going to miss it, I can't imagine it. When I watch her with Kayne, I can see that is how she feels about my brother and me.

I sit in the rocking chair in the corner, adjusting myself so that Kayne and I are both comfy while he feeds. This breast-feeding thing is getting easier each time. My nipples start to feel raw after he's fallen asleep while latched on, but most of the time, it's not bad. According to my mom, I'm "letting him use my boob as a pacifier." She's probably right, but it's going to have to do until I can actually go to the store to get one.

I can tell my mom is debating saying something. She's fidgeting with the books, so I say, "Out with it."

"Well, I was thinking. If you are having such a strong gut feeling about Kirnon, maybe we should reinforce the protection barrier around the pack and coven."

Hey. That's not a half bad idea. At least Kayne would be safe while on our land, and I wouldn't have to worry about it not working.

"You'll have to specifically include Kirnon in the barrier spell. I'm not sure how it will work because he was once a member of this pack. His bonds may still be there, even if only faintly." She just nods before gathering her materials and heading out the door, telling me she's going to get some of the coven elders to help her with the spell.

At least I will actually be able to sleep soundly tonight, knowing he can't get through the barrier. I've heard about mates being able to feel each other's pain, even from far distances. I don't know how that works since he rejected me, but if there's even a chance that he felt the labor pains, I don't want him coming for us. I want to make sure he can't get to either of us.

I know he's the father of my child and deserves to know that he has a son. I had every intention to make sure he knew and was involved. Just because he's a shitty mate doesn't mean he'll be a shitty father, but I just can't shake this feeling. I wouldn't have this feeling for no reason. It could just be my crazy ass making it up because of postpartum emotions. I hope I am; I don't want to believe that Kirnon would hurt either of us, but the truth is I'm not sure if I ever truly knew him in the first place. After everything he's done to me, I can see now that he's obviously not a very good person.

After feeding Kayne, I walk back to the bedroom, going through the motions, burping, changing, and getting him dressed before we curl up on my bed together. I glance at the TV and think about bingeing a show but decide against it, pulling out a book instead and reading him a story. Today, I decide on the story of the three little pigs. He flails his arms around and begins cooing when I make the voice of the wolf.

I'm just about done with the story when he starts fussing. I gently pick him up and rock him. There's no way he can be hungry again so soon, but I try anyway. For the first time ever, he doesn't even attempt to latch on and just continues his wailing. I stand up and begin to pace, talking to him, telling him how much he's loved and that it's okay, but nothing seems to be working.

"Knock, knock," Phoebe says as she enters the room holding Aurora, and Kayne instantly settles, reaching his arms out toward them.

"Hey. I think you must have a magic voice. I couldn't get him to settle until he heard you."

"Aurora was the same upstairs. I couldn't figure out what she wanted until I walked close to the basement stairs. She would settle more the closer we got. Maybe they just miss each other," Phoebe says with a smile, coming and taking a seat on the couch.

I smile back at her and move to sit next to her. "How are things up there?" I ask, pointing to the ceiling.

She laughs and shakes her head. "They're good. You would know if you joined the land of the living every once in a while."

My head falls, "I just can't yet."

She places her hand on my shoulder. "I know and everyone understands why." She lets out a sigh. "It's just you can't live down here forever. We need to figure this out."

I nod, turning sideways on the couch, pulling my legs up underneath me. "My mom is actually working on that right now. She seems to think that we can tweak the barrier spell to include Kirnon so that he can't come on any lands tied to the pack or coven."

She perks up. "Really? Will that work?"

"At the very least, it will warn us when he's approaching to give me time to hide Kayne. Although I don't understand why he would come back here at all."

"Alaric seems to think he will. From what he knows of shifters rejecting their mates, the inner animal almost always disagrees with the rejection and causes problems for the human."

"He really thinks that?"

Phoebe nods. "Yeah. Although he made me promise not to tell you, so don't say anything."

My mouth opens in shock. "He didn't want you to tell me?" Anger and hurt lace my voice.

"It's not that he didn't want you to know; it's that he's worried about you and doesn't want you to stress about this stuff any more than you already are."

Some of my anger fades at her words. I can understand his reasoning even if I don't like it. "Does he think he will hurt Kayne?"

"He doesn't know. Alaric says that when a wolf detaches or is displeased with his human counterpart for long enough, the animal turns feral while the man goes crazy. So, he's not sure what, if anything, he would do."

"Why didn't I know any of this?"

Phoebe chuckles. "I asked the same thing. He said rejections in this pack are so rare that no one thinks to talk about it. The only reason he remembered is that one happened when he was a little boy, and it was his dad who recognized the shifter's wolf going feral and researched it."

I nod, thinking for a minute about when that could have been...Nothing comes to mind, so maybe it was one of those things that was only dealt with by the pack and the coven wasn't involved.

"Any other changes in the 'land of the living'?" I ask, changing the subject.

"Gran's back on her way to Alberta," Phoebe moves a stray curl away from her face as she looks apologetically toward Kayne. "She wanted to say goodbye, but she had to leave before sunrise."

"Why? What happened?" My anxiety—never far from the surface these days—tries to latch onto some sign in Phoebe's face or tone as evidence that something is amiss.

"Nothing happened," Phoebe assures me. "At least nothing recent. She had been waiting to go back and make sure everyone there understood the mage threat. What did she say? 'I hate to deliver and run' and 'now that the next generation of trouble-makers is here safe, I've got somewhere I need to be.'"

"She's a busy lady," I chuckle. "Charleigh and Felicia's brother is here already?" I ask, trying to distract Phoebe from any talk of mages.

"Lennox? Yeah. He, Charleigh, Ashton, and Cybil just went back to her place. I wish you would've come up to meet him; I have a feeling you two are going to get along really well."

"If my mom comes through with this barrier spell, I promise I will." And I mean it. Ever since Charleigh first mentioned her brother, there was something about him that made me curious. It may have been the way she talked about him or what she was saying, I'm not sure.

"Good. I hope it works. You need to get out of this room and socialize."

"We're socializing right now." I gesture between the two of us. She pins me with a glare.

"You know what I mean."

"Yeah, I do," I agree.

I hear the doorbell ring in the distance.

"Oh, that must be our new kitchen table," Phoebe perks up at the noise. "After the other day, everyone refuses to eat at the table saying it's gross even though I've scrubbed it down."

I chuckle. "You have a couple of babies on it and suddenly it's not suitable to eat off anymore."

"Right?" she laughs before standing up and heading to the door with Aurora. "Try to come up for dinner? It will be the first meal at the new table..." She teases.

"I'll try." I tell her although I already know that if my mom hasn't completed the spell, there's no way I'll be joining them upstairs tonight.

With a nod, she breezes out of the room with her daughter bundled in her arms.

"Come on, little man, let's go watch TV." I whisper to Kayne, moving us from the couch to the bed to get comfy for the night.

Chapter Eight

Lennox

I wake up the next morning after spending the night laughing and joking with my family, and a smile crosses my face. When was the last time I laughed that hard? When was the last time I had any sort of fun? I wrack my brain trying to think and come up empty. My smile slips, morphing into a frown.

Has it really been that long since I was happy? I thought I was content with my job. Heck, I enjoyed it most of the time, but after work? The more I think about the last decade of my life, the more I realize that I haven't been living. I've been going through the motions of each day: work, eat, sleep, rinse, and repeat.

"Come on, sleepyhead, we're going for a run," Charleigh singsongs, throwing my door open.

"A run?"

She nods. "Yup. You, me, Mom, Dad, and Felicia are going on a run like old times."

And just like that, the smile is back on my face. I jump out of bed like it's on fire, rushing to the bathroom to do my business while Charleigh laughs and walks away.

By the time I'm done brushing my teeth and getting dressed,

my extremely impatient sister is griping and groaning about how long it takes me to get ready.

"We're going for a run, not to the club," she groans.

"It took me less than ten minutes, Char. Geeze, slow your roll," I say as I walk out of the bedroom, still pulling on my shirt.

I stop next to Ashton where he's holding Cybil. "Soon, beautiful girl, you'll be coming on the runs with us and your daddy too," I coo to her, placing a soft kiss on her head. She giggles at me, and I blow a raspberry on her cheek. The sound of her laughter has to be one of the best things I've ever heard.

"Come on. Come on," Charleigh whines.

"I was saying goodbye to my niece. Patience is a virtue, you know."

She sticks her tongue out at me. "Obviously not one of mine."

I laugh, shaking my head and following her outside to meet our family.

As one, the five of us walk a few feet into the trees where we stop and disrobe for our shift. I spin around, a moment of panic going through me. I've kept my wolf caged up for years, only letting him out once a month to run by himself. How's he going to act around other wolves? As soon as that thought pops into my head, my wolf is there batting it away.

Family, he growls.

Yes. They are our family, I respond.

Never hurt family, he assures me, and some of my panic alleviates. I quickly shift into my rust-colored wolf.

I turn around to search out my family and spot the four of them sitting there waiting for me. My wolf walks up to each of them, nuzzling their necks and rubbing up against them with a whine.

Ready? Charleigh asks through our familial bond, and my head darts to her. When was the last time I heard someone speak to me through a bond? It's been a while, that's for sure.

Without responding, I turn my body and break out in a sprint.

More ready than you, I chuckle at her.

Charleigh, Felicia, and I duck and weave through the trees, pouncing on one another while our parents trot behind us, giving us time to play. I needed this. I don't remember the last time I was this happy. The only time I truly had 'fun' in the last several years was once a month when I was allowed to run as a wolf, and even then, it was always alone, never with a group.

If you stay, you may be able to actually catch up someday, Felicia pipes in through our bond, making me think that I may have broadcasted that last bit to her.

We will see how this goes. No promises that I'll join the pack, but I won't go far again, I tell her, and she comes up, nuzzling my left side while Charleigh comes and does the same to the right. I was worried before I got here that since they both have mates, it would be different than it was when we were younger, that I might feel like the fifth—or even seventh, if you include our parents— wheel, but I'm glad I was wrong.

A pair of black wolves step through the trees toward us, and a low growl builds in my throat while my hackles raise.

That's Alaric and Darren. They're not a threat, Charleigh says, but it doesn't settle my wolf. No. To him, they're large male wolves, getting far too close to my family. Another growl rumbles out of me, and the two wolves stop, shifting back immediately.

I recognize Alaric from meeting him earlier, and I'm going to hazard a guess that the other guy is his brother, considering they look like they could be twins.

"Sorry, Lennox. We caught a scent we didn't recognize and came to check it out. I should've realized it was you when it mixed in with the rest of your family," Alaric says calmly.

I cock my head to the side in confusion. He's the alpha. Why is he apologizing to me? Any other alpha I've met would've ripped my throat out for growling at them, whether I had control of my wolf or not, even if it was justified. Maybe everyone is right. Alaric is different.

I shift back to human so that I can talk to him. "It's me who should be apologizing. I have had to keep my wolf on a tight leash for the past twelve years and haven't interacted with other shifters in wolf form for the same amount of time. Right now, he perceives everything as a threat."

The shocked looks on both Alaric and Darren's faces are apparent, but only momentarily.

"That's horrible," Darren says before stepping toward me with his hand out. "I'm Darren, by the way."

"Lennox," I tell him as I shake his hand.

"You don't need to worry about your wolf causing any trouble here. No one will take his growls as a challenge, but it would be best if you could join us for a pack meeting and run this evening so that everyone can learn your scent and you can learn theirs."

Now it's my turn to be in shock. I'm not a member of his pack yet, so why am I being included in anything pack related?

"Are you sure, Alaric? I'm not officially a member of this pack."

He nods. "Even if you aren't an official member of this pack, you're going to be visiting your family regularly, right?" I nod at his assessment. "Besides, Phoebe and your family really want you to join this pack and how better to convince you than to immerse you into how this pack runs so you can make your decision?"

"Plus, there's always so much good food at the pack meetings. You definitely don't want to miss that," Darren adds, rubbing his flat, muscled stomach.

The three of us chuckle, and I glance around, looking for my family and not finding them. Where did they go?

"They just went to the stream to give us privacy to talk," Alaric tells me, seeing the confusion on my face and points behind me. "It's that way."

"Thanks, Alpha."

"Just Alaric. The only time I ask anyone to call me Alpha is when there are other packs present," he says, and I nod.

"Thanks, Alaric. Nice to meet you, Darren," I say to them both before shifting back into my wolf. When they do the same, my wolf takes a few tentative steps toward them, making sure to store their scents for later as they do the same.

After playing in the stream for what feels like hours with my family—more my sisters than my parents who relax on the dry land—we finally begin our trek back to the cottage.

I can tell my wolf is exhausted from the slowness of his pace and his tongue hanging out of his mouth, but I can feel the joy radiating through him. He enjoys it here too. He catches a whiff of something by a bush and lowers his snout to the ground, trying to follow it with a whine.

What is it? He doesn't answer, just continues his whining and pacing. He lets off a low howl when he loses the trail. Whatever it was that he smelled was here not too long ago, but the scent is so faint that I can't even tell what it was.

Don't worry, buddy. We'll figure out what that was, I tell him and urge him to continue following our family. He tries to protest, wanting to stay here and wait to see if the owner of that scent comes back, but he's too exhausted to fight me. We head toward the cottage. I can't help wondering what that scent is that has him so driven to find it. The way he's acting reminds me of how he acted when we first met Olivia with his overwhelming need to find the owner of the scent.

The day flies by playing with my niece and walking around the pack land, meeting as many people as I can before the run tonight. I try to catalog each person's scent as I meet them, storing them and hoping it will make my wolf feel less threatened by the other shifters.

By the time we arrive at Alaric's, the smell of barbecue has spread throughout the entire area, and I watch as each shifter has their nose in the air, letting it lead them into the back yard.

"Lennox!" Phoebe exclaims, running over to me and jumping into my arms. I hear a growl slip from behind her where Alaric is holding Aurora. She slaps him playfully. "Oh, stop. He's like my brother. I don't growl when you hug Skarlyt."

"I can't help it," he says, as he pulls her back and nuzzles her neck.

"It's okay, Pheebs. I'm an unmated male near his mate. It's natural for his wolf to be possessive. I'd be worried if he didn't growl at me," I chuckle.

"If you say so." She eyes me warily, trying to figure out if I am lying or not.

"Ask Dad," I tell her, and she turns expectantly to my dad.

"It's true, sweetheart," he says, pulling my mom in closer. "I still growl when an unmated, non-family member gets close to Rose."

My mom melts into him, nodding at Phoebe.

"But William has gotten a lot better with age."

Phoebe looks at all of us and then to Alaric. "I guess it's okay then."

"So, Lennox, your parents tell me you work in the oil sands in Alberta. What do you do out there?" Alaric asks.

"I was a heavy equipment mechanic. Basically, I just fixed all the big trucks whenever they broke down. I occasionally had to drive them too," I tell him.

"Was?" Phoebe asks, the only one to catch onto that.

"I put in my notice before I came here. As of right now, I'm unemployed, but I'm sure I'll be able to find something."

"How are you with boats?" Alaric asks.

"Um...I know how to drive one if that's what you're asking."

He nods. "What about fixing them?"

"If it has an engine, I can usually fix it." I look at him in confusion.

"The pack owns a couple resorts, and we provide boats for some of our patrons. Right now, four of our five boats are out of commission, and our pack mechanic is on leave. Would you mind taking a look at them?"

"I'd love to," I tell him with a smile on my face. I guess getting a job isn't going to be something I need to worry about. This pack is looking better and better each day...It's almost too good to be true.

A couple hours later, I'm standing on the back porch sipping a beer when Charleigh comes up beside me.

"Thinking of sticking around?"

I turn and look at her. "Thinking about it. But it feels almost too good to be true."

She nods. "I get how it seems that way, especially when you're used to Christian, but I promise you this is how it is all the time. Ask anyone here. This is the way a pack is supposed to be."

"You're right. This is how it's supposed to be," I say as I look around. There are men and women laughing and joking; some wolves have shifted and are playfully chasing after children. I look around for Alaric, wondering what he's doing. I find him easily standing in the lake, throwing kid after kid into the deeper water—all of them with huge smiles on their faces.

Next, I search out Darren. After we got back to the cottage, Felicia explained that Darren is Alaric's Beta. I'm half expecting him to be in a corner scowling at the pack like Matteo does, but I'm pleasantly surprised when that's not the case. Like his brother, Darren is playing with some of the pack kids. He's currently on all fours giving the little ones rides on his back while laughing and joking with the parents. I'm blown away. I've never in my lifetime seen a pack operate like this. So carefree. So...alive.

"All right, everyone. It's time for our run," Alaric booms out over the crowd.

"What do the kids do?" I whisper to Charleigh.

"The ones who can shift join us. Some close to their shift ride on their parents' back so that they can see what a pack run is like, but the rest all head inside the pack house with some of the moms or non-shifter members to watch over them. There's a large bunk room in the basement that Phoebe suggested we use for them when we go on pack runs so that they're all in the same place."

Every time I think there is no way this pack can shock me any more than it already has, something like this happens and I'm once again floored by the way it operates.

"And Cybil?" I ask.

"Mom and Dad offered to stay with Cybil, Ryker, and Riley so that Phoebe could shift too. Aurora is going to stay with Alaric's best friend Skarlyt." There's that name again...Skarlyt. I haven't met Alaric's mysterious friend yet. Whenever anyone says her name, it sounds like there's a secret in it that I do not understand. Not in a bad way...almost like there's an electrical current in the name that shocks me each time.

We walk down the stairs onto the soft grass. There are hundreds of us sliding out of our clothes and shifting. Within seconds there are hundreds of wolves—not humans—standing there, awaiting the commencement of the pack run.

Alaric's big black wolf turns to address the crowd, but without a pack link, I can't hear anything he's saying.

Alaric is asking the goddess to bless our run and our pack and thanking her for her love and support, Charleigh tells me through our bond.

Are there rules on the pack run? I ask her. In the Ironwood pack, if you overtook the alpha or beta during the run, it would be a severe punishment, and it didn't matter whether they were stopped or not. They stop; you stop. They run; you run. And goddess forbid if you stopped to play with another wolf.

I know exactly what you're thinking and no. If you want to pounce on Alaric during the run, chances are good that he will turn and wrestle with you. The only thing I suggest is stay away from Phoebe. If you thought that Alaric was possessive, you haven't met his wolf. I hear her chuckle through the bond and give a wolfy nod. That I can do.

Seconds later, a long, loud howl goes out from Alaric, and a flaming red phoenix launches herself into the sky. Wow. That's what Phoebe looks like shifted. That is so freaking cool.

When she lets out a loud screech, Alaric howls once again. The rest of us join in this time, and we're off.

We run for hours, every wolf staying together, running, jumping, wrestling. Each time I saw someone fall behind, one of the enforcers, Alaric, or Darren would go back and check on them.

As the night wears on, the run dissolves as older wolves retreat to their homes. Phoebe is still a distant torch in the sky when I turn to follow my family out of the woods.

I finally make it to my bed at Charleigh's, flopping down onto it. I don't even bother getting changed for bed. I'm too exhausted. After the run this morning and then tonight and all the food in between...

Yeah, I'm going to sleep hard tonight.

Chapter Nine

Skarlyt

It's been two days since my mom went to work on the barrier spell. It seems to be a lot more complicated than we originally thought. They've had to weave each spell into each other and anchor them to the four points with a crystal. I wish I could be there to watch the magic happen because this is history in the making. Instead, I've spent every second that I have available scouring through old grimoires with no luck. If there is a direct spell to protect Kayne from his father, it isn't here. There are all manner of protection spells in these old ass books—all with the same loophole. If the subject is linked either by blood or mate bond to the person they need protection from, it won't work. Which means Kayne and I are screwed. I'm not sure if the mate bond still applies to me since Kirnon rejected me, but I don't want to take any chances.

Though, this morning we found a way to link Alaric directly to the barrier spell, and since he wasn't the alpha when Kirnon was a pack member, in theory, it should work to keep him out. They will also link it to my mom, with the hope that her blood running through both Kayne and I will offer extra protection by strengthening our connection to the pack and coven instead of the connection with Kirnon.

"Please let this work," I whisper to the goddess, praying for a miracle that will allow me out of this room. I want to feel the sun on my face, hear the boys laugh, maybe even dip my toes in the water. I shuffle Kayne in my arms so that we're both more comfortable. When I can finally leave to go shopping, the first thing I'm buying is one of those baby carrier backpack things. I need my hands free so that even when he insists on being held, I can still get shit done. Maybe I should ask Phoebe if she has one I can borrow. I could've asked someone to go out shopping for me, but they're already doing so much.

I shouldn't complain. Everyone has been great, leaving me alone when I need to be left alone, talking with me when I need to talk, and holding Kayne when I need a little break. Although, each time my mom comes down, she tries to coax me out of my room with tales of how handsome Charleigh and Felicia's brother is. As if that would suddenly make me want to leave this room. Nine months ago, I would have jumped right on that. Now, he's a shifter and a man; two things that I know just can't be trusted.

"Hey, Skar. Think you can come up and watch the boys swim in the lake for a bit?" I didn't even hear Alaric come into the room. I'm either really distracted, or he was being extra sneaky. "I'll watch Aurora and Kayne for both of you. Phoebe wants to take a shower, and you can get some fresh air."

After Kayne was born, I put up powerful wards to alert me when someone "not of my blood" enters my space, but they didn't activate at Alaric's entrance. Is it because the wards recognize him as my family? I guess since this is his house and all, they probably won't work the same way.

It's not that I'd ever feel that I need warning when Alaric is around, but it proves just how difficult it will be to set this barrier around the pack and coven. If Alaric can get through my wards because of his tie to this house, Kirnon may be able to get through our barrier because of his tie to Kayne.

I know what he's doing: trying to use my munchkins to convince me to go outside. I probably should go upstairs and even venture into the fresh air if only for a few minutes. In my head, I realize that I will probably feel better if I do and having a break from Kayne will probably help as well. As much help as my mom has been, I haven't allowed her to take him out of my sight. She can hold him, bathe him, and even change him as long as she stays where I can see them. I know that's not healthy. I do. I also know that I need to start feeling more like myself than I have been the last few days. You know...maybe have a shower, wash my hair, change my clothes.

"I don't think I can, Alaric," I tell him. What? I'm being honest. I don't think I can physically make myself go up the stairs. My anxiety is through the roof just thinking about it. My palms are sweating, and my heart is pounding so hard it feels like it's going to come out of my chest. Nope. Definitely not. Can't do it.

"What if I bring Aurora down here and stay in your area with them while you watch the boys? I'll even watch him while you take a nice long shower upstairs. You can use the big bathroom after Phoebe," he coos. He's trying to convince me, and I really appreciate his consideration. To be honest, the idea of them staying down here does allay my anxiety a bit. I glance down at myself and admit that using the big shower upstairs, with its rain head and jets in the wall, sounds absolutely heavenly too. Okay, maybe I can do this. Just for thirty minutes.

"All right. All right. Only for half an hour, though. Okay?" I ask, and he nods quickly, a big smile on his face before he rushes off. He comes back a few minutes later with Aurora in his arms.

I hug Kayne a little tighter to my chest, unable to let go.

"We'll be fine, Skarlyt. I promise." I look into his eyes as he talks, the eyes of my best friend, who has never steered me wrong, who's pulled me out of more funks than I can count, the one man I know will never hurt me. I place a soft kiss on Kayne's head and gently pass him over to Alaric.

"I know you will. It's just so..." I begin, and he walks over to sit on the chair cradling a baby in each hand.

"Remember when Kirnon first left you in that hotel room, and you thought you would never be happy again?" he asks, and I nod. "And remember when you fell out of that tree and broke your wrist and said you would never be able to cast a spell again?" Again, I nod. I see what he's doing here. "Same thing with this. I understand you're concerned about Kirnon coming back, and I am too. But you can't stop living. What you're doing right now is letting him control you."

I tilt my head, thinking about that for a moment. Is that what I'm doing? Am I letting him control me without even being in my life? I let out a small sigh. That's exactly what I'm doing.

"Listen. You are a powerful witch, living in a house with the alpha and a phoenix shifter. If Kirnon was stupid enough to come here, which I don't think he would, he wouldn't get far. In this house, in the back yard, on the porch, hell even anywhere on pack land, you and Kayne are safe."

I walk over to the couch and take a seat. "I know that, Alaric. In here, I know that." I say, tapping my head. "But in here," I point to my chest, "it feels like something is coming for him that I need to protect him from. Something big, something dangerous, and my gut is telling me it's Kirnon."

"And that may very well be the case," he says, and I nod. "But...it could happen tomorrow or in ten years. We don't know. All we can do is prepare Kayne the best we can and be ready when the time comes."

"You're right."

"Wait..." He says chuckling, trying to dig through his pockets while still holding the babies.

"What are you doing?" I laugh.

"I'm trying to get my phone to record you. You just told me that I was right," he says, and I shake my head, heading out the door and up the stairs before I change my mind.

If I don't leave right now, I know I won't go. I pause at the stairs and look back toward my room. What if...? No. Nothing can get to them in there. Besides, even if someone managed to get through the wards without me knowing, they'd have to get through Alaric, and that's nearly impossible.

I can smell the fresh air before I even step out onto the deck. It smells so clean and bright, and my mood instantly starts to improve. Nothing beats the feeling I get when I step out into the sun and feel the warmth from the rays soaking into my skin. I take this opportunity to look down at myself and realize that I've been wearing the same clothes since yesterday, and I haven't showered since right after I had Kayne. I must look like complete and utter shit. In the lighting of the basement, it didn't seem so bad, but out here in the direct sunlight? I gently pull my shirt away from my chest and take a sniff. Oh goddess, why didn't anyone tell me I smelled this bad? I run my hand over my hair and feel how greasy it is. I undo my ponytail and comb through it with my fingers before putting it back up. Ugh, I really hope no one comes to the dock. I'm sure they would expect me to look a little worse for wear after delivering a baby no one knew I was having, but this is pretty bad even with that excuse.

The boys see me and instantly rush over from their spot at the edge of the deck where they are waiting and crash into me, wrapping me up in a giant hug.

"We missed you, Aunt Skar," Riley says. He's such a sweet boy.

Ryker just adds, "Yeah, your mom isn't as much fun as you are during our lessons."

A small look of disgust is on his face, and it makes me laugh.

"Aw, boys. I missed you too, and my mom can't be that bad. She's the one who taught me, so you're learning from the master." I try to make light of the situation. I know, based on the amount of research I've been doing and how much Kayne sleeps, I probably could have already resumed their lessons, but, because of their phoenix fire, all their lessons need to be outside, and I just wasn't ready.

They both go to protest, but I give them a pointed look.

"Don't you want to have good control over your magic?" I ask them, and they nod. "Well, how do you think I got so good?" They look at each other and shrug their shoulders. "My mom, silly. She's the one who taught me everything I know."

"Yeah, but she makes it feel like school. When we practice with you, it feels like we're playing a game," Ryker pipes up.

I sigh. I know I'm not going to win this one, but I'm going to try.

"That's because that is how my mom teaches. She wants to push you to be the very best that you can be."

"But Riley is always better at everything than me," Ryker pouts.

"Now, that's not true. Riley is older, so his magic is stronger. Coming into your magic isn't like shifting for the first time. You aren't just standing there all normal one day and then *bam*: you got your wolf. With magic, it comes in slowly." I gather my magic and create a ball of water with my right hand, allowing small drips to pool into my left hand forming a ball. "Like this. It's a slow leak, and you will get small amounts of magic added every day you practice until one day, you're full to the brim. You want to practice and master all forms of magic while you still only have a little bit so that once you have all of it, you won't lose control." With a wave of my hands, I send the water flying back to the lake and look at the boys. "Make sense?"

They nod. "So, Riley has more magic than me right now, but when we both get big, we'll have the same amount?" Ryker asks.

"Sort of. Everyone has different levels of magic. Take my brother Sebastyn and me..."

"You have a brother?"

I nod my head with a smile. "I do, he's younger than me and is traveling far away right now. Next time he comes home I'll introduce you. Anyway, as I was saying, Sebastyn and I have very similar levels of magic but mine is just a tad stronger. He always said it was because I was born first and that I sucked most of the magic out of our parents, but really it could've easily been the other way around. The goddess is the one who determines who has how much power."

"But why would the goddess have given Daddy that much power? He wasn't a good person," Riley asks.

I let out a sigh. "In Tanner's case, his magic wasn't his own. The goddess did give him some magic to start with, but he was greedy and corrupt. The magic he possessed was stolen. He stole it from other supernaturals."

They nod sullenly, and I quickly change the subject.

"Go swim in the lake, and I'll sit on the dock and watch you." That's all it takes. They shoot off like bullets, jumping into the water.

Ah, the water. It looks so nice and refreshing. It's making me hope Phoebe is almost done with her shower, so I can start mine. Instead, I sit there and watch the boys swim back to the dock, jump off again, and repeat the process over and over. Ah, to be young. I'm sure Kayne will be right there with them in a few years, and I know those years are going to fly by faster than I'm prepared for. I look back toward the door, making sure that Alaric isn't coming out with Kayne. I know it's just my anxiety, but I can't help but feel exposed out here. The boys' laughing brings my attention back to them.

The longer I sit and watch the boys, the more I realize that this is exactly what I needed. Sun, fresh air, and watching the boys makes me feel a little more like myself with every minute. All I need now is a nice hot shower and some clean clothes, and everything will be right as rain. Alaric is right. I need to keep living. Hell, my son is a week old and has yet to feel the sun shine on his face. What kind of life is that?

Maybe after dinner Alaric and Phoebe will sit on the deck with me and Kayne. I'm not ready to bring him outside by myself. With the two of them and me, Kirnon wouldn't stand a chance.

Chapter Ten

Lennox

I decide to take a quick break from my sisters and do some of that exploring Alaric suggested on my first day here. Between my sisters and my parents, I haven't had a second alone. If I'm being honest, I just need a few minutes to myself to breathe and become accustomed to being on pack land again. My family is great; they really are. They can be a bit much, though, especially when I've grown accustomed to being alone.

I walk around the pack and introduce myself to countless people in the morning, and they all seem amazing. When I ask about how they feel about their alpha, they all boast that they couldn't have asked for a better one. The raw honesty I see in all their eyes shows me that they're not lying. Alaric is truly beloved in his pack, and—from what I can tell—it's deserved. He and Darren run this pack like a family. No one is better than anyone else, and they all pitch in and help one another. It's how all packs should be run. Add in the fact that they are closely allied with witches, vampires, a bear sleuth, and a mountain lion pride, and damn, this pack is easily the most powerful in the country. Sure, there are other successful packs. The one in Alberta is huge, with over 15,000 shifters, but they are secluded and have no allies. If Alaric wanted to rule over all wolves, all he would need to do is pull together his allies, and it would be a done deal. Not that I think Alaric would ever do anything like that, but maybe he should. A lot of packs, like the Ironwoods, are corrupt, and it doesn't matter how strong, fast, or smart you are. All that matters is who your parents are, who their parents were, and so on.

The longer I stay here, the more I can picture building a life here with a small cottage deep in the forest where I can let my wolf run whenever I want, a job that I enjoy, and my family close. The only way life could get any better than that is if I met a second-chance mate, but I lost all hope of that happening years ago.

"Hey, man," Darren says, jogging up to walk beside me.

"Hey. How's it going?"

"Good. Just finished meeting with the recently shifted pups about when not to shift," he says, and I turn to look at him.

"When not to shift?" I ask. I was under the impression that there were no rules about when to and not to shift in this pack.

"Yeah. Around humans, near the main highway. Things like that."

"Isn't that something that their parents are supposed to teach them?" At least my parents did since neither the alpha nor beta ever got involved in small details like that.

He nods. "It is, and they do. But we've had a few cases of teenagers wanting to rebel against their parents who have shifted at inconvenient times, and we've needed to call in a witch to wipe those memories from humans. Since then, we learned that teenagers are much less likely to ignore advice if it comes from Alaric or me. So, we have a meeting each month with the pups who come of age to reinforce some of the rules."

I chuckle. "Yeah, I've been there a time or two."

"Me too," he joins in with a laugh.

"What about school? Do the pups attend school with the humans, or is there a school here for them?" I ask, glancing around. I haven't seen a building large enough to be a school for all the pups.

"They go to school in Parry Sound until the year they get their wolf, and then they attend a supernatural school here, deep in the forest."

"A supernatural school?" I ask. I've never heard of something like that.

"Yup. It's about four kilometers that way." He points deeper into the forest. "The bear sleuth, mountain lion pride, coven, vampires, and even some local Fae send their kids there. It's easier than chancing an accidental shift in the middle of the human population."

My mouth drops open. "That would've been so cool. Why haven't you guys thought about inviting other supernaturals from across the country?"

"We have," Darren says sullenly. "Every alpha we've reached out to has laughed at us before hanging up. We even built dormitories so that students from outside the area would have somewhere to stay."

"Well, they're stupid. I had to miss an entire year of school so I could get control of my shifts. If I wasn't as intelligent as I am, I would've been held back a year."

"Unfortunately, that's what happens with a lot of shifters and one of the reasons why Alaric and I reached out to the surrounding supes with the idea. It's only been up and running for just over five years, but it's been fantastic. We have teachers from every race as staff."

"So, it's like a private school where the parents have to pay for their kids to attend?" It was sounding really good, but I know quite a few families within other packs that wouldn't have been able to afford sending their kids—my parents included.

He shakes his head. "No, not at all. The pack or coven or sleuth, wherever they come from, puts the money in to pay for the staff and upkeep. All the supernaturals around here have multiple businesses, and Alaric and I said it would be unfair to have individual families pay for their kids while the group finances rise."

"That's amazing. I would like to see it someday."

"When school starts back up, I'll be sure to bring you. If you're interested, we've been looking to add some trade courses for the more advanced students who want to take more hands-on classes. I already talked to your dad about a tool and die course."

"I would love that!" I beam. "Okay, this pack seems too perfect, so what's wrong with it?" I ask, turning to him.

He laughs. "I can see why you would think that coming from a pack like you did and from what you said of your reception at other packs through the years, but we have issues just like every other pack."

I look at him with a raised eyebrow, and he laughs once more.

"Okay fine, we don't have many issues, but it's taken both Alaric and I the last decade to get to this point. Our father wasn't a bad alpha. He was just stuck in the past, which we obviously aren't."

"That makes sense. In the Ironwood pack, Felicia never would've had her own clinic despite being a doctor."

He nods. "If my father was still alpha, she probably wouldn't either. Despite my father being progressive in a lot of things, he still believed that a woman's place was at home with her pups."

"I think that's true of most packs. If the women want to be anything other than teachers or administrators, it's a big fat no."

"So, are you thinking of staying?" he asks, and I look around once more.

"I'm definitely leaning toward yes. It's just hard to stop the nagging feeling that this pack seems too perfect, and I'm waiting for the other shoe to drop if you know what I mean."

He nods. "I do. But I promise you that's not going to happen. It will take time, but I truly believe you'll be happy here."

He claps me on the back, and I nod. "It's beginning to look that way."

"Good. Anyway, I have a couple of land disputes to go and handle, but I'll see you later," he says as he turns to walk away. I am still shocked by the way Alaric and Darren interact with their pack members—even the way they interact with me. As a lone wolf who is not part of this pack, I expected to be kept at arm's length. Instead, they have immersed me into all pack activities, embracing me as one of their own. It feels amazing.

As I walk to the back of the pack house, I stop dead in my tracks and my wolf perks up. There, sitting on one of the Adirondack chairs watching the boys, is the most beautiful woman I've ever seen. Her pure black hair is slicked back into a high ponytail, her face is slender with high cheekbones, and her pouty lips look downright kissable. The sun is shining down in a halo of yellow surrounding her.

She turns in my direction as if sensing me, and my breath whooshes out of me.

Mate, my wolf says.

What? That angel is our mate? Are you sure? I ask in disbelief.

Mate. Claim, my wolf responds.

Well, I was not expecting this today. I had resigned myself to the knowledge that a chosen mate was the only option left for me. This though...This changes everything.

We are stuck in a staring contest, neither of us moving or even blinking for what seems like an eternity, before an enormous splash from the lake distracts us both. I give myself a mental head shake and begin to walk up to her. I see her sitting up straighter and steeling herself for something.

I hope it's not me. I hope she knows that, as her mate, I would never do anything to hurt her. Surely her wolf has already told her that we are mates. The closed-off look on her face gives me pause. If we are true mates, that means she's also been rejected. Maybe she is preparing herself to be rejected again. Shit, perhaps I should be doing that too.

No. If she's been rejected, she knows the pain that comes with it, and I trust in Mother Moon that she wouldn't pair me with a selfish bitch for a second time.

I walk up to her. "Hey, I'm Lennox," I say as I hold out my hand.

She just looks at my hand, then back up to my face saying, "I'm Skarlyt."

She does not make an attempt at shaking my hand before turning back to watch the boys.

What the fuck? Doesn't she realize we're mates? I take a deep inhale through my nose and catch her scent. Hmm, not a shifter. Magic. A witch. A very strong witch.

"Mine," my wolf forces out of my mouth without me being able to stop it.

"Oh, no. Not again," she twists to look back at me with something between exasperation and anger. "I'm not yours, shifter. I'm mine and mine alone."

Not again? What does she mean? Was her first mate also a shifter?

I decide to ask her what she meant. I'm a firm believer in communication. If you have a problem with something, it's only fair to let the other person know. If you want something, it's only fair to let the person who could give it to you know. No one is a mind reader. Unless, of course, she is actually telepathic. Shit. With her being a witch, that is a real possibility.

"What do you mean? We're true mates. My wolf knew it as soon as we locked eyes. Didn't you feel anything?" I ask. I know that witches usually can't tell if they are true mates until they are intimate. Nevertheless, they have to feel something for each other beforehand. Right? How else would they end up in bed together? I'm sure there's not a bunch of witches running around sleeping with random people until they find their mates. That would be crazy.

"You may think we're mates, but that doesn't mean anything to me, and I don't plan on getting close enough to you to confirm that. Ever. No matter how hot you are," she replies, her dark eyes darting back to me momentarily.

Well, at least she thinks I'm hot. That's a step in the right direction. I'm fine with having to work for her affection. I would rather get to know her before we mated anyway. What if she does turn out to be a selfish bitch after all? I dodged a bullet with Olivia. I'm going to make sure that I don't get shit on for a second time.

"I wasn't expecting to get that close to you just yet. I was hoping maybe we could sit and talk, get to know each other," I try reasoning with her. I can tell by her demeanor that her rejection obviously hurt her. Hell, mine did too, but you don't see me shutting myself off to possibilities the same way that she is.

She seems to be contemplating this, and I decide that maybe she needs to hear my rejection story to open up. She's clearly hesitant because she's been hurt, so maybe hearing that I understand will convince her to give me a chance.

"Let me sit down and tell you a story, and then you can decide if you want to get to know me or not. I'll never pressure you into doing anything you don't want to do. If, at the end of my story, you decide that you still want nothing to do with me, I'll never bother you again." I raise my hands in a show of honesty.

"I am supposed to be watching the boys," she offers, lamely motioning to the dock where they are competing to see who can jump the farthest.

"It isn't a very long story," I say with a smile. As far as excuses to not listen to me go, that is a pitiful one.

Still, I wait for her to look at me, her dark eyes wide and sad, and nod before I continue.

"First, I'm Charleigh and Felicia's brother from the Ironwood pack in Morpeth. Our pack holds a meeting once a month for newly mature wolves to run and have the chance to meet their mate—if they are fortunate enough to be from the same pack.

"When I showed up at the meeting after my eighteenth birthday, I saw the most popular female in our pack, Olivia, standing with our beta, Matteo. The second our eyes met, I knew. I could tell she felt it too. I stood there in shock—probably with a big, goofy smile on my face. I felt so lucky to have met my mate at my first gathering and within my own pack to boot. It meant that I'd be able to stay close to my parents and my sisters. I was overjoyed.

"She began whispering to Matteo at her side. I knew they were together. They'd been together throughout high school. They had both turned eighteen a few months before, but everyone knew they either were or would be choosing mates soon.

"Whatever she said to him—he looked at me like he wanted to kill me. I remember being so confused. Surely, they would have expected one of them to meet their true mate at some point, you know? Didn't they want to give Mother Moon a chance to show them their match? I still don't understand..."

"Teenagers always think they know what's best," she says. Her lips twist into a sad smile, and I meet her eyes, silently thanking her for helping me.

"When they came over to me, Matteo began explaining that she was his. Instead of defending me, her true mate, she laughed and rejected me right there in front of everyone. She didn't even know my name to properly reject me. She didn't even give me a chance to introduce myself.

"It hurt like hell," I say, my hand travelling up to my chest, as it always does when I remember the pain. "It hurt me—anyway. It didn't seem to faze her. They just stood there and laughed." I take a deep breath to calm myself before continuing with the rest.

"Over the next twelve years, I traveled around Canada, taking jobs here or there, never being able to stay with my own pack long enough to really put down roots. Every time I did go home to visit my family for birthdays or holidays, Olivia was there. At first, she would flaunt their relationship in front of me. Eventually, she started trying to corner and proposition me. Each time I thought the pain had started to subside enough for me to return home, she would do something to make it come back."

I make a point to wait for Skarlyt to meet my eyes. I try to communicate my need, prove my innocence, through the one look.

"That's why I'm here. I'm hoping that I can finally put down roots and spend time with my parents, sisters, and niece. I hope this is a place where I can belong and live without having the pain of rejection shoved in my face at every corner. I'll never pressure you, but I would at least—please don't..." I stop myself, looking down to where my hands are knotted together. "Please, Skarlyt. Can I get to know you before you say no?"

When I finally look up to see her expression, there are tears sliding down the pale, smooth skin of her cheeks. As much as I want to reach out and wipe them away, I know she's not ready for that.

"I didn't tell you to upset you. I told you because I thought maybe if you knew that I understand the pain of rejection—just like you—maybe, just maybe, you would give this a chance."

All right, the ball is in her court. Putting everything on the line for her was either a smart move or the dumbest thing I've ever done. I watch her beautiful face for any evidence of how I will be judged. At this point, I'm so surprised to have actually been blessed with a second-chance mate that I don't care about playing it cool. I just want a chance—a chance I didn't get the first time.

She wipes her eyes and takes a deep breath.

"Thank you for sharing that with me, Lennox." Her hand, graceful and slender, moves to the place just above her heart before she continues. "It's just that you have had twelve years to deal with your rejection. I was rejected less than a year ago, and I'm not ready. I'm not capable of being anyone's mate right now. I'm a mess," she says as she gestures to her clothing. I'm not sure what her issue is. She looks beautiful.

"I want to be fair to you though. I understand your wolf thinks that I'm his mate, but you both need to know that I'm a package deal. The night that my mate rejected me, he also gave me a gift in the form of my son. So, it's not just me you'd be claiming. You'd be claiming another shifter's son. I think you should take a while to let that sink in before you decide if you want to move forward."

Less than a year? A child? I look at her with fresh eyes and see the exhaustion in her knitted brows, the rosy skin around her tear-stained eyes, and a pronounced roundness in the stomach she has crossed her thin arms across.

"I am up for being friends for the moment and getting to know you. I love your sisters dearly, and I know that you must be a good man if you're related to them. I'm just not sure when—or even if—I'll be ready to be claimed. If, in the end, you decide that it's not worth the wait or whatever, I do have a spell that will deny the bond—not reject it. Neither of us will experience the same pain as last time," she says it matter-of-factly but with an apology in her tone, like a doctor prescribing an amputation. "I just want you to know that there is another option."

Damn, that's a lot to take in. She's right, though. I've had a very long time to get over my rejection, and she's only had a few months. And she has a baby. It doesn't matter to me because I love kids, but it does make things more complicated. I don't know how my wolf will react to fathering another man's pup.

Doesn't matter. Pup will be ours. Mate will be ours. Protect them both.

Well, that simplifies things a bit. My wolf doesn't seem to have a problem with it. Maybe I should ask Alaric about how his wolf handled Phoebe having kids before they met. Perhaps it's not going to be as big of a deal as she seems to think it will be. Am I getting ahead of myself already?

I sit and contemplate that for a minute, staring out at the lake before turning to her. "I want to at least get to know each other. I'll wait forever if I have to. I trust in Mother Moon. If she paired us together after we were both rejected, there must be a reason. I love kids—always have. If you're a package deal, I respect that and would like to at least try. Even if we can ever only be friends, I will honor the Mother's choices for me," I finish, hope laced in my last words.

"Okay," is all she says before turning back to watch the boys. Okay? Okay?

She said Okay.

Can you believe that?

I want to do Charleigh and Phoebe's happy dance so badly right now and scream to the world that Skarlyt agreed to get to know me. Of course, I don't. I can't ruin my chance after just getting it.

It seems things are looking up for me.

After being rejected, the idea of finding a chosen or second mate has always been accompanied with a feeling of dread. I desperately wanted it, but it brought the fear of further rejection—the fear of being vulnerable and having to face the unknown. Instead, it is all I can do to pull my eyes away from Skarlyt's face or contain the stupid grin I know is plastered across my face.

Not only did Mother Moon give me a second chance at a true mate, but I get the feeling that Skarlyt is anything but selfish.

Chapter Eleven

Skarlyt

I turn away from Lennox and watch the boys splashing in the water. To say that I'm shocked is an understatement. I'm dumbfounded that the Mother saw fit to pair me with a second-chance mate so soon after my rejection. According to everything I've read, she waits years before taking pity on those that were rejected, and she usually only blesses those who are deserving and cannot find a chosen mate.

The fact that she deemed me worthy of this is such a blessing, but the fact that he is another shifter does give me pause.

The tale of his rejection though...It seeped into my soul, cutting me deep and carving out a tiny pocket that is already prepared for Lennox—the second-chance mate I wasn't ready for. The way my heart is already thumping inside my chest tells me this is a dangerous game to play. How do I let another man into my heart when it's still broken?

Then I begin to question myself. Who am I to go against a goddess and reject her gift? I would be no better than Kirnon or that bitch Olivia if I did. Even if I'm not ready right now, I'm sure one day I will be. If I act on instinct now and deny the bond, I know I'll regret it. I will never reject him. Even if he turns out to be an asshole, no one deserves to go through the pain of rejection once, let alone twice. If we aren't compatible, I'll simply deny the bond and live my life alone with Kayne.

My head is spinning. My brain is telling me to deny the bond, that I'm just going to end up hurt again, but my heart and soul are telling me I can trust this man, to embrace this gift. Ugh, of course my insides are warring with each other. Why wouldn't they be?

If it's not one thing it's another. With my pregnancy, my heart told me to confide in my family and Alaric, but my head wasn't ready. Is that a sign? Should I listen to my heart this time and save myself the grief of the eventual fall out? Why is this so hard? Maybe I should go talk to Phoebe about it. I know she had conflicted feelings when she met Alaric. Sure, it's not the same, but maybe she'll have some advice.

"Hey, Lennox, would you mind watching the boys swim for a while so I can go talk to Phoebe and take a shower?" I ask, turning back to find him watching me with wide, blue eyes.

Shit. I should probably have talked to Alaric or Phoebe before asking him to watch their kids, but then again, he is Charleigh and Felicia's brother. Chances are that he knows the boys and leaving him with them won't upset anyone. Besides, they're only in the backyard.

"Of course," he replies with no hesitation. No questioning. I didn't even need to use my puppy dog eyes. "You do whatever you need to do."

Wow. If I'm not careful, I have no doubt this one will have me falling in love with him by the end of the week. If the mate bond is subconsciously telling me that I want to be close to him at the same time, I won't stand a chance. Witches may not know who our mates are immediately, but that doesn't stop our souls from pushing to get us closer to their other half.

"Boys!" I yell, and they come running toward us, dripping lake water behind them. They take turns giving Lennox high fives, setting my mind at ease. He's obviously been around them. Probably while I've been hiding in my basement. I wonder what else I've missed. "Lennox is going to watch you now so I can go talk with your mom. Is that okay with you?" I am hoping they say yes, and they both accept with big grins on their faces.

"Do you guys want me to come swimming with you?" he asks them, pulling his plain shirt over his head in one smooth motion. Oh. My. Gods. The body on this man is something out of the movies. The amount of rippling muscles he was hiding under that shirt is astounding. With his shaggy, strawberry-blonde hair, gray-blue eyes, and sun-kissed skin, the action seems casual and familiar —not like he's trying to show off on my account.

He's like a walking, talking wet dream. I just want to trace each one of his muscles with my tongue.

Wait. No Skar. Bad Skar.

We are giving it time, remember?

Luckily, the boys break my mental drooling by screaming, "Yes!" Lennox chuckles as he continues stripping down to his boxers.

Well, that's my cue. I better head inside before I see a soaking wet Lennox with water dripping down his pecs, over his abs, down to the very pronounced "V" below and lose all semblance of self-control. I give myself a mental head shake.

If I'm already starting to fantasize about his perfect body, it definitely won't be long before I succumb to my desires. With or without the mate bond, I don't want Lennox to feel like a rebound. Although isn't that really what we both are?

I quickly walk inside, head straight for the stairs, and hear Phoebe opening and closing drawers in her room. I knock on the door.

"Pheebs, can I come in?"

"Of course, Skar. I'm so glad you're finally out of the basement," she exclaims, wrapping me in a hug before stepping back in a panic. "Wait. Who's watching the boys?" Normally, I would chuckle at her helicopter parenting, but I know she's still not quite over Tanner kidnapping Riley and likes to have someone she trusts watching them at all times, even when they are just in the backyard.

"Lennox was sitting with me on the deck, so I asked him if he would mind watching them while I came to talk to you. I hope that's okay. I figured with him being Charleigh's brother, it would be." I watch her visibly deflate. I guess Lennox was a safe choice.

"Oh yes, of course it's okay. Lennox is a great guy, and he's so good with them," she tells me with a small smile. "Was it something special you wanted to talk about, or just girl talk?" she asks excitedly. I'm not even sure which one she is excited about, maybe both. Either way, I figure I should just pull off the Band-Aid quickly. Here I go.

"Both. Lennox is my mate," I say quickly, and she looks at me with confusion.

"But that Kirnon guy is your mate. I don't understand," she says, her eyebrows pinched together. I keep forgetting that she didn't grow up in our world and wouldn't know about second-chance mates.

"Maybe we should sit down," I say, leading her over to the French doors to sit on the balcony. Once we are both comfy on the outdoor couches, I turn toward her. "Yes, Kirnon was my true mate, the one who the Mother picked for me to spend the rest of my life with. When he rejected me, the ties that bound us together as mates snapped. Sometimes when that happens, the Mother will give those who she deems worthy a second-chance mate. They are still true mates, but they've always both either been rejected before or their true mate died before a bond was established."

"And Lennox *was* rejected when he was just a kid..." Phoebe lists this piece of evidence thoughtfully.

"I met Lennox outside, and that's what he is," I continue. "He's my second-chance true mate, and I don't know what to do. My head says not to give him a chance because I'm afraid of being hurt again, but my soul and heart say that I need to give it a go. I'm so confused. I thought maybe because the pull of the mate bond conflicted you when you first met Alaric that maybe you'd have some advice for me." I finish, looking into her eyes. Whatever I was looking for, I am not expecting what I see reflecting back at me. Hope, excitement, happiness.

"Oh, my gods..." she squeals, and I give her a pointed look that this is serious and not the time for her to have a 'happiness freak out'. She schools her features in understanding before continuing.

"First, I have to say that it is so cool that rejected mates can get second chances." I nod in agreement. "Second, you're right. I was conflicted when I met Alaric and didn't understand my feelings, and, although my situation differs from yours, I can understand what you are feeling. It was the same for me. My heart and soul belonged to Alaric from our first conversation while my head was still married to Tanner, and it was hard to figure out what the right thing to do was. One thing I can say is that no one else can tell you what the right thing is. You have to figure it out for yourself.

"Third, Lennox is an amazing man who was given an extremely raw deal in life. Obviously, because I didn't know about the supernatural world, I didn't know the details of why he started traveling, but I can tell you he was always the most caring and thoughtful guy growing up. He was only a couple of years older than Charleigh and me, so we were always wanting to hang out with him. Not once did he ever complain. Heck, I can't remember him ever even arguing with his sisters. He was always so calm and collected, looking out for us, helping us with homework, projects, even taking us places when we asked, once he got his driver's license, all without complaint."

"It actually makes more sense for you to have been paired with him than that Kirnon guy, based on what I know of him." Her nose wrinkles in disgust at the thought of Kirnon. "But I think you'll find that you and Lennox have a lot in common. I also know that you will never have to worry about him hurting you or Kayne. He doesn't have a temper, and he has no patience for drama. And he always puts his family first, no matter what."

"Okay, Pheebs, I get it. He's perfect," I say, trying not to sound bitter.

"My advice to you is to give it time. Get to know him. Let your head see what your heart and soul already know." She pauses for a brief moment, obviously deciding whether or not to tell me something. "But do not tell Alaric yet unless you want to scare Lennox away. He's kind of gone into 'protect Skarlyt from the world' mode since Kayne's birth. You locking yourself downstairs has just made it worse."

My mouth opens in shock, and I am rushing to defend myself. But she holds up a hand and continues.

"Don't take it the wrong way—I totally understand why you have been staying downstairs. You're worried and scared, rightfully so, but Alaric is also worried about you and doesn't know how to fix it. For an alpha, that is not a very good combination."

Everything that she said is what I was hoping she would say. I feel validated in my desire to at least get to know him despite the shitty situation with Kirnon, but the Alaric thing worries me. I didn't realize that locking myself away was affecting him so much. He's always been my protector, watching over me and taking care of me when I couldn't do it myself, so it makes sense that him watching me retreat into myself just like last time and being unable to fix it would drive him a little nuts. The first time Kirnon left, Alaric had all the time in the world to focus on helping me through it. This time is different because he has a family now. My insides are warring against each other, but his are probably also battling, trying to figure out how to be in two places at once. A pang of guilt runs through me at the thought of making Alaric feel like he needs to choose between me and his new family.

"I'm sorry. I didn't realize I was worrying him that much," I say to Phoebe. I'm sure that it hasn't been easy living with him, especially now that he has a phoenix daughter to protect. The last thing he's needed is for me to give him another reason to worry.

"Oh, goddess no, Skar. Don't be sorry. I told you. I understand why you locked yourself down there. You need time, and that's to be expected. If you still need time, you take it. I'll handle Alaric. It will be fine," she finishes, grabbing and pulling me into a hug. "Now go take a shower because you seriously stink." She laughs and pushes me away gently. I can't argue with that. I really do stink.

"Thank you, Pheebs," I say, getting up and heading to their big bathroom.

I stifle a squeal of delight as I skip my way into the bathroom, still warm and fragrant from Phoebe getting out. I quickly close the bathroom door behind me and speed-walk over to the shower, opening the glass doors and turning on the water before tearing off my clothes and stepping inside.

Once I am inside, my skin acclimated to the almost-too-hot water, I press the button that triggers the jets along the shower wall. I am instantly assaulted with sprays of water from the front and back, while the showerhead above rains down on me.

As I lather the soap and begin to scrub the week's worth of grime off my body, I make a decision. I'm going to give this a go. I'm going to open myself up, as much as I can, to the possibility of a happily ever after with a mate. I didn't think it was a viable option for me anymore.

* * *

Unlike each night before, when I begin to smell the deliciousness coming from the kitchen, I scoop Kayne up into my arms and head to the stairs to join everyone for dinner.

For reasons I do not entirely understand, the stairs make my heart race. I clutch Kayne close and check his small, serene face for any disturbance. He is, of course, completely unaware of my concern. His long, dark lashes rest gently atop his round cheeks.

I take a deep breath and continue to mount the stairs, one at a time, careful to not jar the precious bundle in my arms.

"Are you sure she's okay?"

I pause at the top of the stairs when I hear Alaric.

"Yes," Phoebe sighs. "She's fine. Well, not totally fine, but she will be. You need to give her space. I think meeting Lennox was good for her this afternoon."

"Why?" Alaric growls.

Phoebe lets out a little chuckle. "Because she's still a woman, and sometimes meeting a handsome man who gives you attention helps to make you feel better."

"So, you think he's handsome?"

"Is that all you heard?" Phoebe laughs.

Alaric growls once again, and Phoebe starts to giggle. I can tell things are getting mushy, so I quickly push the door open and clear my throat.

"Oh, Skar!" Phoebe exclaims, stepping out of Alaric's arms.

"Hey," I say, giving her a knowing smirk. If I hadn't walked in right then, dinner probably would've been late. "Can I help with anything?"

"Nope. Alaric will move the playpen into the kitchen so we can put the babies in there while we eat," Phoebe says, turning to look at Alaric who quickly takes the hint.

"Thanks, Pheebs."

"No problem at all. I'm just glad you came up," she says, walking over and wrapping her arms around me.

"Me too," I whisper, releasing her and walking over to a waiting Alaric, placing Kayne down next to Aurora in the playpen. I worried that he wouldn't settle outside of my arms. I shouldn't have. Like magnets, the two babies reach for one another and quickly fall asleep.

"You'd think they were siblings the way they gravitate toward one another," Alaric whispers.

"Or mates," I respond with a smile which he returns. It's been a dream in our families to unite through mating one day. Maybe this generation will be the one.

As always, dinner is eventful, and the boys take turns asking a million and one questions about anything and everything they can think of. Tonight's questions are all about the dinosaurs. Why aren't there any left? How did they all die?

"Aunty Skar," Ryker pipes up.

"Yes, Nephew Ryker," I respond with faux seriousness.

"If you could be any dinosaur, what would you be?"

I chuckle. "That one's easy, I'd be a..."

"Velociraptor," a new voice says from the patio doors, and we all turn to see Lennox standing in the doorway.

I smile. "Precisely. How'd you know?"

He shoots me a panty-melting grin. "Educated guess. They're beautiful, deadly, and the females are fierce as hell."

"What about you, Uncle Lennox? What would you be?"

"Oh, I'd be a T-Rex. Big, bulky, stomping around the forest." He then pulls his arms toward him and begins stomping around the kitchen, pretending that's exactly what he is. We all laugh at his antics. I can see why Phoebe thinks we'd get along.

"Are you hungry, Lennox?" Phoebe asks, gesturing to the food.

"Oh no, thank you." He places a hand on his flat stomach. "Mom just fed me. With the amount of food she had me eating, I don't think I'll be hungry for a week." he says chuckling. "I was hoping Skar might want to take a walk?"

I look up at him, and the vulnerability on his face eats away at any of the walls I had erected. Then I look over at Kayne and remember why I've been staying in this house and shake my head. I turn back to him in time to watch his face fall. "But you can come watch a movie with Kayne and me," I add.

He perks up instantly, a giant smile slipping on his face. I don't miss the looks he's getting from Alaric though. I might have to reign in my bestie sooner rather than later, but then I sneak a look at Phoebe who gives me a smile and nods toward her mate.

Goddess, she's amazing. She can handle Alaric.

"I'll finish cleaning up here," Phoebe says as I begin to help clear the table.

"But you did all the cooking," I argue.

She leans over and whispers. "No, I didn't. Your mom cooked and dropped it off about half an hour ago. All I had to do was keep it warm." We both giggle. I knew that pot roast tasted familiar. "Go. Spend time with Lennox and Kayne. I'll keep Alaric busy."

She doesn't have to tell me twice. With her blessing, I quickly scoop up Kayne and head toward the stairs. "Lennox?" I call out to him when I realize he isn't already following. It is enough to break up the mini-stare-off between him and Alaric.

He hops up and rushes over to me, following me down the stairs.

"So, who's this little guy?" he asks as we reach the bottom, taking Kayne's tiny hand in his.

I beam down at my son before looking up to meet Lennox's eyes. "This is Kayne. Kayne, meet Lennox."

"It's very nice to meet you, little man." Kayne's little fingers wrap around his, and Lennox gently gives it a shake. "So, is this where you live?" he asks, looking around the basement.

"Oh no. Just for right now," I tell him and begin walking toward my room with Kayne still dragging Lennox along by the finger.

"I'm guessing that's because of Kayne's father?"

"Yeah," I whisper, knowing that as my second-chance mate he deserves to know everything but not exactly wanting to go into detail. I shuffle Kayne in my arms trying to free one of my hands to open the door.

"Here, let me," Lennox says, stepping up beside me. But rather than opening the door for me, he scoops Kayne up and cradles him into his chest.

I smile at the two of them and open the door. "Don't mind the mess, I haven't had much company over the past few days—just Alaric, Phoebe, and my mother." But rather than the disaster zone I left before dinner, everything is spotless. Even the grimoire I was searching through is put away. *Mom.* That's the only explanation. I don't know when she had time to sneak down here and clean, but I'm grateful. Although if Lennox is serious about trying to make this work between us, he should probably get used to my messy ways.

"Never mind. It seems a cleaning fairy came in while we were eating," I chuckle.

"Literal cleaning fairy? Or—no, probably not," Lennox says, his mouth hanging open as he takes everything in. "It's a lot bigger than I expected."

"Alaric's made friends with a lot of supes, but we are yet to meet the literal cleaning fairies," I joke, staying a few steps behind him as he wanders around with my son in his arms.

"This is so cool," he says, stopping every so often to read a label on one of the jars. "Phoenix tears?"

"Yeah. They're amazing. I thought all that was a myth—about phoenix tears healing anything. Well, about phoenixes in general, but then I met Phoebe." I stand next to him and pick up the vial of tears, holding it up to the light to let him see the clear liquid in the bottom. "Not only was everything I've read about them real; it hardly even scratched the surface. What those boys can do should be impossible. Males don't inherit the phoenix gene, but they did. They may not be able to shift, but they can produce phoenix fire. I have a theory that when they're nineteen, their tears will heal as well. So, it's going to be tear-jerker movies until I can test it thoroughly."

"I love the way your face lights up when you talk about something you're passionate about," he says, and I blush.

He reaches out and tucks a stray hair behind my ear. We stare at one another, seeming to get lost in our own little world for a few breaths until Kayne starts squirming, breaking the spell we were under. "Thank you."

Lennox clears his throat and walks back to the couch, sitting down and getting comfortable with Kayne.

"I can take him," I say, reaching out, but Lennox shakes his head and looks down at him.

"I'm good with him here if he is. How about it, little buddy? Are you happy to stay here with me and give Mom a little break?" Kayne snuggles deeper into him with an audible sigh, and I chuckle, taking a seat beside them.

"So, I need to tell you everything before we get too close." I fold my legs up underneath me and turn to face him.

"Skarlyt, we don't have to do that right now," he offers me an escape. "If you need a relaxing night watching a movie, this can wait."

"No," I say, my resolve steeling. "You told me your story, so I am going to tell you mine." And then I tell him. I start at the beginning, school, the dance, the hotel, and I end with recent events, Supernatural, my secret pregnancy, the birth of my son just a week ago. Finally, I try to explain how I'm feeling about needing to protect Kayne from Kirnon and the changes to the barrier spell my mom has started.

"Wow." Lennox uses his free hand to push his hair out of his face with a sigh. "Sounds like that guy is a dick. No offense."

"He really is. I don't know how I didn't see it sooner."

"That's usually how it works with assholes. They're really good at hiding their true nature until it's too late."

I eye him warily. "Is that what you're doing?"

"Me? Oh no. I would never be able to keep up a lie like that. Charleigh always tells me I'm the worst liar she's ever met."

I chuckle. "Really?"

"Oh yeah. I start stammering and sweating. The guilt starts rearing its ugly head in my stomach before I even open my mouth. It's embarrassing."

"I don't know. I think that's a good quality to have."

"Not when you're a teenager trying to keep secrets from your parents," he says with a laugh.

"No, I suppose not," I agree.

"How do you feel about twenty questions?" he asks with a smirk.

"The game?" He nods. "Sure. You go first."

He settles more into the couch. "If you could go anywhere in the world, where would it be?"

I wave my hand, answering without any hesitation, "Egypt."

His brows furrow. "Why Egypt?"

"That's another question. You have to wait until your turn." I tap my finger on my chin, trying to think of what to ask him first. "Who's your favorite person in the world?"

"Right now?" he asks, and I nod. "You."

For a brief moment, I am stunned by the sincerity in his voice.

"Okay, before you met me?"

"Cybil."

"Your niece. That's cute."

"Okay, my turn again. Why Egypt?" he asks.

"It's the home of the oldest coven of witches in the world," I begin, imagining all the knowledge they have stored in their libraries. "My brother also happens to be there right now and

119

didn't bother to take me along. The things they know—the things he's learning—probably no one on this continent knows."

"Why didn't you go with him?" Lennox asks, looking apologetic though it's certainly not his fault I was unable to go with Sebastyn.

"You don't seem to know how this game works," I say, with a smile and a wink. "It's my turn now."

Chapter Twelve

Lennox

"Maybe one day we can go together," slips out of my mouth before I have the chance to stop it. So far tonight, I've been pretty good at keeping my comments about the future to a minimum. What I really want to do is look into those gorgeous blue eyes and tell her that I will make all her dreams come true. Because I will. I'll make sure of it.

It's been two hours since Skarlyt and I came down to her room. Two hours of laughing, talking, and a whole lot of questions. It feels completely natural, as if this is how life is supposed to be.

She's so easy to talk to, and her curiosity is adorable. She asks surprising questions, and now I'm kind of curious too. Apparently, the nearby coven of vampires has caught her attention lately, and she's full of questions for anyone from the mysterious group. Especially since she's been banned from asking questions of them since an "incident" that occurred the last time she visited.

The way she explains it, the coven leader gets unjustifiably annoyed with her questions, but from the mischievous sparkle in her eyes, I highly doubt it was unjustified. Maybe between the two of us, we can get some answers.

In my arms, Kayne starts to stir for the first time since we sat down together. He stretches his small, wrinkled arms out of the warmth wrapped around him. Small whimpers come from his mouth. "I think he's hungry," I tell her, watching his pink hands reaching and balling into fists. For the first time since I met her, she looks embarrassed.

"Wow. I didn't realize that much time had passed. He's probably starving," she says, reaching over and scooping him out of my arms. Each brush of her bare skin on mine sends tingles flowing through me. I watch as she gets up with Kayne in her arms, seeming uncertain. Then it dawns on me. She's going to breastfeed him.

"I should go," I say, and she stops mid-stride, turning back to face me.

The relief on her face is apparent. "You don't mind?"

I stand and smile at her. "Not as long as you will let me come over again tomorrow."

She returns my smile and nods. "I would like that."

"Me too." With every fiber of my being, I want to rush over there and wrap her up in a hug, claim her mouth, but I don't. If she were a wolf, it might be different. She would be feeling the mate bond as strongly as I do. Her wolf would also be demanding that we claim one another. I know witches work differently, so I hold myself back.

"Thank you for tonight," she says as she walks me to the door.

"I didn't do anything." I look at her confused.

Her eyes mist lightly. "You did. Trust me."

"Well, then, you're welcome," I say with a smile, bending over and placing a soft kiss on Kayne's head and then Skarlyt's hand. "Goodnight."

"Goodnight," she says, and I turn to leave. "Lennox?"

"Yeah," I say, turning back to her, seeing her biting her lip.

"Do you think that we could keep the mate stuff between us?

Just for a little while?" I knew this question was coming. It's why I haven't told anyone yet. I wanted to scream it from the rooftops earlier. After our brief conversation on the deck, I knew I couldn't. I tried to tell myself it's because she seemed so apprehensive about bonding, but if I'm being honest, I know my sisters will pressure her until we cement our bond. I want her to bond with me because she wants to, not because people are telling her she should.

"Of course." I nod.

She lets out a breath and her shoulders relax. "Thank you."

With that, I turn back, gently opening the door and closing it behind me, pausing outside long enough to hear her step away, whispering to Kayne in a sing-song voice.

"If Mommy's not careful, Lennox might just steal her heart."

With a huge smile on my face, I walk up the stairs to find the house entirely dark and quiet already. I slip out the patio doors, trying to stay as quiet as possible.

"Sneaking out, are we?" A voice calls from the chairs off the side of the deck. I spin and find Phoebe sitting there with a big smile on her face.

"N...no."

"You're still a horrible liar, I see," she chuckles.

I sigh and walk over, sitting next to her. "Fine, I was kinda sneaking out, but only because your mate doesn't seem to want me around Skarlyt."

Now it's her turn to sigh. "It's not you. He's just very protective of her. They've been best friends their entire lives, and she's been through a lot in the last year."

I nod. "I know. She told me, and I get it. I just wish..." I begin and pause. I want to say that I wish I could tell him she's my mate. No matter how strong his protective instincts are toward her, her being my mate trumps it. He wouldn't be able to say anything.

"That you could tell him she's your mate?" Phoebe asks, shocking me.

"You know?"

She chuckles. "I'm the only one. Skar told me right after you two met."

"Then Alaric knows too?"

"Nope. Skar and I agree that he's got enough on his plate right now—not that this is a bad thing. It's just there's been so much happening in the last week that he's a little stressed."

I look back at the house. "That's him when he's stressed?" I ask because he seems anything but. Sure, he started being a little frosty toward me when he realized that I wanted to start spending time with Skarlyt. After hearing her story, I understand a lot better. He's been the constant for her, the same way she's been for him. It's only natural for an alpha to want to protect those he loves, even from their mates.

"Yeah. He's out for a run right now, checking the perimeter."

"For Kirnon?" I ask, and I feel my own hackles rise at the thought of him coming here. "Skar said she's worried about him, and I get it."

"Yeah. Alaric is worried he's lost touch with reality since rejecting Skar. If he finds out about Kayne..." she trails off, unable to finish. She doesn't need to. I've seen what happens when wolf and man don't agree with rejections. The wolf will either take over and go feral, preventing the human from ever taking control back, or retreat entirely, stopping the human from ever shifting which, invariably, makes them go insane. For a shifter, not shifting is probably the worst thing that could happen. The animal is as much a part of us as the human, and I know better than most the stress it puts on your body when you are forced not to shift. Luckily, my wolf understood the reasons we couldn't shift as often as we wanted, and I was spared the insanity.

"I think I might go for a run too," I say, getting up and walking away.

"Be safe, Lennox," Phoebe calls out to me, but I'm already hidden by trees, removing my clothes and calling on my wolf.

Mate, my wolf whines, trying to turn back toward the house.

She needs space, and we need to patrol to keep her safe, I tell him. He huffs but reluctantly turns back to the woods and takes off.

After running for most of the night, I crawl into my bed at Charleigh's just as the birds start to sing, telling me that morning is here. I pick my phone up off the bedside table and set an alarm for ten. It's only going to give me a few hours of sleep, but I would rather be sleep deprived than lose out on time with Skarlyt and Kayne.

* * *

Much to my annoyance, my alarm begins to blare at ten. I snatch my phone off the table, hitting snooze as quickly as possible, and burrowing back under the covers. A moment of clarity hits me, and I jump out of bed. I'm tired, but I get my butt in gear, quickly making my way over to the bathroom and hopping in the shower.

After making myself as presentable as possible, I leave my room and head to the kitchen. I wonder what Skarlyt likes to eat? Maybe that small diner will have something I can bring her.

"You were out late last night," Charleigh says, making me jump.

"You scared me," I tell her. Really, I should've known she was there. If I wasn't so distracted by thinking about Skarlyt, I would've heard her heartbeat.

She raises an eyebrow at me and takes a long, noisy slurp from her mug. "Someone's jumpy."

I scoff at her and walk around where she sits, perched on a stool at the kitchen island behind her laptop. "Just distracted."

"Distracted by what?"

I pause, holding the coffee pot over the mug. I wasn't kidding when I told Skarlyt last night that I'm a terrible liar. If I'm not careful, Charleigh will extract all my secrets. I shrug my shoulders. "Life."

"I know I've already told you, but I'm really glad you're here, Len," she says, and I start to feel bad for keeping this secret from her. It's not only my secret to tell, is it? With that thought, some of the guilt fades away. I finish pouring my coffee, putting in a small amount of sugar and milk before turning around.

"Me too, Char," I finally answer, turning to fully take in her surroundings. The laptop sits open before her, and a notebook off to her right is covered in writing, the pages thick from use. "What are you up to?"

"It's a long story," she says, flipping the notebook shut with a sigh. "So, what's on the agenda for today?"

I lean on the counter, taking my first sip of coffee. "Actually, I was going to go hang out with Skarlyt for a bit." I thought about lying and telling her I was going for a run or something, but at some point today she'll probably end up over at Phoebe's and smell me. No. It's better to be as honest as possible without telling her the entire truth.

She sighs. "That's good. You two have the rejection thing in common. Maybe you'll be able to help get her out of the house. Goddess knows she's been through enough lately. I mean, no one even knew she was pregnant. Could you imagine? Being pregnant and alone after being rejected by the one person who was supposed to cherish and love you for the rest of your life?"

I shake my head. "It was hard enough just being rejected. She's obviously extremely strong to have been able to get through her rejection and a pregnancy without anyone knowing."

"Exactly. But, if anyone can understand, it's you. I wanted to introduce you the first day you were here, but she wasn't leaving her room. I'm glad you two finally met."

I nod and down the rest of my coffee before I can say something I shouldn't. "I'll be back later."

"Okay, Len. I'll probably be over later on. I'm letting Cybil get all the sleep she wants while I get some quiet."

After saying my goodbyes to Charleigh, I head out the front door and make the short walk to the diner.

As I hoped, the diner has an assortment of pastries in the display counter by the cashier. I am staring at the Danishes inside, debating. Does Skarlyt like blueberry, raspberry, strawberry, or chocolate?

"Can I get you something?" An older woman steps up behind the display case to catch my attention.

"Yes, please. I would like two of each, if possible," I tell her, deciding it's best to go big or go home. I'm sure they'll get eaten.

"You are heading over to the alpha house?" she asks, and I nod. "Then you will want chocolate for Phoebe, strawberry for the boys, blueberry for Alaric, and raspberry for Skarlyt. If Constance is still there, she's going to want blueberry as well."

"Okay, then. I will get all of that plus a raspberry for myself," I say thankfully. She nods with a smile and puts the Danishes in a take-out box for me.

The smell wafting to me as she opens up the case has my stomach growling and my mouth watering. "On second thought, put a couple extra raspberries in there, please." If those things taste as good as they smell, I'm going to need more than one.

"Here you go," she says. I pull out my wallet to pay, but she waves me off. "We don't' charge the alpha family."

"But..." I begin, ready to tell her that I'm not family, but she pins me with a look that I know I can't refuse. "Thank you for your help," I tell her with a smile. As she turns to the next customer, I quickly slip a twenty-dollar bill into the tip jar. It might not cover what I bought, but it's something.

I carry my box of deliciousness to the alpha house. I don't even make it up to the porch before Alaric and the boys come rushing out the front door, noses to the sky.

"Is there some for us, Uncle Lennox?" Ryker asks, his puppy dog eyes on full display.

"Maybe," I say, cocking my head. "There might be one for Alaric in there too."

"In that case, come on in," Alaric booms out with a laugh, opening the door and gesturing for me to walk in first. I eye him warily. Yesterday, I felt the ice coming off him when I wanted to hang out with Skarlyt. Today, though, he seems much more welcoming. Maybe Phoebe had a talk with him.

"Skarlyt! Danishes," He yells down the stairs. I hear a faint yelp, and then I see her scurrying up the stairs holding Kayne.

"Where?" she says, her hair still messy from waking up and clothes still rumpled. She looks beautiful, even if she is a little frazzled. I set the box of Danishes down on the island and step up beside her, gently slipping Kayne from her arms so that she can eat.

"Right over there," I tell her, pointing to the box. She looks slightly embarrassed and starts trying to smooth out her clothes and hair. I shake my head. "Don't. You look beautiful just the way you are," I whisper it softly into her ear and look over my shoulder to make sure Alaric and the boys are too busy to overhear.

She scoffs but shoots me a small smile before walking over and devouring a raspberry Danish. In fact, everyone is so busy eating that the only thing you can hear is slight moans of satisfaction and chewing. I really need to try one.

I take a seat at the table and look down at Kayne. His little face is so round and perfect. He looks up at me with those bright blue eyes, and I know without a doubt there is nothing I wouldn't do for him—whether his mom accepts me as her mate or not. His nostrils flare, and he sniffs before snuggling in deeper and closing his eyes.

Skarlyt may have hoped her son would be a witch like her, but this little guy is most definitely a wolf.

"Here," Skarlyt says, sitting next to me and offering a raspberry Danish on a plate.

I move Kayne into the crook of my right arm, freeing my left to grab the Danish off the plate. As soon as my mouth closes over the first bite, I close my eyes and let out a moan. This has to be the best thing I've ever tasted. The perfect amount of flaky dough surrounds cream cheese and what tastes like homemade raspberry filling.

"Good, right?" Skarlyt asks, and I open my eyes to look at her.

"The best thing I've tasted in a long time," I admit.

We each finish our Danish quickly—much to my dismay. Living here could be dangerous. If the diner has those all the time, I can see my bank account dwindling and my waist growing at an alarming rate. I chuckle to myself at that thought. My bank account is pretty large right now because I haven't had anything to spend money on over the past decade, and my shifter metabolism means I have to work pretty hard to gain any weight.

"Want to sit out on the deck?" I ask her, and she looks to the patio doors, then down at Kayne before looking up at me.

"Um..." she begins, but I cut her off.

"We don't have to. I'm happy to do whatever you want to do."

"I would rather hang out inside if you don't mind. Until my mom gets that barrier up, I don't want to chance it," she says apologetically, concerned that I'm going to be upset.

"Sounds good to me. Lead the way," I say, standing up and pulling out her chair for her.

"Hey, Lennox," Alaric calls, making me pause and turn around.

"Yeah?"

"Would you mind taking a look at those boats in a couple

hours?" Shit. I completely forgot. I look over at Skarlyt and then back at Alaric.

"Sure, he will. When you're ready to leave, we'll just be downstairs," Skarlyt answers for me. I was going to tell him I'd rather do it later so I could spend more time with her, but it seems she has other ideas.

Alaric looks at me expectantly, and I nod. "Sounds good."

As soon as Skarlyt and I step off the bottom step, she rounds on me.

"Okay, I have a good one. I've been waiting all day to ask you."

I let out a soft laugh. "Shoot."

She continues walking toward her room. "If you woke up tomorrow and it was a zombie apocalypse, what would you do, step by step?"

"That is a good one," I tell her, following her into the room and settling down on the couch beside her. "Are they fast zombies or slow zombies? Well, I guess it won't matter. Assuming we're still here?" I ask, and she nods. "I would ask the witches to put up a barrier to keep out the zombies around pack land. Then I would go and find as many supes as I could and bring them back here. The vampires are a tough one because technically they're already dead—or undead—so they shouldn't be able to be turned into zombies, so that would help for going out and gathering supplies, but the fact that they're unable to go out in the sun and their need for blood makes it a bit harder."

"For argument's sake, let's say I could come up with a spell to sate their bloodlust."

"Do you have a spell for everything?"

"For argument's sake," she shrugs.

I nod. "Well, that would make a huge difference. In that case, I would invite the vampires here as well and build them a bunker to live underground during the day. Then I would want to ensure we have sustainable food sources for the rest of us: greenhouses, animals, you know, the works. After that, a wall is definitely in order surrounding pack land that we could expand as needed. If everything worked out, we could live out the rest of our days here with no issues."

"The only thing different I would do is put solar panels on as many buildings as possible before the hydro went out so that we would still have energy," she says with a smile.

"I didn't even think of that. Such a good idea." We look at each other for a few moments, seeming to get lost in each other's eyes once more. I would give anything to reach across the couch to her, pull her close and plant kisses all over her beautiful face. Her tongue darts out to wet her lips. and my eyes drop to them automatically, breaking our connection. I shake my head gently to clear the lust-filled thoughts. "I have one for you too. If you found a genie and he gave you three wishes, what would they be and why?"

She chuckles. "I thought mine was good, but yours is better. Okay. So, my first wish would be that I always have exactly enough money in my pockets to buy whatever I need. If I need a house? Bam. Just enough money."

I laugh. "You'd need pretty big pockets for that."

"Yup. After that...I would want world peace, but that would never happen. I'd settle for my loved ones to stay happy and healthy for as long as they're alive. The last wish I'd want to keep in my back pocket for a rainy day. You never know when a wish would come in handy."

"Nope, you have to use all three wishes."

"Fine. Is the genie like the one from *Aladdin* and a prisoner?" she asks, and I cock my head in contemplation.

"I suppose."

"Then I'd wish them free. It doesn't hurt to have some genie magic on your side, and then they'd be my friend for life."

"So true, although you seem plenty powerful on your own. I'm not sure what a genie could do that you can't."

She giggles. "You might be right."

The next two hours fly by just like they did the night before. Before I know it, Alaric is standing in the doorway and ready to leave. As I pass Kayne back to Skarlyt, I quietly ask to come by again later, and she agrees.

I place a soft kiss on Kayne's head and the back of Skarlyt's hand once more before I leave with Alaric. Even these few steps away from her are like torture. It's taking everything in me to walk away from the two of them, even if it's only for a little while.

I'm definitely in too deep already, and I've never been happier.

Chapter Thirteen

Skarlyt

A week goes by, and I'm spending every minute I can with Lennox. He's so amazing with Kayne. He is attentive and so helpful. Even though I wasn't ready to bring Kayne out of the house, he has joined us in my room each day, never complaining. One day, he made us a picnic lunch that we had in the workroom, another time he set up a projector, and we just watched movies in my bed with popcorn all day. I admit I'm beginning to see why the Mother paired us together. He's so different from Kirnon. He hasn't even tried to touch me in any way other than the soft kisses on my hand as we part. I can see that he wants to, but he's respecting my need for distance, and I love that.

"Skarlyt?" my mom calls out, walking into my room.

"In here," I call back to her from my bedroom.

"There's my sweet boy," she says, making a beeline for Kayne, picking him up and peppering him with kisses.

"Nice to see you too, Mom," I joke, and she scowls at me before turning her smile once again to Kayne.

"Have you been a good boy for your mommy?" she asks him, blowing a raspberry on his cheek before looking up at me.

"Yup. He's even sleeping a solid six hours at night now."

"You are? You'll probably sleep even longer tonight after you get to go outside in the fresh air."

My mouth drops open in shock, and she gives me a smirk. "You mean..."

She nods. "Yes. The barrier is all done. It's tied to me, Alaric, and Phoebe as an extra precaution, and it's holding strong. We added in a spell to stop anyone with malicious intent from crossing. So even if Kirnon was able to cross because of his connections to this pack—unlikely—if he meant anyone harm, he won't be able to."

I tug my lip between my teeth. "You really think it will work?"

"I know it will," she says with resolve. "I would never take chances with the two of you."

I let out a small sigh and smile. "I know you wouldn't. Oh, this is so exciting. You want to go outside, baby?" I coo, walking over to Kayne and scooping him from my mom's arms. I can't wait to tell Lennox. Maybe we can surprise him at Charleigh's.

With Kayne nestled in my arms and my mom close behind, I fly up the stairs, straight through the kitchen and out the patio doors. Kayne's eyes close tightly from the sun, and I spin in a circle laughing.

"Well, someone seems happy," a voice calls out from the dock.

I stop spinning and have to shade my eyes to locate Lennox where he sits on the dock with the boys.

"We were going to surprise you," I pout.

"Surprise me?" His head cocks to the side, looking very canine, in the cute way he does, and I nod.

"The barrier is up," I tell him with a smile, walking closer.

He takes big strides, coming up and wrapping his arms around both Kayne and me. I melt into his embrace. It's the first time he's hugged me, and I'd be lying if I didn't say it feels amazing—like I'm right where I'm supposed to be. Holding my son and wrapped in the arms of my mate. *Mate?* Did I really just admit that? Huh. I guess I did.

"Want to go for a walk?" I ask as he steps back.

"Sure. I just need to wait until Phoebe or Alaric get back so they can watch the boys."

"No need. It's time for their lesson anyway," my mom says from behind us, giving me a knowing smirk. Shit. I forgot she was even there. I can feel a blush spreading up my cheeks and step back, putting distance between myself and Lennox and hating every step.

"You three go, and I'll watch the boys," she says, patting my cheek with a soft, warm hand that matches her smile. With no need for further encouragement, we begin our walk.

Lennox and I bring Kayne on a tour of the pack, introducing him to everyone we pass. I know people have been curious, especially considering no one knew I was pregnant. They were giving us time to settle into our new groove, though, and I'm extremely grateful for that.

We end up at my little cottage, and I open up the door. "Welcome home, baby," I say softly to Kayne, showing him the kitchen, living room, bathroom, and two bedrooms. I know he can't understand what I'm showing him, but I'm doing it for myself and Lennox too. I need these few minutes to familiarize myself with my home again. Even though it's only been a couple weeks, my own home feels empty and strange after so long.

"This one will be your room, Kayne," I say, walking him around the mostly empty spare bedroom. "Mommy is sorry. I guess it looks pretty sad." Because I didn't tell anyone that I was pregnant, I'm utterly unprepared for us to move back in here. I don't have a crib, changing table, toys—nothing that would make our home ready for us. I see the painting supplies in the corner, still waiting for me to finish a project I never ever started. Looking around, I realize just how much work I have to do in

F D Fair

order to get this room ready for him, and I begin to feel over-whelmed.

Why did I waste the nine months of pregnancy worrying about not telling people? I could've had all this ready and set up. I could've even cloaked this cabin from the world and kept him safe the whole time. Kirnon knows where Alaric lives, but he's never seen my home. He would never have looked for us here.

I shake my head to clear the thoughts. No use thinking about the things I could have done. I need to plan. I pass Kayne to Lennox, who takes him without a word of complaint, and head into the kitchen. I grab a pen and paper out of the drawer and start making a list.

I like lists. It gives me great satisfaction each time I cross some-thing off. Okay, first, paint the room. Then buy a crib, changing table, toys, etc. Next, set everything up. Then, put a cloaking spell around the cottage to shield us. And then we can move back in.

"What are you doing, sweetheart?" Lennox breaks me out of my list-making endeavors.

"Sweetheart?" I ask before I can stop myself.

"I was just trying it out," he shrugs.

"I'm making a list of the things I need to do and buy so Kayne and I can move back home. I didn't realize just how unprepared I was for his arrival," I reply. Lennox just nods and comes to look over my shoulder at the list.

I can feel the heat from his body coating my back. The way his large frame feels covering mine, sandwiching me between him and the counter, makes sparks ignite in my core, and I close my eyes to enjoy the feeling. All I want to do right now is turn around and claim this man as my own. Thankfully, before I do just that, he replies.

"Tell you what. Why don't we get Phoebe and Alaric to watch Kayne? I'll paint the room, and you can head into town to buy everything, and we'll set it up when you get back. You'll have to

136

sleep at Alaric's again tonight so the paint has time to dry, but if it's something you want, we can have you settled back in here by tomorrow."

What? He just literally came up with a plan to cross every single thing off my list in one day. I've never been able to do that unless I'm cheating and make a list of completely obtainable tasks just to cross things off. Not that I do that. Well. I don't do that often.

I take a breath to steady myself. Leaving the basement is one thing, walking through pack land is another, but venturing all the way into town feels impossible.

"Okay," I say, agreeing and starting the process before I have time to let my nerves catch up to me. I let my agreement provide the momentum to carry me forward.

Alaric and Phoebe are so happy that I am leaving pack land that they jump at the chance to watch Kayne. Phoebe even goes as far as to offer to feed him a bottle if I want to take a little extra time for me. I tell her that I won't be long but decide to pump a bottle for him and put it in the fridge downstairs, just in case.

Next thing I know, I'm hopping in Alaric's truck so that I have enough room to bring everything back with me and driving to town. Cruising down the road with the windows down and feeling the wind blow through my hair as I dance to the music leaves me feeling serene and peaceful.

I realize that I feel lighter since meeting Lennox. I don't want to contribute all my happiness to him, but he's definitely a big part of it. I'm glad I decided to take a chance of at least getting to know him, even if I'm still not ready to be claimed.

I decide that Wal-Mart is my best bet for a one-stop shop, especially since we don't have a Babies "R" Us in Parry Sound. Besides, anything special that I want, I can order online and just have it delivered. Right now, I just need the basics.

I get out of the truck and walk into the store, heading straight to the baby section at the back. Wow, there's more stuff here than I ever imagined needing. Maybe I should've grabbed two carts instead of one. No, I'll get the basics now, and I'll have to get someone to carry out the crib and changing table, so one will be fine...I hope.

It doesn't take long to pick out a matching cherry wood crib, dresser, and changing table combo. I go ahead and pay for it and request to have it brought out to the truck for me while I continue shopping for everything else.

By the time I'm done, the cart is overflowing, and I spent more than I expected to. Between my freelance work as a photographer and making potions and low living expenses—gotta love those pack land perks—I know there's enough in my account to cover however many cute little outfits I want to buy Kayne.

It was a big argument with my mother when I decided to build my cottage on pack land. She thought I should build one closer to the witch community since the coven is just a kilometer away within the same forest. I knew then, and I still know now, that my place is with the pack. Maybe my subconscious knew that I would be paired with a shifter. I know that when Lennox and I eventually claim each other, he's going to want to live on pack land anyway, so the fact that I have a cottage there is perfect. We may have to expand a bit though if we plan on having more kids.

Wow. I shake my head to clear my thoughts. Did I just say *when* we claim each other?

I'm loading up the truck when the hair on the back of my neck stands up, instantly making my danger meter rise. I slowly turn around and instantly wish I hadn't. Fuck. Kirnon is there, standing right in front of me. How did he get so close without me noticing?

"Hey, babe. I missed you," he says sweetly, plastering on the panty-dropping smile he always used with me.

"Babe?" I ask, genuinely confused. Why the fuck would he be

calling me babe? And he missed me? Yeah, okay. Not fucking likely.

"Yeah, I missed you. I wanted to talk to you about our misunderstanding a few months ago, but I couldn't get onto pack land today when I tried to come see you."

So, the barrier did work. Good to know.

"Misunderstanding?" Okay, it confused me before. Now I know it is just fucking nuts. "You're saying rejecting me was a misunderstanding?" I spit at him. Maybe it's because I've already met Lennox or maybe I'm just over him, but for the life of me I can't see what I ever saw in Kirnon. He's not even that good looking. Now that my eyes are open, I can only see him for the man he truly is: a lying, deceiving asshole.

"Yeah, a misunderstanding. I was just so shocked that we were mates that I reacted and didn't think about it. I didn't think I was ready for a mate. I'm so sorry, babe. Forgive me?" he says and moves in for a kiss.

Uh, nope. Not happening.

I step away from him, finding my back up against the truck already.

"No. No, I do not forgive you. Reacting would have been marking me without talking about it. You rejected me because, and I quote, 'I won't have a witch as my mate.' That was not reacting. That was a choice, and you made it. Now you have to live with it. I am not your mate. You will never be mine. You need to leave."

He looks genuinely shocked for a moment before a look of complete evil settles on his face.

"Well...I tried. You always have to do things the hard way, don't you?" he says with a grimace before moving swiftly and stabbing me in the neck with something. My body goes limp before I have the chance to call on my magic, and everything around me goes black before I hit the ground.

Well shit.

* * *

As I wake up in a strange motel room, head throbbing and mouth dry, I can be sure of only two things. Kirnon fucking kidnapped me, and I'm going to fucking kill him.

I look around, my eyes swimming and slow to focus. It's not even a nice motel room. The carpet and bedspread are a dingy rust color, and the small TV on top of the dresser is playing the local tourism channel—nothing but a series of ads on repeat. It's so outdated that the TV isn't even a flat screen—it's still a tube style. Where the fuck did he bring me? The least that fucker could've done is taken me to a decent second location if he was going to kidnap me. Scratch that. Why the fuck does he even want me? He rejected me. Doesn't he remember that?

I hear the toilet flush a second before the bathroom door swings open. Ew, who doesn't wash their hands after they do their business? Disgusting. Just another thing to add to the growing list of subpar qualities he possesses.

"Oh good, you're awake. Now that we're somewhere more private, we can continue our conversation." I think he's snapped. I've always known he was a little crazy, jealous, and possessive. You know, normal shifter crazy, but he is acting downright certifiable. What's his deal?

"Our conversation from earlier? Are you fucking nuts? You kidnapped me, Kirnon. If you think I'm talking to you about anything, you're out of your goddamn mind," I scream at him. I hope there are other people in this motel who can hear me, but from the looks of this place, I don't know who would stay here.

"Now, now, Skar. Let's not be like that. We are going to be together for the rest of our lives, so let's not start off by fighting." I reach down to gather my magic. That's it. I'm really going to curse him now. Mother fucker thinks he can kidnap me and then tries to convince me I am the unreasonable one? I raise my hands with the spell on my lips. I don't feel anything. I can't feel my magic. I look at my hands in shock, turning them over as I search for an explanation. I notice the small silver bracelet on my left wrist. What the fuck is this?

"Ah, I see you've noticed your new jewelry. That's a gift from a friend in Vancouver. You won't be able to access your magic until I remove it. I needed to have some insurance to protect myself."

Fuck. No wonder I can't feel my magic. This is inhumane. I have heard of manacles like this before, but nobody uses them anymore, only dark witches and mages. It's like a war crime. Where did he even get it?

"Why are you doing this, Kirnon?" I plead with him. Maybe if I understand his motives, I will be able to make some sort of deal to get free. There has to be something I can give him in exchange for my freedom.

"Skarlyt, I didn't realize it at the time, but you and I are meant to be together. I was feeling a little lost, so I visited a powerful psychic while I was in Alberta. She told me what was destined for us—the future I can have. You and I are one of the few pairs destined to create true hybrid children," his eyes are glazed and dreamy, but I must not be reacting the way he'd hoped. He slams his hand down, shaking the bedside table, and moves closer to my face. "True hybrids, Skarlyt. A myth—even to us. So, you see, it doesn't matter what my personal feelings toward you are, we have a destiny in front of us, and I'm going to make sure that we see it through."

Ah, so that's why he wants me. He thinks he can use me to further his status within the supernatural community. Wait. Does that mean Kayne is a hybrid? I can't let Kirnon find out about him. I don't know what he would do with him. No wonder my instincts have been going nuts telling me I need to protect him.

"And you think that kidnapping will convince me to forgive you?" I question. Man, this guy is fucking nuts.

"I'm willing to keep you here for as long as it takes. I know, in time, you'll come around to my way of thinking."

"You have snapped, Kirnon. I don't care how long you keep me here. I will never forgive you. I will never take you as my mate. If you think that Alaric won't find me, you're even crazier than I thought." I spit the last sentence with as much venom and promise as I can muster. I know Alaric will come for me because he always does, and I have no doubt, after getting to know Lennox this week, that he will be right beside him.

"Yes, I'll admit Alaric is going to be a bit of a problem for me. Don't worry, though. I've made some new friends who are going to help me. In fact, I have to go meet with them now. You take some time to think about your predicament. If you agree to be my mate, I can make sure that Alaric stays safe." He walks over to me and tries to place a kiss on my mouth. I turn my head away in disgust. No way am I letting that nasty fucker touch me .

"You'll come around, Skarlyt. I promise you," he says as he turns away and walks through the door.

Well, that's just great.

Kirnon is acting crazy enough that Alaric and the pack may really be in trouble, and I need to get home to Kayne soon. Hopefully, by now, they've realized that I'm missing.

Chapter Fourteen

Lennox

I'm just finishing up my second coat of paint when I look at the clock. Five o'clock. Huh, I thought Skarlyt would have been back by now. Maybe she's just over at Alaric's, showing Phoebe all the stuff she bought. Yeah, that's probably it. Hell, Charleigh is probably with them, gushing over all the new baby clothes and toys.

I take my time putting away all the painting supplies and open the windows to let in the fresh air, hoping it will help the paint dry and get rid of the smell. As I finish, I decide that I should probably head over to Alaric and Phoebe's to see if Skarlyt needs help to bring everything back here to set up. Maybe Alaric even has a drill and some bits we can use too, so we don't have to hand tighten all the bolts. Although, hand tightening would take longer and give me more time to spend with Skarlyt.

Yup, hand tightening it is.

I walk the well-worn path through the woods that leads from Skarlyt's cottage to Alaric and Phoebe's house, marveling at how much my life has changed. Not only have I met my second-chance mate but I also found a pack I'm comfortable enough in to call home where I can be close to my family. My wolf even seems more at peace here than anywhere else we've been.

I take a deep inhale, smelling the trees and picking up Skarlyt's raspberry scent as I walk. It's still strong even though she hasn't walked this path in a few hours. Worry slices through me momentarily before I shake it off. She's fine. She's just at Phoebe and Alaric's. I repeat this to myself, but I still pick up my pace.

"Hey, guys," I say to Alaric and Phoebe, who are sitting on the front deck of their house. "Is Skar back yet?"

"We thought she just went straight to her cottage. We haven't seen her, and we already had to give Kayne the bottle she left," Phoebe says at the same time Alaric's phone starts ringing. We all look expectantly at him. "That's probably her now," she adds.

"Hello?" Alaric says into the phone. I can't hear the other half of the conversation, but, based on the way his eyebrows are pinching together, I'm assuming it's not Skar. "No, I didn't...a friend of mine borrowed it for the day...I'll be right there," he says as he hangs up the phone.

"What's going on?" I ask. He looks worried, and I can hear the fear in my own voice. This can't be good.

"Well, that was an officer from town. Apparently, they found my truck parked in the Wal-Mart parking lot, half loaded with baby items and a full cart left beside it," he says, surprisingly calm.

Fuck. There is no way that Skarlyt would leave his truck there, especially if it is loaded with baby items. Where is she?

"I have to go to check it out," Alaric turns to Phoebe, who is already nodding her head with wide eyes. "Lennox is going to come with me." He pauses to look at me, but I am already turning and heading toward my SUV. "But I want Darren, Ashton, and Josh to come stay with you while we're gone." He gives her a kiss before turning toward the driveway as if only realizing now that his truck isn't here.

"I'll drive," I tell him and lead the way to my SUV. What

could have happened? There has to be some logical explanation. I can't just jump to conclusions. Maybe she had to use the bathroom and ran back inside. That's feasible, right? But even as I think it, I know it doesn't ring true. If she'd only been gone for a minute, the officer wouldn't have called.

"Do you know where to go?" Alaric asks once we are seated inside the car.

"Yup," I reply. I don't want to panic, but a bad feeling is pooling in my gut. She has to be okay. She just has to. I just found her. I can't lose her now. "She could've just run back into the store to use the bathroom, right?" I ask him, hoping that he will put my mind at ease.

"I didn't want to say anything in front of Phoebe, but the truck's been parked there for a couple of hours now. They were busy with other calls, so they just got to it. I have a feeling that something happened to Skarlyt."

Well, shit, I wasn't expecting that. That's more of a worst-case scenario situation, and I was trying to stay positive. The bad feeling is just getting worse with every second, and I can't contain it anymore. Why did I suggest that she go to town by herself? I just wanted to cross everything off of her list; she seemed so excited about that damn list. I should have just gone with her, and we could've painted together. What was I thinking?

"She has to be okay. We have to find her. Promise me we'll find her, Alaric," I almost shout at him in panic.

"We will," he says, turning to me in confusion. "But why do you care so much? I know you and Skar have become friends since you got here, but I can smell your panic."

Shit. I forgot she didn't want us to tell Alaric that we're mates yet. I'm silent for a few breaths before I realize that I don't have a reasonable excuse that he will believe.

"She's my mate," is all I say before Alaric goes nuts.

"She's your *what*?" he screams at me, and I have to work to steady the car as I automatically flinch away from him. Yeah, now I realize why she didn't want him to know yet.

As calmly as possible, I simply say, "She's my second-chance true mate. We found out that day while watching the boys at the lake. She said she wasn't ready, and I agreed to just be friends and wait until she was ready to try." I turn my head to look at him. "I promise you, Alaric, I will never hurt her the way that bastard has hurt her. I'll wait forever for her to be ready if I have to. And if, in the end, she doesn't want me, I'll leave and let her live her life in peace.

"I just found her though. I haven't even gotten the chance to kiss my mate yet, and now she's missing. I understand you're upset, and she's your best friend, but can we leave our issues out of it until we get her back. Please?"

He nods stiffly in agreement, still obviously seething from the revelation. I know he's her best friend. He probably feels protective and maybe even a little betrayed right now, but we have bigger things to focus on—like finding my mate.

We pull into the parking lot, and it doesn't take long to find the truck and police cruisers. Alaric hops out before I can even put the car in park, but I follow quickly after. I immediately detect the scent of another male wolf, and I can't stop the growl that slips out.

"Kirnon," is all Alaric says.

What would that fucker want with Skarlyt? He rejected her. He made the choice not to have her in his life. If he thinks he can have her now, he's got another thing coming. If she chooses not to complete the bond with me, I'll let her live her life in peace, but I won't step aside for that asshole. No fucking way. I quickly replay everything she told me about him. There's no way she would've left with him on her own. She especially never would have left Kayne. Hell, she had the witches create a new barrier spell specifically to keep him out. No, something else happened here.

Alaric is talking with the officers, but I walk around the truck, trying to commit the scents to memory. The cart is still full of cute baby clothes and toys Skarlyt bought for Kayne. I can picture us sitting on the porch of her cottage with him in this little rocking swing. I can see us making breakfast in the kitchen with him sitting in his highchair and throwing food at us. There are so many possibilities before us, and I hope they are not lost now that Skarlyt is.

As I'm looking in the bed of the truck, I notice something glinting in the sun under the back tire and crouch down. I reach out to pick it up and then stop myself when I see it is a syringe.

"What's this?" I ask the officers.

One of them, a woman who is about five foot nothing with bleach blonde hair, comes over to look. She crouches down, taking out a pair of latex gloves and grabbing the syringe.

"I don't know," she says, carefully placing the syringe in a clear bag. "It's a good find, though. Our lab can test—at least for fingerprints."

I step closer to see if I can smell whatever was in it. I take a big whiff and have to smother the growl that tries to slip out. A sedative. So, she was taken. Someone drugged her and then took her. What the actual fuck?

"Alaric, can you come over here?" I shout to him. He walks over to me with a questioning look. I simply point toward the syringe with my head. His puzzled look quickly turns murderous. I know that same look is reflected on my face.

Someone took my mate. That someone is not going to live. I promise you, Skarlyt, wherever you are, I will find you, and I will mow down anyone who gets in the way. We will both get our happily ever after, no matter how many lines I need to cross.

"So, you said Skarlyt Moon borrowed your truck, correct?" The second officer, an older man with a balding head and protruding gut, asks Alaric.

"That's right."

"And she left at what time?" the officer asks.

"She left her cottage around twelve-thirty," I pipe in.

"And you are?" he turns to me as he writes something in his small notebook.

"Lennox Johnson," I supply, looking down at his name tag: Rogers.

"And who are you to Miss Moon?"

"I'm her m—"

"Boyfriend," Alaric supplies, cutting me off from calling her my mate. I had already taken a whiff of the two officers here, and both are human. Humans understand the "M" word, of course, but they generally just think it's creepy.

The balding man eyes me warily but writes that down in his notebook too.

"Okay. She's only been missing for a couple hours. It's possible she ran back into the store or went to get a bite to eat," he says, and I don't even try to stop the growl from slipping out this time. Neither does Alaric.

"What about the syringe?" I question.

"We don't know for sure that it's connected to Miss Moon's disappearance. Drug use is a sad reality, even here in Parry Sound. I know you are both assuming the worst already, but until we know for sure she was kidnapped, there's not much more we can do."

"That's not good enough," I growl, barely containing my extremely irate wolf from clawing his way out.

"Calm down, Lennox. We'll find her," Alaric says, stepping up and putting his hand on my shoulder.

"Sir," Officer Rogers puts his hand up as if he can force me to calm down. "Sir, I need you to take a deep breath and calm down."

"Her purse and phone are in the cart," the blonde officer at least tries to appease me with some actual help, but I cannot waste the time to respond politely. "If she had them with her, we could try to track the phone. Would she have anything else on her?"

"You don't understand. We need to find her. I need to find her," I tell Alaric, pleading with my eyes for him to understand.

"I do understand. Probably better than most. I love Skarlyt too. Don't forget that."

Love? Do I love Skarlyt? Yeah. I guess I do love the quirky, curious little witch. She's burrowed into my heart and made herself a home there. Her and Kayne both have. A pang of sadness goes through me at the realization that I love her and haven't even gotten the chance to tell her.

Find mate, my wolf growls.

We will, buddy. If it's the last thing we do. We will find her, I reassure him.

Alaric's phone starts ringing, and my head jerks toward him. Maybe it's Skarlyt. Maybe she got free and found a landline.

The two officers step away, happy to give us some space for the moment.

All my hopes are dashed when Alaric answers, "Hey, love," telling me right away that it's Phoebe.

"Whoa. Whoa. Calm down. What happened?" I move closer to him so I can hear what's being said.

"The barrier alarm went off. Darren has the entire pack in the bunker, but I've been watching the monitors. Alaric, it's Joe. He's here, and he brought a lot of friends," Phoebe says. I can hear the fear in her voice, and my throat tightens.

My family is there. My parents, sisters, and my niece. Shit.

Kayne. Kayne is there.

I've never been more conflicted in my life. I feel like I'm being pulled in separate directions. I need to find Skarlyt, but I need to ensure that the people I love at the pack are safe too. I'll never be able to forgive myself if something were to happen to any of them, and I know for sure Skarlyt will kill me if I can't promise Kayne is safe when we find her.

"We're on our way," Alaric says, hanging up the phone before turning to me. "We need to go."

I shake my head, still unsure of what to do. "I can't just stop looking for her."

"And we won't, but we need to go make sure everyone else is safe first. Then we can gather a bigger group to look for Skarlyt." I try to interrupt, but Alaric is already waving stiffly to the officers and turning to finish loading his truck. "We've got an issue back at home, so I'll just be taking my truck back since you can't do anything else right now."

"An issue?" The older officer's brows knit in concern as Alaric lifts the contents of the cart—more than a human man could—and tosses it in the bed of the truck.

"I've got a newborn at home, and she's fussy." It's a lame excuse, and he's clearly dismissing the officers. "Rogers, you know how to get ahold of me if you need me?"

The officers seem happy to for an excuse and wave us off as they get in their car.

"Alaric," I try to slow him down, but he's already got the driver's side door open. "He took Skarlyt somewhere. Maybe—"

"The people attacking the pack," he interrupts me, "could be using her as a hostage. They've done it before."

I hadn't even considered that. It is a very big coincidence that she goes missing just before a massive attack is launched on the pack.

Protect pup. Find mate.

Even my wolf feels the need to go make sure Kayne is safe. Gods I hope I'm not making the wrong choice.

Hang on, Skarlyt. Just a little longer. Please.

Chapter Fifteen

Skarlyt

I've spent the last couple of hours trying to figure out a way to leave this stupid room. I obviously tried the door first. Kirnon must have put a barrier spell on it to trap me in here. I can feel the magic coating the handle, and I feel like my skin is on fire as soon as I touch it. The magic is strong enough that he never could have pulled it off himself.

How he found a witch that would help capture another witch is beyond me. We usually stick together, but, based on my new jewelry, I shouldn't be surprised. If they were willing to give him bracelets to block my magic, they would probably be willing to help him trap me as well. Whoever they are, I'm putting them on my list too.

I tried the phone next. That fucker cut the end that plugs into the wall. I tried to connect the loose wires for a good half hour before figuring out it was futile. Then I banged on the walls for another hour. Either no one heard me, or no one bothered to answer.

Once I had yelled myself hoarse, I grabbed a couple of the metal coat hangers out of the closet, twisting and molding them into something I could stab him with and hid them around the room for easy access. One under the mattress, another under the sink in the bathroom, and the last one behind the TV. Let's see him try anything with me now.

I finally sit down on the bed, wiping my stinging red hands on my legs.

"Great. Just great. I'm fucking stuck here."

I need to get back to Kayne. I need to get back to Lennox. Oh, Lennox. He's probably so worried. I hope he doesn't think I ran off on him. I would never just run away. At this minute, though, all rational thought is gone. The panic is starting to catch up to me. All I can picture is Lennox being so angry with me when I do finally escape that he rejects me just when I've come to the realization that I want him in my life.

No, Lennox wouldn't do that. Kirnon would. I really need to try and separate the two. Kirnon literally kidnapped me, and Lennox is probably in my room right now making sure my son gets to sleep. Ugh, why did I wait to claim him? If we were bonded mates, this wouldn't be a problem. He'd already know where I am, and we'd be home with Kayne. Stupid Skarlyt.

I hear Kirnon coming in the door and can smell the McDonald's from here. I'm not a big fan of McDonald's usually, which he should know considering we dated for years, but right now it smells like heaven. I don't know how long I've been here, but my growling stomach is evidence it's been a few hours at least. When was the last time I ate? I don't remember eating lunch or breakfast for that matter. I was too excited about the barrier being up to stop and grab something to eat.

"Honey, I'm home," he says, coming through the door in a suspiciously good mood. What's that about? When I don't respond, he crosses the room and grabs me by my neck, raising me up against the wall. "You are supposed to welcome me home," he spits in my face.

Yeah, no, thank you.

I can't talk because of his hold on my neck, which is starting to hurt almost as much as my boobs. I haven't been away from Kayne this long before, and I know he's probably hungry because I feel like I'm about to burst.

He leans his face into the crook of my neck and sniffs. "Mmm, you smell good enough to eat," he says. Ew. No. But he doesn't stop there. He glides his tongue from my collarbone up to my ear, making me cringe. How I ever let this asshole touch any part of my body is beyond me. "Maybe we'll save the McDonald's for dessert. I have a brilliant idea to work up an appetite."

Oh, my goddess. No. I try to protest and squirm out of his hold. I reach my hand down to try and get the makeshift weapon I hid under the bed, but he just tightens his grip on my throat, beginning to kiss my neck. If the growing bulge in his pants is any indication, I'd say he's getting off on me struggling.

I have to think of a way to stop him.

He starts making his way down my throat toward my breasts. He pulls my shirt down roughly, freeing one of my fully engorged breasts and causing a rather large stream of milk to shoot out from the pressure right into his face. Ah, that feels so good. The milk that shot out of my too-full breast lessened the painful, engorged feeling a little, giving me a moment of relief.

Another bonus is that it catches him so off guard that he releases my throat and backs away as he tries to wipe the milk off. I'd laugh if my throat wasn't so raw. Watching him claw at his face, not knowing what is on it, is hilarious.

I kick out my leg, taking the momentary distraction as an opportunity, and try to aim for his balls. He's flailing around a bit, so I miss and curse internally. I slowly inch my hand closer to the metal hanger I have stashed under the bed, but I freeze at his next words.

"What the fuck was that?" he screams at me as I adjust my

breast back into my bra and shirt. "Was that breast milk?" Nope, still not answering. I can see that he's growing more furious as the wheels in his head are turning.

"Are you fucking pregnant? Who is the father? I'll kill whoever dared to touch my mate." He's straight up screaming at me now. If it wasn't for this barrier spell, I'm sure that the manager would have called the cops. I want to shrink back away from him. I know he's stronger than me physically, and I don't have the power to beat him without my magic, but I refuse to cower to this piece of shit. I stand there with my chin raised in defiance. He can do whatever he wants to me, but he cannot find out about Kayne.

"Wait, no. You get breast milk after you have a baby." Oh shit, he put it together too fast. I was hoping he was still too disinterested in the workings of a woman's body to know. I can see him counting months on his hand and whispering under his breath. He's going to figure it out. What can I do? Think, Skarlyt.

"You're delusional. What the hell do you know about breast milk and babies?" Good one, Skarlyt. I mentally face-palm myself.

"You do, and it's mine, isn't it?" he asks. I shake my head over and over, but I know it's a lost cause when I see the smirk that crosses onto his face.

"It is. Is it a boy or a girl?" he asks before switching gears. "Never mind that. It doesn't matter. Where is it?"

It, he says...like Kayne is a thing and not a tiny person. My son is already only a tool for him to use. I shake my head once more, refusing to give him anything. He grabs me by my neck again.

"I'll find it. Don't you worry. We'll be one big happy family, and you'll never leave me, or I'll kill it. Do I make myself clear?"

I cannot get air into my lungs, so I pray silently, sending the Mother every ounce of my pleading heart.

Mother, please keep my baby safe. Don't let this evil man get his clutches on him. I don't know what he intends for my beautiful boy, but as long as this man is alive, he will never be safe.

154

I know she won't answer me. It's nothing personal; that's just not how she works.

Still, I hear a musical voice, warm and deep, saying only *"I promise, daughter,"* just as everything turns black, and I lose consciousness.

So much for eating today.

Chapter Sixteen

Lennox

I 'm speeding back to the pack land after Alaric's phone call with Phoebe, and I'm ashamed to say that, as much as I want to be there to protect my family, I want to find Skarlyt more. Before we left the parking lot, I tried to reason with Alaric that maybe we should split our efforts. Alaric is right, though. Whoever kidnapped Skarlyt is connected to the attack occurring on pack land. It's too much of a coincidence.

That is why we're both driving like madmen down the highway. We couldn't tell the cops why we were leaving. How do you explain to humans that your shifter pack is under attack by other supernaturals? They'd look at us like we were crazy. That's the one thing I'll miss about the Ironwood pack. Some law enforcement there knew our secret. It made dealing with certain things a whole lot easier. Maybe I can convince Alaric to do something similar here. Maybe bring a couple of officers in on our secret. Getting a couple of shifters to join the force would be even better.

As I speed down the driveway, I watch out the windows for any sign of the attack. I see small signs of movement on either side before we cross the barrier. I hope it's just some animals, but I've never seen movement like that out here before. It is pretty normal for local animals to avoid a shifter pack; they know that we're predators and tend to stay clear. The only animals that generally venture close are other predators, like bears or cougars. If a family of deer wander through, they scatter once they catch a whiff of wolves.

I continue to scan the woods as I drive. The main square of pack land is deserted. I can see signs that people were in a hurry to leave. What is normally a playground full of kids is completely empty. A couple of empty swings move slowly, blown by the wind. Some of the cabins have their lights left on or their doors swinging open. There are bikes, toys, and stuffed animals abandoned on their porches. It looks like a ghost town here.

We pull up to Alaric's house, and I can see that the back yard is full of shifters. There must be close to four hundred of them here. I knew this pack was large, but I obviously didn't know the totality of it.

Alaric's brother, Darren, comes running up to greet us. We have gotten close over the past couple of weeks. He's a solid guy, and I can easily tell why he's Alaric's beta. He's very pack driven, always coming through for random requests for anyone. He'd make an amazing alpha if he ever started his own pack.

"There's a mixture of mages and vampires roaming on the other side of the barrier," Darren says.

"Vampires?" Alaric questions.

"Yup. It seems like the mages are attacking the barrier on rotation, taking turns testing each side for weaknesses while the vamps are just patrolling through the trees."

After what Skar told me about the amount of magic they use to power that barrier, I doubt there are any weaknesses to find, but I don't know who or what is on the opposing side.

"But that doesn't make any sense. Roderick would never attack us," Alaric says.

"The scouts I've sent out haven't recognized anyone, so I'm thinking it's a different coven helping them."

"Hopefully, that's it. I'd hate to go to war with the local vamps," Alaric says matter-of-factly. As if it's not even a question. If it were the local vamps, he would go after them. There's none of the backhanded politics that determine Christian's choices.

The three of us walk around the house into the back yard, meeting up with the rest of the shifters.

"You all right?" Darren asks, sliding up to me while Alaric explains the situation to the rest.

I shake my head. "Not really. As long as we get through this quickly and I can go find Skarlyt, I will be."

He nods and places his hand on my shoulder, comforting me as if he knows our secret even though it's impossible. "We will," he promises. I hope it's a promise he can follow through on, not something he's just saying to placate me. We turn our attention back to Alaric as he begins issuing orders.

It doesn't take long for us to get mobilized, and I follow Alaric and his team through the woods to the eastern border of the pack. As we approach the border of the pack land, I hear a low growing in Alaric's chest before we even clear the trees.

"Joe," he bites out, striding toward the mage standing on the other side of the barrier.

"We were told you'd be distracted," he begins. "A little birdy also told us that you have a baby phoenix ripe for the picking."

The mage, Joe apparently, has some balls.

The next thing I know, Joe is on our side of the barrier with a silver rope wrapped around him like a lasso. I don't even know where it came from, but if it will stop him from using his magic on us, great. Even better, he may know where Skar is.

I look around quickly and see several of the witches are holding the same sort of silver ropes. I can only assume that they've enchanted them to help fight mages. Based on what

Charleigh and Felicia told me of the pack's last run-in with them, it's a smart move and seems like the witches have learned some things.

The lasso pulled him so forcefully to our side of the barrier that he stumbled and landed face first in front of me. Perfect. Easy access.

"What do you mean you were told we'd be distracted?" I question him, grabbing him by the front of his shirt and lifting him into the air. He's squirming within the enchanted rope and is certainly more fat than muscle, but my rage makes it easy to lift him high enough that his feet kick helplessly at the ground.

"We were told that someone has taken something of yours, and that you'd be too busy looking for her to protect the baby phoenix." So, he does know who took Skar.

"Where is she?" The words grind out through my clenched teeth. I'm vaguely aware that there is fighting going on around me, but I can't focus on anything other than the fact that Skarlyt was taken by someone working with these fuckers, and I'm going to make him tell me where she is. I'm not above torture. Not with Skarlyt missing.

He just laughs in my face, showing his square, yellowing teeth in a manic grin.

Man, this guy really has a death wish, and I'm just about to oblige when Alaric comes up.

"Phoebe warned you, Joe. She gave you a chance, and this is how you use it?" He turns to me. "This one is Phoebe's. They have history."

I nod in understanding, even though I'm not too happy about it, and hand him over to Alaric. If this is one of the mages from Morpeth who made Phoebe's life hell for years, she deserves to exact her revenge. Hopefully, she'll be up for a team effort. She can make him suffer while I ask some questions.

"Just because Tanner is gone doesn't mean there aren't more of us ready to take his place. We have more members than you think, Alaric. A lot more." His voice has the frenetic energy of a zealot, and his eyes are wide and hateful. He is probably planning to say more, but I can't help the way my fist connects with his face. It feels so damn good, but the silence is the best part. Alaric raises his brow at me in question. I simply shrug.

"You only said not to kill him. Besides, I don't think he was going to give us any answers. Not yet anyway."

Looking around, I see a few wounded both sides. Wolves are dragging pack members back to our side of the barrier while vampires and mages retreat on the other side, doing the same. I knew Alaric is a different type of alpha, but I don't realize just how different until I see what he does next. As he steps away, he raises his voice to address not only our side but our enemies as well.

"We have the leader of the mages. You have twenty-four hours to gather your dead. We will not attack you during that time. We will place any of your members on your side of the barrier. If you attack us in those twenty-four hours, consider any future deals off the table.

"I would also like to sit down with the leader of the vampire coven present. I have a feeling they've been misled. Have them meet me in this exact spot at midnight tomorrow, and we'll talk." He says this to everyone, not stopping to look at a singular person. I can see the shocked faces on the other side. I'm sure they've been told all kinds of stories about this alpha. It will be interesting to see what can come out of a meeting with the vampire leader.

The sun is peeking over the horizon by the time we make it back to the house, and Skarlyt has been gone for nineteen hours. An entire night. Although I'm pretty much dead on my feet, I don't have time to sleep. The urge to find her is overwhelming.

Once inside the house, Alaric pulls me aside.

"I have to lock down the pack," he says, looking at me with disappointment.

"Not with me in it, you don't," I bite back.

"I can't risk you leaving now and getting captured. Because of the temporary bonds we created when they put up the barrier, you can be used to let them across, the same as Skarlyt, which is why I honestly thought she would be with them. I can't let you go out there yet. I'm sorry," he says calmly. I know I'm not thinking rationally, but I can't help it. I allow my wolf's dominance to push forward and growl out.

"I am not a member of your pack. I will not be staying here. I am going to find my mate. I don't care what you have to do. Break the bonds if you have to, but I am telling you: I am not staying here." He looks taken aback and surprised at the level of dominance I just emitted, so I soften my voice a bit.

"Listen, Alaric. I respect you as an alpha. I respect you as Phoebe's mate. I appreciate you taking in my sisters and my parents and showing them what a real pack should be like. I also appreciate and respect the fact that you are Skarlyt's best friend. Let me be perfectly clear. My mate is in danger, and so is her pup. I can't do both. I need you to take care of your pack, your mate, your pups, my sisters, and my mate's pup while I go find her. Don't try to tell me that you wouldn't do the same."

With the last statement, he realizes exactly what he was asking of me.

"On two conditions. First, you wait a couple of hours before you leave to make sure there is no one lingering to attack. Second, you take Skarlyt's mom, Constance, with you when you go. She should be able to trace Skarlyt's magic and help you locate her.

"You go and get my best friend back, and I promise I will keep our family safe," he finishes, clasping me on the shoulder.

Our family? Huh. I guess I can see that. With him being mated to Phoebe, and Charleigh and her being like sisters, and Skar being my mate, and her and Alaric being best friends...Yeah, we're one big happy family.

"Okay, deal," I say and follow him into the house.

Once we're downstairs, I see an older version of Skarlyt barreling toward me. The same woman from earlier who offered to watch the boys. I should've introduced myself then, but I was too excited about Skarlyt being out of the house. The fact that her body had melted into mine the second I wrapped her up in a hug had nothing to do with it...no, absolutely nothing.

I don't know whether or not I should be afraid, but I take an involuntary step back as she approaches. She just throws her arms around my neck and begins sobbing into my chest. I look to Alaric for help. He just shrugs his shoulders and continues on into the safe room.

I pat her back for a few moments before saying, "Are you okay?" I seem to have caught her off guard because she stiffens, backs up and wipes her eyes.

"No, I'm not okay. My daughter is missing. I'm scared, but I'm also happy because I found out that you are her fated mate. From what your sisters have told me over the past hour, you're a pretty amazing man."

When she looks up at me, a fire in her bright blue eyes, I instantly see the resemblance. It is the same fire that is in Skarlyt's eyes when she is upset or excited about something.

Wait, did she just say that I'm Skarlyt's mate?

"How did you know that Skarlyt's my mate?" I ask.

She scoffs. "Not that I needed anyone to tell me after watching the two of you this morning, but Phoebe let the bomb drop while you and Alaric were out. Now, what are we going to do about finding my daughter?"

"You and I are going to be leaving in a couple of hours to go find her. Alaric said something about you being able to track her magic," I explain to her, and she immediately perks right up.

"What? I mean I can. But what about the attack?"

"Well, Alaric has to lock the pack down, and I refuse to stay here instead of being out there searching for Skarlyt. So, Alaric and I made a deal. You and I will be leaving pack land in a couple of hours to search for her, and we're not coming back until we find her. I promise that I will stop at nothing until she's back with us," I tell her, looking directly into her eyes so she can see my determination.

"Stood up to Alaric, then? Not bad. I better go get my things," she says before rushing off.

I make a quick stop to see my sisters where they sit with Cybil between them in the crowded safe room. When she catches sight of me, Charleigh immediately storms toward me.

"Mate?" she demands.

"Yeah." I rub the back of my neck, not knowing what to say. The fact that I kept this a secret from her probably feels like a betrayal. Add in the fact that Phoebe already knew and, well, I'm probably in trouble.

Instead of yelling at me like I thought she would, she throws her arms around me.

"I knew it! I'm so happy."

I wrap my arms around her waist. "Me too. But first I need to find her."

Charleigh steps back as the rest of my family join us. "You better. Skarlyt's awesome."

"She really is," Felicia agrees, leaning into Josh.

"If anyone can find her, it's Constance. Alaric told us the plan. It's smart bringing her along," Josh adds.

I nod, reaching over to grab Cybil out of Ashton's arms. "Keep my princess safe, will you?" I say to him.

"With my life," he nods.

"I have something else to ask you all," I say as I look at each of them.

"Anything, son," my dad says, clapping a reassuring hand on my shoulder.

"I need you to protect Kayne as well."

"Obviously we will protect Kayne," Charleigh says with a roll of her eyes.

"I know. But..."

"He's your pup," my dad supplies, and I nod in agreement as tears spring, unexpectedly, to my eyes.

"Thank you," I whisper as I hand Cybil back to Ashton. I turn toward Phoebe where she sits on a couch with two babies in her arms. I lean down, scooping Kayne out of her arms and snuggle him into me.

"I'm sorry, Lennox," Phoebe whispers.

My head snaps up to her. "For what?"

"For telling them about you and Skar being mates. I didn't mean to. It's just that he was so hungry and wouldn't eat the formula and wouldn't latch on for me. I was starting to get worried. So, I asked Charleigh to try, but she refused. She thought it was best if I kept trying because she didn't want to step on Skarlyt's toes. I finally told her that you and Skarlyt are mates so she'd give it a try."

I sit next to her and place my hand around her shoulders, pulling her into me. "It's okay. I understand. Besides, it's not me who wanted to keep it a secret."

She chuckles. "I know."

"Did it work?" I ask.

"Did what work?"

"Charleigh feeding Kayne; did it work?"

She smiles. "Yup. Charleigh's going to have a hard time keeping up with two babies, so the sooner Skarlyt is home the better, but he won't starve."

I lean my head down, placing my forehead on Kayne's and take a deep inhale. Memorizing his scent, pine with a hint of rasp-berry just like his mom.

"You be a good boy now while I go get your mommy," I whisper, placing a soft kiss on his head. He snuggles in deeper to me as if sensing that I need a hug, and I give him a soft squeeze before handing him back to Phoebe.

"Don't worry about us. We'll be fine. You just go get Skarlyt and bring her home," she demands.

I nod as I stand. "I won't return without her."

"Good," she says, turning back toward the two bundles in her arms, effectively dismissing me.

I walk back out of the bunker, pausing momentarily at the door to look back at my family, my pack, and my heart swells. Finally, I found something worth fighting for. The only thing that would make this better is having Skarlyt here at my side.

"I'm ready when you are," Constance says, appearing beside me in a way that is eerily similar to her daughter.

"I'm ready," I tell her.

Both of us turn and walk up the stairs. It's already been almost an hour. By the time we're done loading up, Alaric's two-hour request should be up.

Even if we are too early for his taste, it's time to go find my mate.

Chapter Seventeen

Skarlyt

"Rise and shine!" I hear Kirnon call as he rips the covers off me. I don't even remember going to bed last night. My hand reaches up automatically to support the throbbing pain in my neck. Wait, I do remember. He choked me until I passed out. I feel the warmth of a stream of sunlight on my face. Damn it. He must've drugged me again. Mother fucker. As the events of the previous day start to come back to me, all I can think about is the fact that he knows about Kayne and my son is no longer safe.

I open my eyes and look at his unusually cheerful face. "What are you in such a good mood about?" I spit at him before rolling to the opposite side of the bed and standing up. The motion, a little too quick, sends my head spinning.

"Well, my dear Skarlyt, it seems you don't mean as much to Alaric and that pesky pack as I once believed. I thought that they would be so distracted by looking for you that my new friends could steal the baby phoenix without too much trouble."

My mind is still reeling. The baby? Aurora? What "friends" could he have made that even know about Phoebe's daughter?

"It didn't happen, by the way," he explains as he rips back the second curtain . "Alaric gave up searching for you as soon as they attacked the pack. I thought for sure he would have at least kept a couple of different wolves in town looking for you, but there isn't even one. It really is fortunate for me. It means I have longer to convince you to come to your senses."

"Come to my—" I start to yell at him, but my throat is still too raw to accommodate my anger. No one is looking for me. At least, that's what Kirnon wants me to think.

"I also stopped at Wal-Mart looking for those pad things you had in your bra, and the woman at the store said I should buy you this pump thing to 'keep up your supply' while away from the baby. Whatever that means."

I want to pick up the pump and throw it back in his face after everything he's said, but, at the end of the day, I would want Alaric to stay and protect Aurora and Kayne. I'm also pretty grateful that he bought me a breast pump. Not only will it help with how painfully full I am and release some of the pressure, but I'll still be able to produce milk to feed Kayne when I eventually figure out how to get back to him.

I say *when* I get out of here because I am leaving this place. Whether it's over Kirnon's dead body or not is ultimately going to be his choice.

"Can I take a shower?" I ask him, making him realize for the first time that he hasn't been as great of a host as he believes. If I want to escape, I'm going to have to make him think that I'm coming around to the idea of being his mate. It's the only way he will let his guard down.

"Also, if I'm going to be staying here with you, I'm going to need some clothes, a toothbrush, some food maybe." I try to keep my voice light and airy, but I know I don't entirely succeed. Either he doesn't notice or doesn't care because he simply smiles like he's just won the lottery and hands me a pen and pad of paper from the bedside table.

"Make a list of everything that you need, and I'll run out and grab it while you're in the shower."

I take the pad and paper from him, making a list. I take a little extra time to list the most expensive brands of everything just to inconvenience him. When I'm just about done, I have a brilliant thought and add tampons and pads to the list. Just because Phoebe's tear did wonders and I'm no longer bleeding, doesn't mean he needs to know that. I do my best evil laugh, in my head of course. Don't want him to know I'm an evil genius.

I give him a quick kiss on the cheek as I saunter to the bathroom, taking the breast pump with me. The feel of his skin on my lips makes me want to vomit, but I am able to keep it down. I will try to be agreeable with him so I can get home to my family, but I will not let it go any further than that small peck. As soon as I enter the bathroom, I lather my hands with soap and begin to scrub my lips, desperate to get the oily feeling of him off my skin. I take a peek at myself in the mirror, noticing the slight bruising around my neck and let out a soft curse, wishing I had my magic to help speed the healing. Without it, I need to pray that it heals quickly and nothing major is permanently damaged.

With the stage set for me to pretend I am coming around to his side of thinking, it's just a waiting game. This is a matter of *when* I get out and not *if*. I just hope Kayne still remembers me by the time I do.

I pull the breast pump out of the box. He even got the good one. Perfect. After reading the instructions and plugging it in, I take a seat on the toilet. I lift my shirt above my head and pull down my bra to expose my nipples. My boobs are rock hard and so sore that I am terrified to put any pressure on them.

I grab one of the pumps, turning it on and pressing it up against my nipple. A stream of milk flows out before the suction even latches on, giving me a little relief. The first couple of draws from the machine are a mixture of pain and pleasure, as it sucks my nipples inside and the milk flows out.

By the time I'm done with both breasts, I have over eight ounces of milk and my boobs feel like a million bucks. I screw the cap on the bottles of milk and rinse out the machine quickly before cracking the door open a sliver and taking a peek.

Good. He's gone. I rush out of the bathroom, straight for the mini fridge in the corner and place both bottles of milk inside before heading back to the shower.

I find myself wondering what Lennox is doing as I wash out my long black hair. Kirnon said no one is looking for me, but I find that hard to believe. If there's one thing I know about Lennox, it is that he would never give up searching for me. Unless...A small sob lodges in my throat. Unless he thinks that I left him on purpose. I crouch down at the back of the shower, hugging my knees as sobs wrack my body. I just want to go home.

I've never missed anyone as much as I miss Lennox and Kayne. Even in the dark days after I was rejected and discovered I was pregnant, I never felt this bad. I keep hoping that I'll open my eyes, and this will all just have been a nightmare. I'm not really here. I'm home nestled safely in my bed with Kayne. Lennox will be over in the morning for breakfast, and we will finish setting up Kayne's room in the cottage.

When he's ready to leave for the night, I'll ask him to stay, tell him I'm ready to be claimed, that I've fallen hopelessly in love with him and want to spend the rest of my life with him. Then, after we've put Kayne safely in his new bed, I'll show him just how much I care and appreciate him.

The more I envision this daydream, the more sobs wrack my body. What if I never escape? What if I never get to run my fingers through Lennox's strawberry-blonde surfer hair? Kirnon is crazed enough to kidnap me. I don't want to take my chances that he won't hurt or even kill me in his anger. What if I don't get to see Kayne perform his first spell or shift for the first time? There are so many things I will miss out on if I can't find a way out of here.

No. None of those things are options. My only option is to get out of this hellhole. My only option is to get away from Kirnon and back with my loves. I'll do whatever it takes to make that happen. Even if I have to pretend to be complacent.

Ugh. A shiver flows through my body despite the warm water rushing over me, and I wonder what it will take to make Kirnon think that it's safe to let me out, or even better, take off this damn bracelet.

Solidifying my resolve, I stand. "I'll do whatever it takes." I wash the tears from my eyes and make quick work of the rest of my body, hoping to have a little longer to myself before Kirnon comes back. I don't necessarily want to put my dirty clothes back on, but it will be better than waiting around in a towel for him to return.

Throwing my underwear in the garbage, I slide my pants back on before clasping my bra and placing the breast pads inside. At least I won't have to worry about leaking through my bra anymore, although it's already pretty wet. If I didn't need to worry about Kirnon taking it as some sort of invitation, I would just throw it out and go without until he brings me a new one. But that's not my life right now. No, right now, I need to have as much clothing as possible between me and him.

After slipping my shirt on, I walk out to the room and look around once more at the dingy motel he brought me to.

By now, I've placed it. Parry Sound is only so big, and even a roach motel I'd never go to is hard to forget entirely. This is the Sunset Motel. We are still close to the store where Kirnon grabbed me—where Alaric's truck is still waiting. If I could get out of the room, I could probably run there on foot. We are also too close to the edge of town, just a few turns from the highway that could take me far from home in no time at all.

I'd never step foot in this place by choice, but I'll take it if the other option is being crammed into Kirnon's trunk. Seriously. Shag carpet, a comforter that was probably popular in the eighties, dust everywhere, and yellow nicotine stains on the wall.

Who would stay in a place like this?

Chapter Eighteen

Lennox

Constance and I load up my SUV and are ready to leave pack land around midnight. However, I didn't anticipate the number of books that she would need to bring with her. It feels like we load the entire back seat with only books. Maybe I should suggest to Skar that she digitize some of these so that they can be more portable. I've already had to call and change my reservation at the motel so that we can be on the main floor. No way am I lugging all those books up the stairs.

Luckily, they had a set of adjoining rooms on the bottom level available. Although, now that I'm here, I don't see why I bothered with a reservation at all. This place is a dump. I look over at Constance. "Are you sure this is the right place?"

She simply nods. "Yes. We can't stay on pack land tonight, and there is no one here to interrupt us while we do what we need to do." I guess I can't argue with that logic...

We walk up to the check-in desk, and I tap the little bell on the counter.

"Can I help you?" an older man asks as he walks behind the desk from a back room.

"Yes. We have a reservation under Johnson," I tell him.

"Ah yes. Two rooms, right?" I nod. "You're in luck. We have the two end rooms available right now."

As if luck had anything to do with it. Pretty sure we're two of the only people to have stayed here this decade.

"Thanks," I say, plastering a smile on my face.

I take the keys from him, finding the one for the end room and handing over the other to Constance. As I open up the door, my sense of smell is assaulted. It smells like mothballs and musk mixed with shit. On a positive note, the way this room smells should mask any magic we produce. The negative side is that I think I might be sick. The dingy, rust colored carpet and bedspread have visible stains. I'm glad I brought my sleeping bag. Otherwise, I'd just sleep in wolf form. Constance won't be able to, though, so I've made sure to bring a spare one for her just in case.

I prop the door open to air out the room. I do the same with the small window beside the door and turn on the bathroom fan. Hopefully, the smell won't be as terrible by the time I need to sleep. There is absolutely no way I would be able to sleep with that stench. I'd rather sleep outside. Thankfully, by the time I bring my bags into the room and set myself up, it has already started to dissipate.

I open the door to the adjoining room, and I'm shocked by what I see. The space is ten times the size of my room with a beautiful bed, sitting area, and work area similar to Skar's basement at Alaric's. It even smells like an ocean breeze.

"Wha...who...how?" is what chooses to come out of my mouth in front of my mate's mother. I'm usually a lot better with words, but I was expecting to find her room looking as pitiful as mine.

She just shakes her head at me, chuckling. "One of the joys of magic. We can't make something out of nothing, but we can remodel almost anything into something new. It's not usually permanent since we have to create tiny pockets in space to make room. But this will serve our purposes."

"Why did you let me reserve two rooms if you can do this?" I ask, looking at the enormous space she's created.

"Don't be ridiculous," she scoffs, "I will not be caught at some sleazy motel, sharing a room with a boy half my age."

I shrug and nod in response and walk around the space, trying to see if I can feel where the extension starts and stops while Constance continues setting up the workspace.

"If you are going to be my daughter's mate, you have an awful lot to learn," she says as she pauses to watch me walk around.

"I've been around witches before but never long enough to learn anything about their magic. My old pack beta made sure to contact all shifter packs in the country and warn them away from me. In turn, they told their allies as well. Let's just say I've been on the outside of the supernatural world for the last twelve years, but I can't wait to learn more," I tell her with honesty.

She seems satisfied with my answer and goes back to setting up her workspace.

"I never liked Kirnon," Constance admits matter-of-factly after a few moments of silence, "even when they were kids. Skarlyt has always been extremely curious. She can be overwhelming at times, but he tried to turn her into something she's not." She stops as abruptly as she started, and I am still searching for the words to reassure her that I understand when she continues. "But not you. I think you can also be...overwhelming. Even though we are in what my daughter would call an 'extremely shitty situation,' you're trying to stay positive. I know how I'm feeling right now, and it seems like you're feeling all that and more. That shows me how much you already care for my daughter."

Wow. I don't know whether to be offended or impressed by her calling me overwhelming. Of course, that's what I latch onto.

I'm going to take it as a compliment since that seems to have been her intention.

"I care for her more than I ever thought possible, and I haven't had the chance to tell her yet," I respond, and her eyes start to mist briefly before she turns back to what she was doing.

I go back to walking around. I don't have much I can do to help her set up her workspace. I guess I'm here to act as the muscle whenever she needs me.

An hour passes while she sets up, and we're both exhausted when she suggests we sleep a bit. I protest, but she wins by explaining that her magic will work better after she's had some sleep. She hands me a vial and I take it, looking at her in confusion.

"It's to help you sleep," she says, as if it's the most normal thing in the world to just pass potions around.

"I probably need to be alert—"

"I will be alert," she cuts off my protest. "You will be a distraction with all your pacing and hand-wringing."

It's harsh, but I know it's true. I quickly swallow the potion and head to my room. Either the room smells better than when I left, or my senses are confused after being assaulted by the oily, herby tincture I just swallowed. I probably should have at least asked what was in it, but Constance Moon doesn't leave much room for uncertainty.

I crash onto the bed with surprising force, already fighting to keep my eyes open. I intend to turn off the lights and set up my sleeping bag, but I cannot seem to rise again. I promise myself I'll get up in just one minute to change clothes and pull the grimy covers from the bed, but my eyes drift shut instead.

After what must've been a few hours of the best sleep I've ever had, I wake feeling perfectly rested despite still being face-down, breathing in the dusty mattress. Once I am up, I run to town to grab us food before returning to a now awake Constance. We inhale our McDonald's as if we haven't eaten in days, but really I think we both just want to get back to finding Skarlyt. The sun is setting which means Skarlyt has been missing for more than twenty-four hours now, and that's twenty-four too long.

"Lennox, can you unload all my books for me, please?" Constance asks while she's stretching a map across a desk to study it. Thank the goddess she is giving me something to do.

"Can't you just magically move them in here?" I ask her. I am only curious, but, judging by the look on her face, I should've rephrased it. Goddess knows my mother used to love saying that to me. 'It's not what you're saying, it's how you're saying it.' I used to hate it, but after spending some time with Phoebe's boys the last week or so, I know what she meant. I have even been tempted to say it a few times myself.

"I'm not trying to be a smart aleck; I'm just genuinely curious," I add quickly before I destroy any of the progress I've made in the relationship department today.

"Of course I can, but you need something to do in order to focus your mind," I simply nod and head out the door. She's right. I do need something to do other than pace and worry about what is happening with Skarlyt right now. Is she hurt? Is she sad? Her boobs must be killing her since she hasn't fed Kayne in over a day. Is she eating?

When I come back into the room on one of my trips to and from the car, she says, "I need to meditate and try to focus my mind on reaching Skarlyt. When she was little, we were able to speak into each other's minds during meditation. We haven't tried speaking telepathically since she was little, but if there was ever a time to try again, it's now," she finishes and walks over to her meditation pillow and sits down cross-legged.

"Is there anything I can do to help?" I offer.

"Just stay as quiet as possible," I nod and zip my lip closed, bringing a brief smile to her severe lips.

I watch for a moment as she closes her eyes and settles in

before I continue to unload the car.

On my next trip in, I see that her eyes begin to flutter and open as I'm bringing the last of the books inside, so I ask, "Any luck?"

She shakes her head no, and tears start to mist her eyes once more. I can't help that my posture deflates with what feels like defeat, but she hops up and claps her hands saying, "No, it didn't work, but it doesn't mean we don't have more things we can try."

The next few hours consist of us trying locator spells, sight spells, and basically any other kind of spell Constance can find that would help us locate her.

"It's almost like there's a barrier surrounding Skarlyt that I can't get through. Like there's another witch helping him and nothing I'm doing is working," she says, slamming her fists on the counter. "The only thing left to try is blood magic."

"I thought that wasn't an option," I argue, "because of the whole 'corrupts your soul' thing."

"You're right, it does, which is why it will be the absolute last resort. It's addictive, like a drug. Use it once, and it calls to you, enticing you to use more and more until your soul turns black and there is no trace of your former self."

"Yeah, let's avoid that. Skarlyt would hate me if I let that happen to you," I tell her.

She just shrugs her thin shoulders as if Skarlyt doesn't really have a choice in the matter.

"Let's head to Supernatural first," she suggests, "we will see if Trevan can help us."

"Who's Trevan, and what is Supernatural?"

"He is the Fae who owns Supernatural, which is a bar downtown that caters to supernatural customers. He's also friends with Skarlyt, so, if there are any Fae tricks that can help us, he'll know," she tells me before grabbing her purse and heading to the car. I hope she's right and the Fae can help us.

On the drive to Supernatural, I try to think through this

kidnapping the way they do in the police procedurals my mom
and dad watch constantly. He took her from the store's parking
lot. He left the truck, so he either has a car of his own or carried
her away. That would have gotten attention, so probably he has
a car.

I study the buildings we pass and try not to lose hope. If he
was on foot, he could only have taken her so far away. If he has a
car, though, they could be anywhere by now.

"Do any of these spells work if she's—I don't know—across the
country?" I ask.

"Yes," Constance says. Her eyes are closed, but I know she's
searching for her daughter in some way I cannot see. "Most of my
methods for searching work regardless of distance. Don't worry,
though. I think she's still close to home."

"Why do you think that?"

"Honestly?" She opens her eyes to look at me, and I break my
attention to the road long enough to nod at her. "Whatever those
asshole mages attacking the pack want, they are connected to
Kirnon and this kidnapping. Taking her far away would be smart
because it'd lessen our chances of finding her. They've got her
powers blocked somehow, but transporting her for long would give
her chances to escape. Honestly, they'd have to be smart and brave
to try to get her far away from Parry Sound," she explains with
disgust, "and I don't think any of them have the brains or balls
for it."

"Brains or balls, huh?" I ask. I am not sure I agree with her
reasoning, but it does make me feel better. She only smiles in
response.

I park the car in front of an extensive, unmarked building, and
we head inside. It isn't crowded at this hour, but the scene looks
like it is straight from a book about Faerie. There's green everywhere with colorful flowers sprinkled throughout.

"Constance!" some guy with aquamarine hair yells, coming

out from behind the bar and pulling Constance into a giant hug. I'm guessing this must be Trev.

"Trevan. It's so good to see you," she says, squeezing him back for a minute before stepping back and gesturing to me. "Lennox, this is Trevan. Trevan, this is Lennox, Skarlyt's mate."

Trev's eyes go wide as I stick out my hand to him. Trevan slaps it away and pulls me into a bear hug.

"We don't shake when we're family. If you're Skarlyt's mate, that makes you family. Say, where is the little witch?" he asks with a laugh while releasing me.

"Well, that's why we're here. Skarlyt's been taken, and my magic is being blocked by something. I was hoping you could help," Constance pleads with him.

"Taken?" he seems to hesitate. "You know I rarely get involved in these things. Since it's Skar we're talking about, let's go to the back room and see what we can come up with," he states before he claps his hands together and leads us there.

Thank Mother Moon, let's hope he has something that can help.

"So, you said that she was taken?" Trevan asks.

"Yes. Kirnon took her," Constance supplies.

"Kirnon? Hasn't he done enough?" Trevan growls. Having a growl come out of a blue-haired Fae who looks like a supermodel on steroids is about the strangest thing I've ever seen. Though most Fae like to stick to their own world, he has chosen to make earth his home. He's even gone so far as to build this bar. I don't have to know much more about him to know he's a pretty strange guy. In a good way.

Trev quickly gets to work; he is still pulling out herbs and whispering spells without success when my phone rings. I glance at the screen and see that it's Alaric before I quickly swipe to answer.

"Hello?"

"Lennox? I have some news."

"What news?" I ask, okay, more like growl.

"I met with the leader of the vampires tonight, Drake. Seems he was misled into thinking that they would be able to walk in the sun by helping the mages and has effectively switched sides."

"So false promises from the mages? Are you sure it's not a trick?" I have to ask. It's not normal for any supernatural faction to switch sides mid-battle, especially vampires. When you are immortal, it helps to have a reputation for being loyal.

"I'm sure. His sister was taken when she was younger by hunters. All I needed to do was remind him of that, and he agreed to help us."

"I'm not sure if I trust anything coming out of his mouth as he was just attacking the pack, but if you trust him, I'll take the information. Constance and I struck out, so we came to see Trevan. He's not having much luck either."

"Is there news about Skarlyt? Does he know where she is?" Constance cues into my conversation and starts peppering questions. I give her a soft look shaking my head but holding up a finger hoping that she'll give me a minute.

"Go ahead, Alaric."

"Drake said that Skarlyt is being held at the Sunset Motel on Highway 169."

"What?" I shout in frustration. That's where we're staying. I go to toss the phone and run to her, but I hear Alaric yell.

"Wait. There's more. I don't think Kirnon will hurt her. Apparently, he's been going on and on about the fact that he and Skarlyt have been blessed by the goddess to produce true hybrid children. That's why he wants her. If you go in there half-cocked, we may lose her if he gets away. We need to be smart about this. With the vampires out of the fight, they've agreed to patrol the barrier on the outside for the mages so that we can come meet you. It should only take us about half an hour to get there."

"I can't wait that long, Alaric," I growl out.

"I know it seems like a long time but please. Just wait for me."

"You have thirty minutes," I growl out just before hanging up the phone.

Chapter Nineteen

Skarlyt

I hear another car pull into the parking lot and run to the window. Maybe the barrier only works for sound, and they will be able to see me. I yank the curtains open and watch as a familiar SUV pulls into the parking lot.

They found me. They found me...I jump up and down, waving my arms. I know I must look crazy, but I don't care. They found me...

I watch as they don't even look in my direction and drive all the way to the other end of the parking lot before pulling into a spot. What the...Oh, maybe they're getting a key from the clerk. Yes, that makes sense. What makes little sense is the fact that instead of Lennox and Alaric getting out of the car, it's Lennox and my mother. What the hell are those two doing together? I expected Lennox to come but thought that Alaric would be coming with him.

I watch as they walk into the office and exit a few minutes later with room keys and walk to the last two rooms on the other end of the building. Away from me rather than toward me. They're staying here? Why would they be staying here? I thought they were here to rescue me. Now, I'm not so sure. Whether or not they know how close they are, they are clearly looking for me and getting closer all the time. Thank the goddess!

Kirnon did say he has people attacking pack land. With an impending threat to the pack, Alaric will have no choice but to lock it down. Maybe Mom and Lennox left before that happened in order to look for me, and that's why they need a room. At least, that's what I'm hoping for.

With my mom being so close, maybe we can do the telepathy thing we used to do when Sebastyn and I were kids. I get myself comfortable on the bed and close my eyes. I start to picture my mom clearly in my mind. Her straight, jet black hair with small streaks of gray, her bright blue eyes with laugh lines beginning to form at the edges, her favorite blue maxi dress with her favorite leather sandals that don't quite match but she says she doesn't care because they're comfortable. Just as I think I start to feel something, I'm pulled back. Stupid fucking bracelet. I need to figure out a way to get this thing off.

I have lost a few hours of time to intense meditation, but the constant, cold weight of the manacle keeps me grounded here.

Maybe if I pretend that I'm cooperative or if I can think of a way to be helpful with my magic, Kirnon will take it off. Not likely, but I won't know if I don't try.

I rush back to the window as the sun begins to set and watch Lennox carry books back and forth from the car to the room. He looks so sexy when he's sweating like that. Why didn't I want to claim that man again? Oh yeah, because I was too heartbroken by the one that's holding me hostage here. I stand and watch out the window for a while after I see him go in and close the door, willing him to come out again and look up to see me.

I stay there until I see Kirnon pulling in. Shit, I hope he didn't see me standing at the window. I can't have him thinking that I was trying to escape or bring any attention to the new tenants at the end. I pull the curtains closed quickly and sprint back to the bed, flicking the TV on and changing the channels like I am at all interested.

A few minutes pass and Kirnon comes in carrying a bunch of bags in his thick arms. As he drops them roughly on the bed, I can see that it's mostly women's clothing for me.

"Oh, thank you, Kirnon," I say, lacing it with sweetness.

Now that I know Mom and Lennox are so close, I need to lay it on thick. All I need is for him to either take this bracelet off or let me out of the room, and then it's only ten steps to them. Between the three of us, I think we can handle Kirnon.

He smiles back at me. "Now that's the welcome I was expecting. Glad to see you're starting to come around." Not exactly, but I'll let him believe that I am.

I grab the bag and head straight into the bathroom. I need to make sure, even though I'm acting compliant, that I am not leaving an opportunity open to have to touch him in any way. I pull the clothes out of the bag, doing a happy dance at the thought of having clean clothes.

I quickly undress before hopping in the shower once more to clean myself again after wearing my dirty clothes all day. Once I've pulled on the clean underwear and bra, I feel a little more like myself. I glance down at the bag, finding the tampons and pads and tear open the boxes. I may have no need for them right now, but Kirnon needs to think I do. I make quick work of making it look like I'm using them by wrapping them in toilet paper and stuffing them at the bottom of the garbage and leaving the wrapping on top. Once I'm done, I am satisfied that I've left enough clues to convince this man—who knows very little about the female body—that I'm actively bleeding. I hope it's enough to keep him away from me. His wolf should be able to smell that I am not, but he's let me get away with this illusion so far. Huh. I wonder why.

"Hey, Kirnon. Do you think we could watch movies and order pizza like old times?" I ask as I come out of the bathroom. He pauses for a moment, taken aback by my request, before quickly pulling his phone out of his pocket and dialing.

"Yes, I'd like a large meat lover's pizza and a large pizza with just cheese and pepperoni delivered to the Sunset Motel, room eight."

The person on the other end of the phone says something, but I don't pay attention. Instead, I move to the bed, building a pillow wall in the middle in case he decides to climb up here with me.

"Pizza will be here in forty-five minutes. Here, drink this," he says, handing me a small vial.

"What is it?"

"It's a healing potion. For your neck." He points to my bruised neck. I take the vial out of his hand and bring it up to my nose and inhale.

"There's no point in me poisoning you, Skarlyt. It's just a healing potion, I promise." As if any promise of his would actually mean anything to me. But after smelling nothing but the herbs required for a healing potion, I pour it into my mouth and swallow. Instantly, the bruises all over my body from Kirnon's rough treatment fade and the throbbing in my neck disappears.

"Thanks," I say with a smile before placing the empty vial down on the bedside table and going back to arranging the pillows.

"What's this?" he asks, gesturing to the pillow wall.

"I like to have pillows to throw my legs over. Like a body pillow," I tell him with a shrug.

"You can throw your legs over me," he says.

I suppress my gag and give him a sweet smile. "Other than the one night with you, I've slept alone for twenty-eight years, Kirnon. I like my space."

"You know, Skarlyt, I do regret that night," he says, and I look over at him in shock.

"You do?" I hate how vulnerable I sound right now, but I've always wondered if he regretted leaving me like that, alone in a hotel room, crying as he walked out.

"Yeah. I didn't understand then why my wolf was so enamored with you. I thought that it was just a phase."

Tears swim in my eyes, but I blink them back. "So, it was your wolf, not you, who wanted me?"

"That's not what I...Damn it. Why is it always like this with you?"

"It's a simple question, Kirnon. Was it you or your wolf who wanted me?"

"My wolf," he growls, and a few stray tears fall. I angrily swipe them away. I spent years pining for a man who didn't want me. Years of crying myself to sleep. For what? The man sitting in front of me is nothing special. He's not like Lennox.

"So why do you want me now?"

"Because we are fated to be together. Because we will produce hybrid children. True hybrids. Can you imagine? Our children will be able to perform magic and shift into wolves. They will be the strongest supernaturals in existence. Surely you want that?"

"But we're not fated anymore. You rejected me. Once that bond is broken, it can't be repaired." His face morphs into a sneer.

"I have a witch who can recreate the bond."

"That's—But it won't be blessed by the goddess. Who knows if your impossible hybrid children would result from a manufactured bond? Seriously, Kirnon, think about this logically. Why would you want to do this? Just to have the strongest children? Tools for you to use to...what? Take over the supernatural world?"

"I've been assured that the bond will be just as strong as before. Of course, I want to be at the top of the supernatural hierarchy. Why don't you?"

"Because I think all people should be equal. Because it isn't fair to have one person controlling millions," I argue.

"What about packs? They have an alpha. One person who controls them all."

I scoff. "Only horrible alphas *control*. A good alpha leads—never controls."

"Like your precious Alaric? He's just too weak to control anyone."

"If you think that then you don't know him at all," I say, quickly snatching the remote and turning on the TV. I'm done with this conversation. So much for trying to reason with him.

I am not sure where he got these ideas from, but he's completely delusional. He's obsessed with our children being hybrids, but there's no evidence they are or will be.

We spend the next couple of hours watching movies. I hear Lennox or my mom pull out of the parking lot in the SUV at one point. At least, I assume it is them since they're the only other guests I've seen here. Hopefully, tomorrow I can figure out a way to get their attention.

I must fall asleep while watching movies because I wake up to a full bladder and sore boobs begging to be emptied. A glance out the window tells me not much time has passed. It's still night, and the moon is high in the sky. Her light is streaming in through the cracks in the drapes. I do a quick search for Kirnon around the room and can't find him. Where did he go? On second thought, who cares?

I rush over to the window to see if Lennox's SUV is back yet. Nope. Wait, what time is it? They have to be coming back soon, right? Glancing over at the clock, I see that it's just after midnight. Where could they be?

I look down at the table and find a note from Kirnon, still attached to the Sunset Motel notepad.

Went for a run. Be back soon.

So that's where he is. Out for a run.

I try to push my over-analyzing thoughts out and head to the washroom. I might as well take advantage of being by myself and not having to pretend for Kirnon. After quickly using the bathroom, pumping, and then taking another shower, I sit back on the bed and choose the Hallmark channel. That's one good thing about this shitty motel. It seems they still pay for the decent channels. They have some great specials on right now, and. at this time of night, it's all the reruns that I've missed. Perfect.

With commercials playing in the background, I get up and head to the door again, studying it at a distance like a formidable enemy. I muster all my confidence, all my "manifest your hopes into reality," and just reach up to unlock the door. The lock sticks a little, but it turns over without issue.

Feeling more confident by the second, I twist the doorknob and pull it open.

A shriek comes from the old hinges as I pull inward, but I feel no pain or difficulty.

Oh, my Mother. Can I actually make it out of here?

I push my hand up against the barrier, meeting resistance at the barely visible net stretching across the doorway. I try to get through, but my luck has run out. Excruciating pain radiates through my hand, up my arm, and spreads throughout my body. It feels like a thousand needles are being pushed into my skin at the same time. I drop to my knees and pull my hand to my chest, cradling it until the pain fades.

"Son of a bitch," I whisper, gripping the door and slamming it closed before going back over and sitting on the bed. This is ridiculous. On one hand, the fact that I can open the door now means that the spell is becoming weaker, but the pain is much more intense than it was when I just touched the handle.

With my mate and mother so nearby and the promise of an

impassable but open door, I am more frustrated than ever. I know they're going to find me, and I know that I can't do anything until this bracelet is off or I can step outside this barrier. Instead of wasting my energy doing something that I know won't pay off, I choose to relax and plot my escape for the second Kirnon decides to let me out of this room or my mom and Lennox find me.

With the goddess's intervention and them staying here, I have faith that's exactly what's going to happen. Between Lennox's shifter senses and my mother's magic, I have no doubts that they'll be able to break through whatever is keeping me hidden here.

As long as Kirnon doesn't realize they're staying here, he will hopefully keep me here—close enough to be found. If he finds out how close they are, though, he will move me faster than you can say Mother Moon.

Please, don't let that happen, I pray.

Chapter Twenty

Lennox

When Alaric told me that Skar could be at the same motel we had spent the whole day at, I almost lost it. How could she have been that close without me knowing? How could she be that close without Constance sensing it?

"What did he say?" both Constance and Trev ask at the same time.

"He said that Kirnon has a room at the same motel we checked into earlier and he's sending a group to meet us here before we head over there in case it's a trap," I reply. Constance just sucks in a breath and nods, seemingly lost in her own thoughts. I don't blame her. I'm sure she's wondering the same as me. How did we not feel her that close? Something must be very wrong to keep her concealed from us so well.

I know that I just told them that we're waiting for the cavalry, but I'm getting out of here as soon as I can.

"I need some air," I say, turning to walk out the back door.

"I'll come with you," Trev says to me. He gives me a look that says he knows exactly what I'm going to do, but I can't let him come.

"No offense, Trev, but I really just need a minute alone." I really don't mean to snap at him, but I'm just so frustrated, mainly with myself for not scenting her earlier. A pang of regret flows through me at my sharp words. He's been nothing but helpful, and I can see why Skar is friends with him. Heck, maybe after all this, we could be friends too.

Trev nods in understanding. "Don't do anything stupid."

Of course, I'm going to do something stupid. My mate is in danger, and I've been close to her all day without knowing it. I wonder if she knew how close I was and couldn't tell me. I wonder if she tried to get my attention and thought I was ignoring her. I really hope not. I don't know what is going on in that room. If she's chained up or locked in, or both, but I need to get her out of there.

I try to avoid the more dangerous thoughts. If Kirnon brought Skarlyt to the Sunset Motel but neither her mate nor her mother could sense her there today, she's either long gone or—I stop that thought before I can complete it. Skarlyt is fine. She's going to be fine.

As soon as I'm outside the doors of Supernatural, I shift. No one is there to see, and I don't care that I'll be naked when I arrive. I will move faster as a wolf, and that is all I care about.

I try to scent the air for evidence of my mate or another shifter. We are too close to pack land, though, for me to be sure of any unfamiliar scents. This asshole broke my mate's heart and then kidnapped her. Once she is safe, I will find him and make him pay. All this for the hope of hybrid children? I do not doubt Kayne is special, but that is true regardless of whether or not he is a hybrid. Either way, Kirnon is never getting his hands on my pup.

I'm right, and it's only about five minutes later when I'm coming up around the back of the motel. I slip through a door, propped open for smoke breaks by the smell of it, that leads toward the lobby. I shift back into a human and grab a towel from a stray housekeeping cart. It is rough and barely large enough to wrap around my waist.

I walk up to the front desk, startling the young girl who has replaced the crusty, old man from earlier. She looks to be about sixteen and drops the book she's holding when she glances up to find me half-naked in front of her. If I wasn't in such a rush, I would be embarrassed by the way she can't seem to take her eyes off my abs. As it is, this might just work in my favor.

"Hey, there. My girlfriend locked me out of our room at the end. Is there any way you could give me a spare key?" I ask, giving her my most charming smile.

"Well...we are supposed to ask for ID," she starts to say.

"I'm Kirnon, and all my ID is back in the room. Obviously, I just got out of the shower. You would be doing me the biggest favor if you could bend the rules, just this one time. I would really appreciate it." Even having his name come out of my mouth makes me want to puke, but after double checking the name on the reservation, she nods and hands me a key.

Yes. Thank the goddess she didn't notice how sweaty my palms were or my fidgeting hands. Even lying for a good reason is difficult for me, so I am shocked it is so easy. Is it possible that being naked is the key to a convincing lie?

"Thank you," I boast, adding a saucy wink before rushing out toward the room. She better be in there. She better be okay. She better not be hurt. I am going to kill Kirnon one way or another, but if she's hurt, I'll make it a slow and painful death.

I walk up to the door and insert the key, feeling so nervous about what I may find inside. I steel myself and command myself, "Just do it."

I quickly turn the key and push open the door. Skarlyt is

laying on the bed in front of a movie playing on the ancient TV. She is sitting at attention, her eyes wide and staring at me. I start to take a step toward her, ready to grab her in my arms and never let go when she shouts, "Don't move," and I freeze.

"What do you mean?" I ask her, scanning the room around her for a threat.

"There's a barrier spell on the room so that I can't leave. I'm not sure if you'll be able to leave if you cross it, and I don't want to take that chance," she replies, coming up to the barrier and placing her hand on it until it makes her wince. I move mine up so that it's mirroring hers.

"Are you okay? Are you hurt?" I spout the questions off rapidly. I need to know. She looks okay, but she's wearing clothes and there could be marks underneath. Even now, I cannot get her scent. Whatever the barrier is made of, it is incredibly strong. My eyes roam all over her body, checking the patches of skin that I can see.

"I'm okay, Lennox. I promise. How's Kayne?" She sounds sincere that she's not hurt.

"He's okay. Missing you, obviously, but healthy and safe. Charleigh has been having to feed him because he apparently won't drink from Phoebe, and everyone said that you didn't want him to drink formula. To be completely honest, she's freaking out that you're going to be pissed at her, even after Phoebe dropped the mate bomb on everyone." She gives me a soft smile before looking at our hands where they rest between us, almost touching.

"And Alaric?" she asks.

"He's on his way to Supernatural to meet with your mom and Trev before coming here. He wasn't too happy to find out through me that we're mates, but I didn't have much of a choice about telling him once you went missing."

She nods in understanding, although she looks a little sad.

"He's probably so pissed..." Before she finishes whatever she was going to say, my SUV flies into the parking lot, driven by a crazy woman.

"Uhh, I should probably tell you that I left your mom and Trev at Supernatural and came to get you myself without waiting for Alaric. I kind of didn't tell anyone." I try to say everything super quickly so she can understand what happens next.

"*Lennox*," Constance shouts at me, chiding me like she's the scariest teacher I ever had. "How dare you...If you would've just told me you wanted to come, I would've come with you. Instead, you snuck out and had us worried sick," she finishes with an exasperated sigh as she comes to stand beside me.

"I'm—" I begin, but I am cut off.

"Oh, my baby girl. Are you okay?" she turns to ask Skar, her voice and manner entirely different.

"Yeah, Mom. I'm fine, I promise. I just need you to take down the barrier spell and take off this bracelet. Also, you can't be mad at Lennox, Mom. You know if it were Dad in danger, you would've done the same thing." Constance just gives us both a small nod before raising her hands and begins whispering a spell.

"How long do we have?" she asks, her eyes still closed as she focuses on the spell.

"He went out for a run," Skarlyt says, eyes on the road behind me for any sign of movement.

"Don't worry about that," I growl. "You take your time. If he comes back, I'll take care of him."

Skarlyt offers me a charmed smile, but Constance just hums and continues her work.

After a few moments with no change, Constance curses under her breath.

"I knew this magic felt familiar."

Skar looks at her mother in confusion. "What do you mean?"

"The signature on this magic is from my second cousin, Hazel. You remember Hazel?" She waves her hand in the air as if we should know exactly who she's talking about and how she would know.

"That's a good thing, right?" I ask. I don't know anything about magic or signatures. If it's anything like the scent of a shifter, though, everyone smells unique. I'd know any of my cousins by scent alone.

"It's a wonderful thing," she says with a dangerous smile and pulls out her phone to bring it up to her ear.

"Hazel? Hello. It's Connie. How are things in Vancouver?" she says casually to whoever is on the line while pacing back and forth on the sidewalk. "Good, good. Well, I'm not so good actually. You see, some shifter decided to kidnap my daughter. You'll never believe this. He had the audacity to even put a binding bracelet on her and locked her in a room with a barrier around it. Imagine my surprise when I get here and find that it's your signature on the spell." She's quiet for a few minutes, listening to whatever Hazel is saying over the phone. "Okay, then. Just tell me what loophole you used, and we'll drop it." She nods a few more times before saying, "Thanks, Zel. Don't worry; we'll be having another talk real soon, dear," and hangs up.

"Okay, long story short, there's more to it than just a witch helping capture another witch. Kirnon apparently held her daughter captive until she helped him." I grit my teeth at the thought. Who does this guy think he is? "I'll tell you more when we are back with the pack, but she did tell me where to look for the weakness," she says, while coming back to stand at the door. She raises her hand back to the barrier, wincing as it makes contact, and focuses her attention on it. I am watching closely, but I still can't tell exactly what infinitesimal change occurs just before the barrier drops.

I know it is gone because Constance doesn't hesitate to run the two steps between them and grab Skarlyt, bringing her in for a hug.

Skarlyt collapses into her mother for a moment before she surprises me by jumping up into my arms, wrapping her legs around my waist, and fusing her mouth to mine. Oh, Mother Moon. I have dreamed about this every day for the past two weeks, and those dreams didn't do it justice. Her mouth is so soft and eager. When I push my tongue into her mouth, hers matches mine with enthusiasm. I walk us toward the wall, pushing her back up against it. Now that I have my mate, I don't want to waste another minute.

Claim mate, my wolf demands, and I don't disagree. I want to take her back into that room and not leave until we are both fully claimed and mated.

We're forced to pull apart by the sound of vehicles pulling into the parking lot. Guess the cavalry has arrived.

"All right, love birds. Time to break it up," Constance says, and I begrudgingly place Skar back on her feet. I don't have the strength to let her go, though, so I keep my arm placed firmly around her while adjusting the too-small towel around my waist to hide my growing member.

"Skarlyt," Alaric yells as he comes running up. He doesn't even pause at my arm around her but scoops her up into a hug. I know they're best friends and that he's a mated wolf, but I can't help the growl that escapes. My wolf and I just got our mate back, and I just kissed her for the first time. Watching another male touch her is extremely difficult, even when I know it's platonic.

"Sorry," Alaric says to me, placing her back into the crook of my arm. "I remember how hard it was with other men touching Phoebe in the beginning."

"In the beginning? Try all the time," Darren scoffs, coming up and placing his hand on Skar's shoulder, not attempting to take her from me. "Good to have you back, Skar."

"All right, everyone. Let's get back to the pack where we can all be safe. Then we can start searching for Kirnon," Alaric says, clapping his hands together and ushering everyone out.

"He left a note that he went out for a run, but I don't think he'd be stupid enough to confront all of you at once," Skarlyt pipes in, and I nod in agreement.

"I'm going to hop in with Alaric and let you two have some alone time on the drive," Constance says before beginning to walk away.

"Wait, Mom. Do you think you can remove this before you go?" Skarlyt yells out, holding out her wrist.

"Oh, yeah. I forgot." She walks over to Skar, grabbing her wrist that has the bracelet on it.

"A daughter of the Moon demands you let go," she says forcefully to the bracelet, and it opens up, falling to the floor.

"Seriously?" Skar says, looking between the bracelet on the ground and her mom. I watch as she lets out an audible sigh, raising her hands in the air and calling on a gust of wind to whip around her. I can tell she's insanely happy to have access to her magic again.

"Yes," Constance says, gingerly picking up the bracelet between two fingers like it's dirty and then walking to Alaric's car and hopping in.

Skar begins to walk to the passenger door, but I beat her there, opening the door and helping her inside. I know it only takes two seconds to walk around and hop in the driver's seat, but I can't help but feel anxious the entire time.

Once we're driving out of the parking lot, I grab her hand, planning to hold it the whole drive home. I don't think I'll be able to let her get too far from me for a while.

"Do you want to talk about it?" I ask, squeezing her hand in reassurance.

"Not right now," she says, leaning over the center console into my side. A slight wave of her hands and the console morphs into a seat which she slides right into. I wrap my right arm around her, pulling her in close. "Right now I just want to be held by my mate," she whispers.

I lean over and drop a soft kiss on her head, drinking in the scent of her. Although it's mixed up with the strange motel and unfamiliar clothes, it's just like coming home. "Me too, sweetheart. Me too."

Fifteen minutes into the car ride, her head perks up. "Lennox?"

"Yes, Skarlyt?"

"I have to tell you something." I glance down at her, worried at what she might reveal but trying to keep my face neutral.

"You can tell me anything," I whisper, looking from the road to her and back.

"I love you." My jaw drops open momentarily, and I pull the car to the side of the road, throwing it in park before turning to face her.

"And I love you, Skarlyt Moon. You are my second chance at happiness, but I think this is how my life was meant to be. I used to curse the Moon goddess for letting me be rejected by Olivia, but now...now I thank her. Because I never would have found you."

"Oh, Lennox," she whispers before reaching up and pulling my face to hers. She kisses me passionately, pouring every ounce of love into it. I can smell her arousal, and I push the seat back, lifting her so that she's straddling me.

I grip her hips and press her down onto my fully engorged cock, already peeking through the towel around my waist. She releases my mouth with a gasp, her eyes rolling back with pleasure. I kiss down her neck, my canines elongating, proof that my wolf is ready to claim this woman here and now.

Reluctantly, I pull back. "As much as I would love to continue what we're doing. I don't want to claim you in this car, and there's a little boy who's waiting on us," I whisper. The statement clears the lust-filled fog from her brain.

"You're right. But soon," she promises.

"Definitely soon," I promise her back, pressing one last soft kiss to her mouth before slipping her back so that she's sitting next to me.

After re-adjusting the seat, I pull the car back onto the road and continue making our way to pack land.

Chapter Twenty-One

Skarlyt

When we pull up in front of Alaric's house, I don't wait until the car stops. I push open the car door, jump out, and sprint into the house. I can't wait to see Kayne.

As I rush in, I vaguely register all my friends and family waiting to greet me, but I can't stop. I zero in on Kayne, who is being held by Charleigh on the couch. I walk up to her and reach my arms out. Tears are already pooling in my eyes as she places him in my arms. I pull him close, inhaling his scent. He still smells like a baby, my baby. I don't know why I thought he would smell different. It's only been two days, but those days were absolute hell for me. I sink to the floor as sobs start wracking my body, and I press soft kisses all over his face.

He looks bigger. His hair is a bit longer and there's more of it. His cheeks have filled out a bit as well. By the looks of him, he didn't go hungry while I was gone.

I feel someone picking me up and sitting down on the couch with me and Kayne in their lap, and I know it's Lennox. I can tell by the way my body is relaxing into his. He says nothing, and I don't need him to. Just him holding me is enough to re-start the stream of tears falling down my face. We sit like that for a few minutes before I feel strong enough to raise my face to look at the room.

I move my eyes to Charleigh. "I can't than..." I try to thank her for everything she's done, but my throat is thick with emotion, and I'm unable to finish.

She understands what I mean and simply waves her hand at me. "You don't need to thank me, Skar. You're family, and Kayne's family. I know you would do the same for me." She's right, I know she is. The fact that she kept my child alive and healthy by feeding him from herself is a kind of primal, maternal gratitude I have no words for. I wouldn't have expected someone else to do it, especially when letting my baby go hungry until he's willing to accept formula would have been the easier option.

I nod and move my gaze over to Phoebe. I don't even try to say anything. She simply throws herself on the couch next to me and wraps me in her arms, then she's crying too. "I'm so glad you're back. I was so worried about you."

I try to lighten the mood and say, "Does anyone have a vial handy for these tears?" She immediately starts laughing. Mission accomplished.

I'm not ready to talk about what happened over the past two days, but being in this room surrounded by my family and friends makes me feel like everything is going to be okay.

"Okay. I need to know what happened here last night," I demand, looking around the room.

It's Alaric who starts. "Joe brought a bunch of mages and vampires here to try and take Aurora."

"What?" I exclaim, looking around the room. I knew Aurora was in danger, but what the hell?

"He's locked in the cells," Phoebe whispers.

"Joe is?"

"Yup. He didn't take my warning seriously. After Kirnon told them we would be busy searching for you, they thought it would be easy to just swoop in and steal a baby phoenix." She gets up briefly, rushing over to grab Aurora from the playpen before sitting back down. "But he obviously doesn't know what lengths family will go to for one another."

"Definitely not this one anyway," I tell her, glancing around the room. "How did we get ahold of Joe? The ropes?"

"The ropes," Alaric confirms, and I give myself a mental high-five. "The coven was incredibly brave and resourceful. The ropes you designed caught him, brought him through the barrier, and dampened his powers until we could get him into the cells."

"Damn straight," I am proud of my coven and the ropes I designed, silver and iron wrapped up in enough magic to keep any mage contained—or so I had hoped.

"We aren't going to waste any time on Joe tonight, though," Alaric says, in the same tone he'd tell the boys to leave the cake for after dinner. "He's contained, the mages have fled for now, and the vampires are on our side. The barrier is stable, and we know it can keep Kirnon at bay."

I move to protest. Surely, we need to do something right now, but Alaric interrupts me.

"It is late, and we are safe for the night," he places a hand on Phoebe's shoulder, and I see her relax under his touch. "We all need some rest. *You* need some rest, Skar."

The desire to keep going, keep moving, is so strong I barely notice it. I am tired, though. There's nothing to do right now, but if I do nothing...if I do nothing, I know where my thoughts will go. I know I will have to face the trauma of the last few days the moment I am alone.

"The girls did something for you, Skar..." Lennox says, cutting into our conversation before my thoughts can carry me away.

I look around at him, then back at Charleigh, Felicia, and Phoebe. "What?" I ask.

"Well..." Charleigh starts, but Phoebe finishes for her.

"We thought that when we got you back, you might want to stay in your own home. So, we brought all Kayne's stuff to your cottage and set it up for you. I'm sure you'll want to rearrange everything, but..." I don't even know what to say. I'm floored. The fact that they thought about what I would want when I got back is amazing. To set up Kayne's room for me...Cue the tears again.

"You didn't have to do that," I try to tell them, but they all just wave me off while Phoebe jumps up and begins dragging me along with her. I reach back for Lennox's hand and realize that sometime between the SUV and the house he must've put on clothes because he is no longer sporting that way too small towel. Bummer.

There's a large group to join us on our short walk to my cottage. Everyone reaches out and touches my shoulders at one point or another, but I hardly register them, focusing instead on the baby in my arms and my mate against my side. This right here is heaven. It doesn't matter what happened in the last two days. Hell, nothing that happened before this matters. The rejection. The pain. The kidnapping. It was all worth it to have this moment.

As we step up to the cottage with Kayne still in my arms, Phoebe opens the door and Lennox scoops me up in a bridal hold, carrying us both over the threshold.

"Welcome home, sweetheart and my little prince," he whispers into my ear. I look around as he sets us down in the living room. Not only did they do whatever they did to Kayne's room, but I can see that they cleaned. My entire cottage smells fresh, and my floors are sparkling. There isn't even a speck of dust to be seen.

"Did someone dust in here?" I ask the rather large group of people that came with us.

"I thought you might want to come home to a clean house, and

I enjoy dusting," Felicia says sheepishly, with a shrug of her shoulders, before her eyes go wide. "I hope—you didn't *need* the dust, right? Do witches—"

I grab her into a hug, sandwiching Kayne between us. I'm sure she doesn't know, but I detest dusting unless I have to—which is never. It doesn't get done, obviously.

"Thank you." I have no other words, and I don't think I'll be able to say them enough. Not only did they search for me and not give up, but they made sure I could come back to my own home when I did. I look around at this vast family that I've found.

"Thank you all for everything. For coming for me, for setting all this up for us...Just thank you," I say loudly to everyone.

"Does that include me?" I hear a familiar voice call out. I turn around and try to find out where it's coming from when Sebastyn walks up the steps.

"Sebastyn!" I cry out and run into his open arms. "I can't believe you're here," I say to him as I squeeze him as tightly as I can without crushing Kayne.

"I missed you, too, Skar," he says with a little chuckle.

Stepping back, I adjust Kayne so I can introduce them. "Kayne, this is your Uncle Sebastyn. Sebastyn, this is your nephew, Kayne." I hold Kayne out so that Sebastyn can hold him. It's awkward at first, since I don't think Sebastyn has ever held a baby before, but he gets the hang of it after a minute or two.

"Hey, little man," he whispers to him, placing a soft kiss on his head before raising his eyes to look at me.

"What are you doing here?" I ask him. Not that I'm unhappy that he is, just that he was traveling the world, doing everything he wanted to do before finding his mate.

"Mom called me when you were taken, and I hopped on a plane to come help. Guess I'm late to the party, though," he tells me and begins to look around. Oh, I guess he doesn't know some of the people here because he's been gone so long. Maybe I should introduce him.

"Everyone, this is my baby brother, Sebastyn. Sebastyn, this is everybody," I say, and he just raises his eyebrow at me.

"Okay, fine. This is Phoebe, Alaric's mate, and their newest addition, Aurora. The two extremely sleepy little munchkins at their side are Ryker and Riley," I say, gesturing to them before moving on.

"This is Charleigh, Phoebe's best friend, and her mate and daughter, Ashton and Cybil. Beside them is her sister, Felicia, Josh's mate. You remember Josh, right?" I know I am over-whelming him, but I slow down as I save the best for last. I step back into Lennox's side.

"And this is their brother, Lennox. He is my mate." Sebastyn's eyes go wide with shock for a moment, but he recovers quickly and pulls Lennox into a hug.

"Nice to meet everyone," he says as he nods at them.

"Welcome back home, bro," Darren says, clasping him on his back. "Any chance you're gonna stick around?"

"Actually, I wasn't going to, but now that I'm home, I'm not sure I want to leave again," Sebastyn replies. "I clearly miss out on a lot when I'm gone."

That is the best news I've heard all day. Sebastyn has been traveling for the past three years, hitting every major city and some of the smaller ones as he travels across the world. I've missed him. And, if the huge smile on his face is anything to go by, it seems like Darren is ready to have his best friend back too.

"Okay, I need you to see the room, Skar. I'm going crazy with anticipation." Phoebe snaps me out of my thoughts of Sebastyn being home by grabbing my arm and pulling me to the bedrooms. As she opens the door, I suck in a breath. It's exactly how I imag-ined it. Someone even painted stars on the dark blue part of the wall with little bursts of magic coming up onto the light blue. It's gorgeous.

"Do you like it?" she asks nervously.

I turn to face her. "I love it. Thank you." I whisper the last part as I pull her into a hug. I've cried enough tears over the past few days to last me a lifetime, and I don't want to cry anymore.

Charleigh walks into the room next to us and pulls me over to the corner, where Kayne's crib is, and points to the wall. Right there, at the head of his crib, are paintings of wolves, a phoenix, and multiple bursts of magic.

"This is our family," she says, pointing to each wolf. "The red one is Lennox, and the green-blue magic is yours. Obviously, Alaric and Phoebe are the black wolf and phoenix, and the boys are the two bursts of red magic. I'm waiting to see if Aurora also has a wolf before I paint her too. Then, over here, are me, Ashton, Felicia, Josh, and Darren. I didn't realize you had a brother, so I'll add him in there too."

Wow, her attention to detail is amazing. The wolves are perfect. Even the rust-colored spot on Alaric's chest is there. Looking at the wall and then out at the room, I can feel the love that went into every detail.

As if he can sense that I'm beginning to feel overwhelmed, Lennox steps up to me, Kayne now happily in his arms, and says, "All right, everyone. Let me get Skar and Kayne settled in, and we'll come by Alaric and Phoebe's tomorrow afternoon or, more accurately, later today."

Everyone gives me hugs goodbye, making me promise over and over to come see them later in the afternoon until only Sebastyn is left.

"I can't believe you're a mom," he says to me in disbelief but with a smile on his face.

"Yup, I am. We have so much to talk about, but I'm mentally drained, so it is going to have to wait until tomorrow," I say to him, pulling him in for another hug. After only seeing him a handful of times over the past three years, it's nice to be able to hold him instead of watching him through a screen. "I really did miss you, though, Seb. You can't run off again anytime soon. Your nephew will need you to teach him all the tricks we used when we were kids because, as his mom, I'm supposed to get him in trouble for those things and can't teach him myself."

He chuckles at me before giving me one last squeeze. "You can count on it." He turns and strides out of the cottage.

I turn and head back to the room, watching from the doorway as Lennox gets the rocking chair ready for me. "He's probably hungry," Lennox says, handing Kayne to me once I'm seated. I pull out my breast and Kayne latches on quickly, instantly relieving some of the built-up pressure. Ah, that feels so good. It only takes him about ten minutes to completely drain that one before I switch to the other. I wonder if I pumped enough while I was with Kirnon. Probably not. I have some catching up to do.

Once he's finished eating and has been burped, I gently place him in his crib and turn on his sleepy time music. The girls even got the right playlist set up on the speaker.

I close the door tightly and pad my way next door to my room. There, I watch as Lennox carefully arranges candles throughout the room, humming to himself. After a few minutes, he finally notices me standing in the doorway.

"I know you said that you wanted to wait...but I was hoping that after the last two days, you might be ready. If you aren't, that's okay. I just need to hold you tonight." He's babbling, but it's cute. Instead of answering, I walk over and merge my lips to his in a hot and needy kiss.

I pull back, gasping for air, and turn toward the bathroom. I kick off my shoes and slowly take off my shirt, throwing it across the room. I'm trying to do a sensual dance for him, but the clothes Kirnon brought me—boxy, generic, and not quite the right size—do not help. I desperately need to take a shower and wash off the last two days. Despite having showered while I was in that flea-bitten motel, I instantly felt disgusting again after sitting on that bed. I unhook my bra, shimmying the straps down my arms, and turn toward him, tossing it in his direction.

"Coming?" I ask in my most seductive voice. It definitely isn't up to par with my previous expertise because it's been a while, but it seems to do the trick. He watches me in a state of shock before removing his own clothes in quick succession and following me into the bathroom. Seeing how small my bathroom is with the two of us in it, I realize that my tiny shower probably won't work for what I have in mind, so I whisper a minor spell and create a replica of Alaric's big shower—bench seat and all. Now, this is more like it. I might have to make this one permanent.

I step into the shower and let everything from the last two days wash away down the drain. I'm home with my baby and my mate. I'm safe on pack land. Kirnon can't get to us. I allow all the pain and longing I've felt dissolve and bring my focus to the present.

I hear Lennox step into the shower, and I feel him begin to lather up my back with soap. Ah, that feels so good. I've never showered with someone before. I always thought it would be too intimate, too intrusive, but it feels right now that I have Lennox here. I turn to face him, putting soap in my own hands and lathering them up. I begin to wash his chest and broad, muscled shoulders.

As I move my hands downward, I notice his extremely large cock standing at attention, and my pussy starts to clench. It's extremely intimidating because of the size, and I'm worried that it's not going to fit. However, if the Mother paired us as mates, I know it will turn out all right.

I wrap my hand around his thickness and begin stroking him. My fingers don't even touch either because of my small hands or the girth of his cock. He doesn't seem to mind as he presses himself closer to me and captures my lips, pushing his tongue into my mouth and coaxing mine to dance. He moves his hands slowly down my body, teasing me with gentle touches as he approaches exactly where I want him to be.

He presses a feather light touch to my swollen nub before moving to sit down on the bench, causing my hand to lose contact with him. I almost protest, but he quickly presses his mouth to my sex and begins slowly licking me.

I know it won't take me long. Over nine months with no sexual activity has made sure of that. I start to move my body so that he focuses on my clit, but he holds me tight and slowly moves his mouth exactly where I want it. He doesn't need directions, obviously, because he starts to suck and flick my clit with his tongue slowly and then gradually gets faster in time with my breathing.

I cry out with my release. Oh, my goddess. I'm probably biased, but if there was an award for the best oral sex, Lennox would win hands down. Maybe it is the "mate" thing, but I've never had a man be so in tune with my body before. He knows exactly what I want without me having to say anything.

I drop to my knees in the shower, hovering my mouth over his cock, blowing on it before engulfing him in my mouth. I rarely like giving head. I have an overactive gag reflex, but I'm actually enjoying myself. I move slowly up and down, watching his body for clues for what he likes. I adjust my suction in time with the movements. A sharp inhale shows me that he likes it when I run my tongue along the underside of his tip, tracing along the deep vein there.

"Skar, babe. If you keep doing that, I'm not going to last and I want to be inside you when I cum," he says, his voice gruff and low, as he gently lifts me up and off of him. I go to raise my leg up onto the bench, giving him room to guide himself into me, but he shakes his head and turns off the shower. "The first time I have you will be in a bed," he says as he steps out, grabbing us both a towel.

Being the impatient witch that I am, I simply wave my hands and a powerful gust of warm air flows around us, drying us both in seconds.

He looks at me with a smile. "Well, that's handy."

It sure is.

I don't give him any more time to think before I throw my arms around his neck and fuse my lips to his. I throw every ounce of longing I've felt for the past two days into that kiss. I show him all the passion I've felt for him since day one, and he meets me back with just as much. He lifts me up, his strong hands supporting my ass, and wraps my legs around his waist while walking us farther into the bedroom. As we finally make it to the bed and he lowers me down, he pauses to look into my eyes.

"Are you sure?" he asks, and I can tell that if I told him that I wasn't ready right now, he would stop. He wouldn't expect anything in return. He would simply hold me until I fell asleep.

Which is exactly why I say, "I'm sure, Lennox. I'm your mate, and you're mine. I want us to be joined together forever. I know it's only been a couple of weeks, but I've fallen in love with you."

"I love you too, Skar," he responds before lining himself up with my entrance and slowly sliding in. There is a small pinch of pain and an extreme feeling of fullness as he seats himself all the way in. Thankfully, he pauses for a moment to allow me to adjust to his size before starting with small, smooth movements in and out.

Once the pressure starts to subside and a feeling of utopia takes over, I begin meeting him thrust for thrust, both of us slamming our bodies together. As I wrap my legs tighter around his waist, I feel my release coming, so I shift my body weight and flip us so I'm on top.

I slowly move myself up and slam down onto him over and over, his cock hitting that delicious spot inside of me. I place my hand on his chest and don't have to reach far for my magic that's waiting to mark our mate. Unlike with Kirnon, I want this. I need to mark the man underneath me as my mate.

As I find my release, my magic pulses and I lean down to give him access to my collar bone so he can mark me as well. As soon as I feel his canines slip into my skin, my body begins to burn in utter bliss, my orgasm reaches a height I did not know anyone was capable of. We stay there like that for a few minutes after he retracts his teeth and licks at the wound, just holding each other. Finally, as bonded mates.

A feeling of completeness washes over me as I roll off of him. I have a mate. A sweet, wonderful, sexy mate who won't hurt me or reject me. He slips out of bed, heading to the bathroom.

"Thank you, Mother Moon," I whisper into the air as Lennox comes back with a washcloth to clean me up. He's so gentle as he glides the washcloth over my swollen and thoroughly used pussy. Just another reason to love this man. I glance at his collarbone and see a crescent moon mark sitting there and smile, reaching up to touch my own. We're both wearing each other's marks. What an amazing end to a thoroughly shitty day.

I roll over as Lennox climbs into bed and snuggle into him. I lift my head to make sure that the baby monitor on the table beside my bed is on before drifting off. My last thought as I relax into my mate's arms is another grateful prayer and a simple question.

How did I get so lucky?

Chapter Twenty-Two

Lennox

Waking up next to my mate has to be the best feeling in the world. I roll over on my side and just watch her sleep for a few minutes, until tiny little hands start moving on my chest. I look down and meet Kayne's bright blue eyes.

"Come on, buddy. Let's let Mommy sleep for a little longer," I whisper to him as I scoop him up into my arms. I guess he woke up to eat at some point in the night, and Skar just brought him into bed with us. I must have been sleeping too soundly to notice.

I carry him out to the living room and place him on his back on top of a soft blanket to stretch out for a bit. Grabbing the diaper and wipes, I change his bum quickly before pulling out some of his toys. I know he's not quite old enough to play with them yet, but I pass different ones to him anyway. The crinkly ones that make a lot of noise appear to make him happy, so I squeeze a few for him. He seems to get frustrated after a while because he can't grab the ones he wants himself, so I move him to his swing.

I study his sweet face and sleepy eyes for a moment, searching for some evidence of him being a hybrid. I try not to think about what that will mean for him, how much more difficult it will make his life.

"Do you think Mommy would like breakfast in bed?" I ask him quietly. He looks up at me. "Yeah, I think so too, buddy."

I set him up with vibration, music, and rocking motions on low and turn him to face the kitchen. Maybe Skarlyt will like pancakes? Should I go with the classic: bacon and eggs? I should probably check out her food situation first to see what she has.

Looking in the freezer and cupboards, I find everything I need for pancakes, bacon, eggs, and some hash browns to boot.

Screw it. I'm just going to make them all. As I'm cooking, I envision what life is going to be like in the future. As Kayne grows, I'm going to teach him to fish, hunt, and play ball; everything that my dad taught me. We're going to go on boys-only fishing trips. Maybe we can even invite Alaric and his boys. Oh, man. It's going to be so much fun.

If we have more kids—if they're girls—we can change them to family-only fishing trips and make it a tradition. At some point, I'm going to take Skarlyt to Egypt, with or without our kids. She deserves something just for her.

The woman of my dreams pokes her head into the room, "Good morning."

I spin, "Good morning, sweetheart. You need to go back to bed. Kayne and I have a surprise for you."

"But it smells so good," she half whines with a pout on her lips, but she turns and walks back into the room anyway.

"That was a close one, eh, buddy?" I say to Kayne. I quickly load Skar's plate up with eggs, bacon, hash browns, and a couple of pancakes, and set it down on the counter to free my hands to grab Kayne. I pick up the plate once more before walking into the room to bring Skarlyt her breakfast.

"Aw, Lennox. I've never had anyone make me breakfast in bed before," she coos to me.

"It was all Kayne's idea," I tell her, nodding to the little man in my arms and passing her the plate. "And you better get used to it because it will be a regular occurrence from now on." And it will. The goddess was generous enough to bless me with a second-chance mate, and I'm going to make sure that she is well taken care of and happy for the rest of her life.

I place Kayne down on the bed next to Skar, secured with a few pillows. I run back to the kitchen, making my own plate so we can enjoy our breakfast together. This is my idea of heaven: in bed, eating breakfast with my mate and our pup. I can't believe just how lucky I am. I never thought this day would come for me.

An anxious feeling starts to come over me, and I know I need to bring it up now before it festers, so I just spit it out.

"Skar, how would you feel about me adopting Kayne once we have dealt with this whole Kirnon business?" I hold my breath as she finishes chewing slowly and puts her own plate off to the side.

"You don't have to do that, you know." That's not really the response I was going for...

"I want to. I want us to be a family, and if you want to have more, we can. If you want to stick with just Kayne, that's okay too, but my wolf and I are in agreement that it doesn't matter whose DNA he has running through his veins. Kayne is our pup," I finish, looking into her eyes. "Unless there is a reason why you don't want me to."

She throws her arms around me, and I hope that means she's happy. "I would love that," she says in my ear before pulling back and giving me a kiss. Kayne takes that moment to start fussing, and we pull apart with a little chuckle. I thought it would take a little longer for him to be a cockblocker, not that I mind. After all, we have the rest of our lives together.

"He's probably hungry," Skar says, getting comfy before scooping him up and giving him his breakfast. "You know..." she begins. "I haven't registered Kayne's birth yet. He doesn't have a birth certificate yet since it was a home birth. It's just an idea, and you can tell me if it's too much, but how would you feel about just listing you as his father on his birth registration once it's filed? I was going to leave the 'father' space blank with the way Kirnon was acting. I don't want him to be able to take him from me legally in any way. If you're serious about adopting him and we can deal with the Kirnon situation, this would bypass all the legal stuff," she says as she looks into my eyes.

I didn't think about that. Ordinarily, I would never want to take the spot of anyone's father, but Kirnon is an asshole who doesn't deserve to have anything to do with Kayne.

"I think that's a great idea," I say, giving her a quick kiss, and I begin cleaning up the dishes.

We spend the next few hours doing normal, everyday family stuff like cleaning up after breakfast and playing with Kayne. It's absolute bliss and something that I never thought I would get the opportunity to do after Olivia.

"We should head over to Alaric's soon. If we don't, they will be banging down the door shortly," I tell Skarlyt. As much as I want to hole up in this cottage with the two of them forever, I know that I have to share her with her friends and family.

"I know you're right, but is it so bad to want to spend some alone time with my family?" she pouts.

I walk over to where she's sitting on the floor playing with Kayne and sit behind her, wrapping my arms around her middle. "Of course not. But the sooner we go, the sooner we can come back." I place a soft kiss on my mark and feel the shivers roll through her body.

She turns her head to look up at me, "Don't start something you can't finish."

"Oh, I can finish," I tell her with a smirk, standing up and lifting her into my arms. "We'll be right back, little buddy."

I leave a sleepy Kayne in his bouncy chair and sprint with

Skarlyt in my arms to our bedroom and throw her on the bed. "Now what was that you said about not starting something I can't finish?"

She just smirks at me as I slowly crawl up her body, leaving kisses on every bit of skin until I reach her lips. I fuse my mouth to hers at the same time that I grip her legs and pull her flush against my cock. I want her to feel just how much I want her.

I move my mouth down the side of her neck, giving my mark a few extra licks for good measure before gliding the rest of the way down her body. Her breath hitches as she turns her head away, inviting me to do as I please.

She's still in the sleep shorts from the night before, and the thin material does nothing to conceal the scent of her. I hook my fingers in the waistband and pull them down her body in one swift motion, exposing her glistening wetness. I drop the shorts on the ground and dive in. She tastes amazing, and I hook my arm under one soft, supple thigh and pull, bringing her closer.

"Lennox," she growls, desperate now that I'm lazily moving my tongue, and I chuckle. I could stay here all day, and I contemplate teasing her for a little longer but decide against it. We do have somewhere to be after all. I latch onto her clit, sucking and flicking it with my tongue, faster and faster. I slip two fingers inside of her, coaxing her toward the edge. She explodes with my name on her lips, and her pussy desperately gripping my fingers.

Her body goes lax as I pull them out and pop them into my mouth. I refuse to waste even a drop of her heavenly goodness. I shimmy my pants down and line myself up with her. She is too breathless to speak, but her eyes burn into me as she pushes herself closer to the edge of the bed, opening herself up to me, welcoming me inside. I push in hard and fast. If I didn't know that she was perfect for me before, the way she meets me thrust for thrust would prove it.

Just like the night before, we both tumble over that edge far too quickly. After, we hold each other as we catch our breath. I wish I could spend all day every day here in this bed with her, but alas, it cannot be.

"You go hop in the shower, and I'll pack a bag for Kayne," I tell her with a soft kiss, pulling up my pants and helping her stand.

"I love you," she whispers, standing on her tiptoes and planting a soft kiss on my lips.

"And I love you. To the moon and beyond."

I step out of the room, quickly checking on Kayne and finding him fast asleep, before heading into his room to pack. A couple diapers, a set of clothes, baby wipes. Is there anything else? I look around, but I'm pretty sure Phoebe would have anything we need. I place it all in Skarlyt's diaper bag and head to the living room.

"Your turn," she says, walking out of the bedroom dressed in a pair of skinny jeans and a tight blue shirt that makes her eyes pop even more. Damn, my mate is beautiful.

"He's all packed up, but you should double check just in case I missed something," I tell her, giving her a kiss as I walk by.

My shower doesn't take long at all and soon the three of us are out the door walking the well-traveled path to Alaric and Phoebe's.

There's a flurry of activity as we walk up to the porch. I see Darren standing by the door and ask, "What's going on?"

"There's activity at the border again, so we're moving everyone into the safe room," he responds. Shit. I didn't think they'd be attacking again so soon.

I turn to Skar, but she places a finger on my lips. "It's okay. I'm going to take Kayne downstairs. Don't worry; I'll stay safe."

Thank Mother Moon. I half expected her to want to run into danger with me. With what I know of her already, that is exactly what she would be doing if it weren't for Kayne. I nod and give her a thankful kiss before she walks into the house.

"What's the plan?" I ask, turning to Darren.

"Once everyone's inside, Alaric will probably send most of us to the border. The monitors detected movement near the main driveway. Then, I guess we'll see what's going on. Full disclosure, though. I didn't want to say anything in front of Skarlyt, but it looks like it's Kirnon."

A growl escapes my mouth. That fucker. How dare he come here? I'm going to rip him to shreds if he thinks he's getting anywhere near my mate or pup.

Alaric walks out of the house just as my growl finishes. "My sentiments exactly. Let's go see what this fucker wants and tear him apart if he's even thinking about Skar."

I walk to the front of the large group with Alaric and Darren. It's probably not where I'm supposed to be, but I cannot force myself to walk any slower.

"Since Skarlyt and I completed our mating, I guess I should officially petition to become part of your pack," I say to Alaric, going for a nonchalant tone.

Alaric lets out a small growl and then stifles it.

"Sorry. Skarlyt having a mate is still a touchy subject. Even though I know you're the complete opposite of Kirnon, the shit he put her through is still fresh in my mind. But, yes, I guess we should make it official."

He stops in his tracks and turns to me.

Oh, I guess we're doing this now. Okay.

"Do you, Lennox Johnson, pledge your allegiance to the West-wood pack?" he asks.

The shifters around us halt also, watching in quiet, if confused, respect.

"I do," I respond, turning my head to the side, showing him my neck in a sign of submission. His canines lengthen, and he bites in, snapping my bonds to the Ironwood pack and replacing them with ties to the Westwood pack.

"Wow." It takes a moment for me to adjust. This is so much different from my bond with the Ironwood pack. Even without having met them all, I can feel almost every pack member. I can feel joy from some, fear from others. Then, I feel the excitement radiating from my sisters. We have our familial pack bond, but now it's been strengthened.

"And do you pledge to protect the pack as an enforcer to the best of your ability?" Alaric continues, surprising me.

"Enforcer?" I ask, and he nods. Tears threaten to fall at the warm feeling spreading through my body. With my old pack, the idea of being an enforcer was unimaginable. My family was nowhere near powerful enough for Alpha Christian to even consider that.

"I do," I answer, raising my chin up to meet his gaze.

Can you hear me? Alaric says in my head through the now-functioning bond.

Yeah, I can, I respond.

"Good. Let's go," Alaric says, and we resume walking to the border, pausing briefly as his phone begins to ring.

"Skar, what's wrong?" Alaric's tone is alarmed, and I am instantly on edge. He waves me off a second later and silently mouths "they are fine" to me.

At Skar's request, he steps away, speaking low. The conversation is not long, but I am anxious to keep moving toward our destination. I know better than to eavesdrop, but I cannot help but overhear something about Joe and Phoebe.

"Everything good?" I ask as he hangs up and moves back toward our group.

"Yup. We just need to figure this out quickly and head back to the house. Sebastyn and Skarlyt have an idea to deal with our mage issue."

I nod my head, agreeing that I want to get this over with sooner rather than later. The sooner this asshole is gone, the sooner I can get on with my happily ever after.

"Where is she?" I hear someone yelling up ahead. The voice,

half crazed, repeats the question until we get close enough to answer.

"She's none of your concern, Kirnon. If you're smart, you will leave now before I let her mate tear you apart," Alaric says, as a disheveled man comes into view. I don't know what he looked like before, but right now this guy looks like shit. His straight, black hair is overgrown, hanging in stringy clumps around his face. His clothes are baggy on his thinning frame and look like they haven't been washed. I would hate to be close enough to smell him.

"Mate?" he screams, voice getting shriller by the second. "I'm her mate."

"No, you're not," I growl out loudly. "You're nothing to her. You don't deserve to even walk on the same earth as her. Really, I should thank you. If you were a real man, it would be you who got the honor of being her mate instead of me."

He looks shocked. I don't know what he thought he would accomplish by coming here.

"I challenge you for the right to be Skarlyt's mate," he roars.

Oh, shit. He should not have done that. There's no way he can or will win. My wolf is already on edge after he kidnapped her. He's not going to show any mercy. I glance at Darren and Alaric, waiting for both of them to nod in agreement before I begin taking off my clothes.

Kill. Protect mate, my wolf growls, and I hum in agreement.

There is no way that I'm letting this man walk away today. He will never have another chance to take my mate, or worse, my pup.

No. This ends here and now.

Chapter Twenty-Three

Skarlyt

After leaving Lennox with Darren on the front porch, I walk into the house and follow the throngs of people heading to the basement.

"What's going on?" I ask Alaric as I pass him.

"There's some activity at the border. It looks like the mages are back for their leader. Don't worry. The barrier is holding, I'll come get you if there's anything you need to know." He pulls both Kayne and I in for a hug. "I'm really glad you're safe, Skar."

"Me too," I whisper.

Once he releases me, I head down the stairs to find my mom and brother in a heated discussion.

"We need to warn the coven, but I don't think we have time," my mom says.

"I can go warn them," Sebastyn reassures her.

"How?" I question. My brother looks at me with a smirk.

"I can teleport."

"You can what?" I ask in awe.

"Teleport. There's no time to explain. I need to get going. It takes a lot of magic, so I'm going to need to rest when I get back."

Without further explanation, he disappears. There's a small flash of his magic right before he leaves, and I pout, wishing I could do the same.

"He's going to need a strength potion to revive his magic," my mom whispers to me, and I watch as she rushes to my work room. I walk over to Charleigh and Phoebe.

"Can you guys watch Kayne for a few minutes?" I ask, and Charleigh opens her arms. I pass him over, thanking them quickly before dashing away.

Walking into my work room, I find that it's back to its original glory, although my mom seems to have extended the workspace a little for her task. She has a grimoire out on the counter and is rushing back and forth gathering the ingredients.

"You get the herbs; I'll mix," I tell her. I look over what is needed and begin placing them in my bowl to grind.

~ *Ginseng*
~ *Sage*
~ *Rosemary*
~ *Peppermint*

Grind into a powder and mix with moon water.
(For an extra boost, add in a few phoenix tears)

The last note has been added in pencil in my mother's handwriting. Good thing we have some phoenix tears. There are over one hundred witches in our coven, and he's definitely going to need an enormous boost. Mom gathers the ingredients while I start grinding them up with my mortar and pestle. I step away as she brings the moon water to a boil and pours it over the top of the powder. I run to my safe in the wall and open it up, gathering up a vial of Phoebe's tears. I know I can trust my mom with the code, but I have told no one except Phoebe and Alaric where I've been keeping the tears. They can be used in a variety of dangerous spells, and I prefer not to worry about the wrong people getting their hands on them. After it's all mixed up, she brings the potion to a boil.

"We just need to infuse it with our magic," she tells me, closing her eyes and I do the same, pushing all the positive magic I can reach into the potion.

When we've done all we can, we fill one vial to the brim and pour the excess into a second and rush back into the bunker. We get there just as Sebastyn blinks back, looking extremely drained.

Seb takes the vial wordlessly, downing it like a shot, and I notice the difference immediately as he straightens his back.

"Wow, that was powerful," Seb says, handing the empty vial back to me.

"Phoenix tears," I shrug.

Phoebe's phone starts ringing and she pulls it out of her pocket with a frown. She swipes up, tapping the button to put it on speakerphone.

"Hello?"

"Phoebe?" A woman's voice says.

"Sarah? Is that you?"

Sarah? Isn't that the woman married to Joe? Phoebe told me a bit about her; she said she's a good woman but in a horrible marriage.

"Yeah, it's me. I was wondering....Well...Have you seen Joe at all? He was talking all this crazy stuff about coming after you a couple weeks ago, and I haven't seen him since."

Phoebe looks at me in panic as if asking, 'what do I say?' That's a tough one for sure. What can she say? 'Yeah, I have your husband locked in a cellar that is designed to siphon his magic and keep him weak?'

"Uh, about that," she begins.

"It's okay, Phoebe. I don't need to know what happened. I just want to know. Am I...is he gone?" she asks with a sliver of hope in her voice.

I blow out the breath I'd been holding as I waited for her response.

"Yeah, hun, you are," Phoebe replies, exhaling the same tension I was feeling. I hear the other woman crying on the other end of the phone. I really hope those are happy tears and not sad ones. I know Phoebe, and she wouldn't want Sarah upset. Heck, she wouldn't want anyone upset.

"Thank you," she replies softly.

"Aw, hun, I didn't know it was that bad. If I'd known, I would have come for you. You know that, right?" Phoebe asks, and I can see how much she truly cares about this woman.

"I know. It's just...What do I do now? I have no one here. You know how the other wives are. If they find out Joe is gone, I don't know what they'll do with me." Phoebe sucks in a breath. I already know what she's going to say, and I wholeheartedly support her. If anyone has an issue with it, I'll stand right beside her to defend this woman. I haven't even met her, but I can tell of her from this phone conversation that she's someone who should be protected.

"Okay, hun. This is what you're going to do. You're going to pack up anything that you want to keep, and you're going to drive to Parry Sound. You can stay with us until you get back on your feet. You get to town and get a motel room under a different name. You call me at this number when you check in, and I will come get you as soon as it's safe here. There are some...complications right now, and it's not safe for you to come straight here."

"Are you sure? Is your mate going to be okay with this?" she asks, the anxiety in her voice is palpable.

"Oh, hun. We've been lied to for so many years. Real men don't treat their wives the way we were treated. Alaric is my partner. We share every decision. If I tell him I need to do this, he will support me and help you in any way he can."

A small smile graces my lips as I think about my own past relationships. If I were with Kirnon, I'm sure I would have been conditioned the same way as Sarah, never being able to make a decision on my own. Phoebe is right, though. Lennox is my partner. I know with my whole heart that he will stand beside me no matter what. Even if he disagreed with me, he would protect me with everything he has.

"Really?" she asks.

"Really. Just pack your stuff and drive. It's about a six-hour drive if you don't hit Toronto traffic. Take the 407, and I'll pay the fee if you're short on cash." From the look Phoebe is giving me, I can tell that her gut is telling her something and it's really never good. "Sarah, hun, I need you to leave now! I've got this feeling that they are coming for you, and I don't know how to explain it. Just take basic necessities. I'll help you buy whatever you need when you get here. Oh, I almost forgot. Take off any jewelry—just in case they have trackers on it."

I hear Sarah suck in a breath and pause for a minute. "I'm on my way. I don't need anything here. I'll see you in a few hours." I can hear her car door close and the engine turn over.

"See you soon. Drive safe," Phoebe tells her before hanging up the phone.

"Did I do the right thing?" Phoebe asks me, and I pull her into a hug.

I push her back a little so that I can look into her eyes. "Absolutely, and if anyone tries to say anything, I will stand beside you."

She lets out another shaky breath with a nod. Gods this woman is amazing. She has a heart of gold. We're so lucky that Alaric found her and brought her into our lives.

I glance over, finding my brother looking deep in thought, and walk over to him.

"You know we're going to need Phoebe, right?" he says as I reach him.

I nod at him solemnly. "I really wish we could find another way, but it's looking that way." The last thing I want to do is put Phoebe in danger. If it's the mages that are attacking again, though, she may be our only shot.

"Unless you have access to the leader of their coven, there really isn't another way," he says, and I immediately perk up. "What? You don't, do you?"

"Actually…" I begin, looking around before continuing, "say we did…How would that help us?"

"Well, in theory, all mages are connected through their coven leader. Sort of like how a pack is linked with its alpha. When a coven leader dies, just like when an alpha dies, every member feels it. It might be enough to get them to leave and give us more time to come up with something." If what Sebastyn says is true, we literally just hit the jackpot, a surefire way to get the mages to back off with minimal fighting.

"One sec," I say, rushing to grab Phoebe and heading back over to the secluded corner where Sebastyn is still standing. He waves his hands and I watch as a translucent blue barrier erects around us.

"Soundproof?" I ask, and he nods. "That is so freaking cool, Seb. Once this is over, you and I are going to have a few things to talk about." He shrugs. giving me a smirk. I narrow my eyes to emphasize my point. His smirk just gets bigger, and he winks at me.

"Okay, what's going on?" Phoebe asks, looking between us both.

"Well, Sebastyn just had an idea on how to get the mages to leave. At the very least, it will buy us time to train you more, but we need to get Alaric in on this conversation too," I say and begin dialing Alaric's phone number on speakerphone.

"Skar, what's wrong?" he answers.

"Nothing's wrong; we're all fine. Seb just has an idea that should help us with our current problem. Can you step away from everyone for a minute while we explain?"

"Sure...Okay, I'm away from everyone. What's the idea?"

"I'll let Seb explain it since it was his idea." He shoots me a panicked look, and I smile. Payback's a bitch, Sebastyn.

"Hey, Alaric. I have reason to believe that mages are connected to their coven leader the same way that a pack is connected to their alpha. With that said, if a coven leader dies, the entire coven should feel it and leave to regroup until they can elect another. It should buy us the time we need to train Phoebe or find another solution. When I told Skar this, she got excited, so I'm guessing you have the leader hidden somewhere." I watch the surprised look on Phoebe's face.

"Yeah, we do actually, but I want to question him on a few things before he dies," Alaric says.

A brilliant idea pops into my head. "What if we could make a truth potion?" I look over at Sebastyn, and he nods his head. All the truth potions I've ever made haven't worked; they always seem to be missing a key ingredient. If Sebastyn has learned how to teleport, chances are that he's learned some tricks about the truth potions as well.

"Okay. I am sending Darren back to you now. I'll be there as soon as I can. Then, we will go have a little chat with Joe," Alaric says and hangs up the phone.

Phoebe looks at us both and asks, "Theoretically, if Joe was married, how would it affect his wife when he dies?" I know exactly where she's going with this and look to Sebastyn to explain. He seems to be the expert on mages.

"Same way it will for the coven, except she might feel some of his pain if they are true mates. Why?"

"And say she was driving at that time...What would happen then?" My eyes ping back to Sebastyn, awaiting his answer.

"I suppose, theoretically, she'd probably crash the car." Her eyes get wide, and a worried look appears on her face. "Why are you asking these very specific questions, Phoebe?"

"Well, Sarah, Joe's wife, was my friend before when I was married to Tanner. She...uhm...She called me about an hour ago, and she's on her way here." A look of anxiety flashes on Sebastyn's face, and my eyebrows furrow together in confusion.

"Can you call and ask her to pull over at a rest stop or something?" She doesn't answer me. Instead, she just picks up her phone and dials a number.

"Hey, Sarah. Can you stop at a rest stop or something for a bit?" Sarah is obviously talking because Phoebe is quiet for a few minutes before saying, "Well, something's going to happen soon, and you might feel weird. I don't want to give you the details, but I need you to pull over just in case you feel some pain." I can tell she doesn't want to tell her that we're about to kill her husband, but she's probably going to have to.

"Sarah, calm down. Everything is going to be fine. We are going to try something with magic and the mages, and I don't know how it will affect you. I promise you everything will be okay, and I'll call you as soon as it's done. I just want you to be safe," she finishes telling her and begins nodding as she listens. "Sure, hun. Don't worry. I can have Charleigh take the phone. She'll keep talking to you, so you won't be alone. Will that work?"

"Where exactly is she?" Sebastyn asks, tapping Phoebe on the shoulder, and my confusion grows even more.

"Sarah, where are you right now?" She pauses, then pulls the phone away. "She said she's just coming up to Woodstock."

"Perfect. Tell her to get off and head to the Pittock Conservation Area. Tell her to park at the Husky Trail parking area, and I'll meet her there." Phoebe relays the information and gives nods, confirming that she will.

"Okay, hun. My friend Sebastyn will be there shortly. Just pull off there, and he'll see you soon," she says before hanging up and looking at him. "Thank you, Seb. This means a lot to me."

"You're welcome, Phoebe. Nobody should be alone during that, especially since we don't know how it will affect her." Sebastyn drops the barrier, and I give Phoebe's shoulder a squeeze.

"She'll be okay."

Phoebe just nods, tears threatening to drop as she walks back over to Charleigh and the kids.

Together, Sebastyn and I make quick work of the truth potion. It looks like the missing ingredient was an elderberry. Sebastyn had to pop over to Supernatural to grab one from Trev who, thankfully, gave one up without argument.

We walk back into the bunker to wait for Alaric, Darren, and Lennox. I just grab Kayne from my mom when a wave of anger hits me. I know that it's coming from Lennox. I need to see what's going on. What could have happened to make him this angry?

"I'm just going to take a peek at the cameras to see what's going on," I say as I hand Kayne to my mom.

"I don't think that's a good idea," Phoebe says to me just as I start walking away.

"And why is that?" I turn and ask her. She doesn't want to answer and starts looking around at everyone around us. I don't let up, though, and I stare straight at her until she relents.

"Because Alaric told me that it looked like it was Kirnon at the border," she says, looking down at her hands.

"What?" I say, but I don't stay to hear what her answer is as I begin to march over to the monitors. Sure as shit, there, in the middle monitor, is Kirnon. He looks like a bag of crap standing off against my mate. Oh, fuck. Are they going to fight? I watch as Lennox begins to undress, handing his clothes to a waiting Darren before shifting into the most beautiful rust colored wolf I've ever seen.

Kirnon, on the other hand, strips down and looks like he's trying to...Well, if I'm honest, it looks like he's trying to take a shit. After a few minutes, he shifts into a sickly looking black wolf. Even from here, I can see his ribs and his wolf's matted and dirty fur .

"Mom, come look at this," I yell to her in the sitting area.

She rushes over with Kayne in her arms and stares at the screen with her mouth hanging open. "Oh, Mother. He's split his soul," she says in a whisper.

"He what?" I ask.

"He split his soul. It's what happens to a shifter when their inner beast doesn't agree with a large life decision. It doesn't always happen, but it can. Whatever Kirnon did, it was a while ago. Now, his wolf is dying."

Shit. That doesn't sound good.

"Is there any way to separate their souls permanently?" I have to ask. As much as I hate Kirnon, I have a feeling that it was the decision to reject me that caused his soul to split. If I can do something to save his wolf, I have to try.

"Well, there is one spell in your great grandmother's grimoire in your room that can grant the beast's half of the soul dominance over the human. It essentially kills the human half, which allows the beast to live a full life in that form only. I've never seen it done before. I've only heard stories, and, even then, it doesn't always work. The Mother has to agree with the decision and bless the shifter half of the soul," she explains.

"But there is a chance?" I just need to make sure.

"Yes, I suppose there is a chance."

That's all I need to hear as I let myself out of the safe room, calling back to my mom, "Keep Kayne safe for me."

I rush to my workroom, grabbing the grimoire and flipping to the soul splitting spell page. It seems easy enough, only an incantation. It doesn't even require any ingredients.

I run down the road faster than I've ever run before. I need to make it there before Lennox tears him apart, and I know he will. I need to at least try to save Kirnon's wolf. If I had thought about it, I could've had Sebastyn teleport me and saved myself all this running.

Once I'm within hearing distance, I yell out "*Stop!*" causing everyone to turn and look at me. A small whine leaves both Kirnon and Lennox's wolves as they watch me approach, with the latter prancing up and rubbing himself on me. I take a quick minute to stroke his fur and really admire him in his wolf form.

"I need to try something first, okay?" I say to the wolf. I know Lennox can understand me. He definitely doesn't look happy that I'm here, but he nods. Walking up to the barrier, I say, "Kirnon, you have committed the worst act imaginable to your wolf. You have caused your soul to split, thus sentencing him to death." I raise my hands in a placating gesture, and step forward.

"I want to talk to him now," I say, projecting my voice across the space between us. "I want to speak to the wolf. The wolf who is trapped inside this man, the wolf who has been mistreated and ignored, the wolf who could have been mate."

I am watching him closely, so I see the exact moment when his eyes shift in an indescribable way, and I know that the wolf has taken control.

"I am so sorry for what he's done to you," I say, and I am shocked by the tears springing to my own eyes. "He has hurt me too, and I cannot keep my family safe if I let him leave here today."

The wolf, so pitifully thin and weak, whines in a high tone. Lennox and Alaric both step forward, but I know the wolf won't hurt me. Kirnon is the danger.

"I can help you," I say, taking another step forward and

extending my hand. "He's already so weak that shifting back may be hard for him. I can help you shut the door on him forever."

The wolf pads closer to me and surprises me by nuzzling his head against my outstretched hand. I can feel the tension in Lennox behind me, but happy tears streak down my face at the sign.

I close my eyes, throwing all my intent into this effort and praying to the Mother to help me as I whisper the spell.

"What was both, is now one. What stood on two legs, now stands on all four. The beast is now bound, and the man is no more."

She must hear me and find my cause justified, because the next thing I know, Kirnon's wolf lets out a whine, then a sigh. Before my eyes, he starts to change. His frame fills out to a healthier weight, his fur becoming shiny and smooth, and his eyes even begin to clear.

He drops on his back, showing his stomach and neck to Alaric and Lennox as a sign of submission. Thank the Mother. I was worried that we were going to have to kill him. I hate Kirnon with a passion and he doesn't deserve a second of my pity, but this beautiful creature has done nothing to deserve the death sentence that he was given.

"I've never seen that before," Alaric says, breaking the silence. "Do you think it's safe to let him in?" he asks.

"I'm not sure," I respond. Turning to Kirnon's wolf, I begin to speak. "How about you go out into the woods and try to make a life for yourself? If you need us, we will be here. Just howl. Now's your chance to live your life your way." That seems to satisfy him. He gives me a small nod and turns, trotting into the forest.

Next thing I know, I'm being pulled back into a large chest with arms wrapping around me tightly. "You scared me," Lennox whispers into my ear.

"I know, babe. I'm sorry. I had to try and save his wolf. He didn't do anything wrong," I respond, turning to look him in the eyes.

He goes to say something but stiffens, thrusting me behind him.

"Mages," Alaric says before posturing himself in front of me as well.

Chapter Twenty-Four

Lennox

T
he next few minutes flash by in a flurry of activity. I see dozens of men step out of the trees and begin to throw magic at the barrier. Alaric goes into full alpha mode, shouting out instructions to everyone.

"There are more mages than I expected. For a supposedly extinct race, there's a whole lot of them," he says, coming up to where Skar and I are standing, throwing me a pair of shorts.

I glance down at myself, realizing for the first time that I'm naked and send him a look of gratitude before pulling them on.

"Who told you they were extinct?" I ask him. In all my travels, I've heard rumors of groups of mages. Sure, they have been in hiding and tried to keep their numbers some big secret, but I've known there were covens of mages all over the world.

He turns to look at me with wide eyes. "Everyone. I've always been told that they died out with the last phoenix shifter over fifty years ago. Are you saying that's not true?"

"I'm not sure about the group of mages involved with the phoenix shifter fifty years ago, but in my travels, I've networked with a lot of supernaturals, and mages have always been around. They're hiding, but definitely not extinct." I can tell that's not what he wants to hear as a look of concern crosses his face. But it kind of makes sense, I'm sure he wasn't networking with the types of people I was, and I don't think any of the legitimate groups are aware of the mages.

"What am I supposed to do? Lock my mate and pups up for the rest of their lives because we're constantly going to be attacked? How do we defeat them without Phoebe's help? I can't let her out here with them, but I don't see how I have much of a choice with this many."

I feel for him; I really do. If it were my mate and pups, I would be feeling the same way. Heck, I already want to lock Skar and Kayne up in our cottage and live the rest of our lives alone in peace, but that's just not how the world works, and it's not any way to live.

"Send Darren to Phoebe and have them deal with Joe together. Maybe Sebastyn's plan will work." Skarlyt pipes up.

"What plan?" I ask looking between them both.

I don't get an answer though. "Darren?" Alaric calls to his brother.

"Yeah?" he says, jogging up. It's hard to hear him over the sounds of blasts of magic breaking against the barrier.

"Go back to be with Phoebe. She needs support if she's going to deal with Joe." Darren turns to leave, but Alaric growls out, "Don't let that bastard near my mate though."

"I won't," Darren promises and takes off running back toward the house.

Maybe what we need now is time to regroup and plan how to neutralize the mage threat. Just as I open my mouth to tell him, more people step out of the forest. Only these aren't mages, they're vampires. I glance at the sky, realizing it must be later than I thought as the sun seems to have dipped behind the trees. Goddess, I hope they're on our side.

"Oh, good. Drake's here with reinforcements," Alaric says, walking up to the barrier. What's he doing? I know that he came to some sort of agreement with them, but I can't help how hard it feels to trust them with everything that has happened so far.

"Skar, I want you to go back to Kayne, please," I say as I turn to look at her. I know she's going to protest. Heck, I would too, but I can't focus on the battle and her at the same time.

She goes to disagree, but I stop her by holding my finger up, asking for a minute. "Listen, it's not that I don't think you're capable. You're probably one of the few people that actually stands a chance out here. Kayne already lost a parent today with Kirnon being bound in wolf form. If you and I both stay and fight, he could potentially lose three, and that's not really an option I want to face right now. He needs you more than he needs me. If you need me to go with you in order for you to return, I will." She deflates. Any argument that she had on the tip of her tongue is lost because she knows I'm right.

"I just don't know what to do. I can't just sit in that room worrying about everyone, knowing that I could help. I'll be hiding away like a coward." I had a feeling she would feel this way. She's so strong and used to taking on the world that she sees it as cowardice instead of bravery.

"It's not you being a coward, Skar," I tell her, rubbing my hand down her cheek. "It's selflessness. You're putting the needs of our son over your own. It's staying safe, and hopefully coming up with a plan while down there to beat these assholes without having to risk everyone's safety. If anyone can come up with a kick ass plan, it's you."

"I didn't think of it like that. I guess I could go back and try to come up with something," she relents, giving me a quick kiss before turning to run back to the house.

Whew. Now that I know she's going to be safe, I can focus on actually helping the pack defeat these fuckers once and for all. We just need to figure out how.

I walk up to Alaric where he is talking to a vampire with long blonde hair.

"We estimate that there are at least two hundred of them surrounding your property. They have shelters raised and are ready to wait you out. I don't know what other options we have if you refuse to bring the phoenix out," he tells Alaric.

Alaric growls loudly. "That's my mate who just gave birth to my pup. Would you ask your mate to run headfirst into danger after just giving birth?"

"I don't have a mate yet, Alaric, so I can't imagine what kind of decision that would be. I'm not trying to upset you. I'm simply stating the facts. Mages are hard to kill. Even with us outnumbering them five to one between us, the losses on our side are going to be huge.

"I understand you wanting to find another way. I do. I just don't see one at this point," the vampire finishes. I know he's right, and so does Alaric. Neither of us like it, but it's hard to find another option when there just isn't one.

Although the mages have a constant barrage going against the barrier, it seems to be withstanding them. Thank the goddess for everything Constance and the coven did to reinforce it. Even if they never break through, it's only a matter of time before we cannot stay inside any longer. I think back to Skarlyt asking me for my zombie apocalypse plan and realize just how much I left out of my plans.

"I have some of my people working on a plan," Alaric explains to the leader of the vampires, Drake. "Let's try to give it a few minutes." He's grasping at straws. We both know it, but for now it's what he needs, so I let it go.

"Maybe whatever Sebastyn has planned will work," I supply, hoping to add to his hope. Two weeks ago, my logical brain would've been thinking along the same lines as Drake. knowing it would be easier just to have Phoebe out here to obliterate them. Now, with Skarlyt and Kayne, I know how Alaric feels.

"If you're going to let the clock run down on this, can my people at least cross the border? The mages are focused on you and the barrier for now, but my people are completely exposed on this side." Drake's voice is silken and calm, but I can tell he's uncomfortable.

Shit. I didn't think about that. Although it's great that they are here to help us, I didn't think of the consequences there would be with them being on the other side. I was only focused on the benefits that the barrier is providing to us.

I look around at the vampires scattered throughout the woods. They aren't warriors. They're normal people who have lives and families at home waiting for them too. I share a look with Alaric, and he nods.

"Yes, you're right. I can't expect you to stand in danger while we sit back here, safe for the time being. I'll send a team to the eastern border. Have your people meet there, and I'll have some wolves and witches on standby to bring them across."

"Thank you," is all Drake says before flashing away, running so fast that he is almost a blur.

"Are you sure about this?" I whisper to Alaric once Drake has left. I really hope we're making the right decision to work with them, and they aren't double crossing us.

"No. But I don't see how we have a choice. His father is a good man and leader. I have to trust that he raised his son to be the same."

I nod, but I know that's not always the case. A father's influence can produce an opposite effect. Look at Ashton and Christian. If Alaric's theory was correct, Ashton would be a womanizing asshole with a god complex. If he was, I wouldn't have let him near my sister. Hell, he would've rejected her just because of her standing in the pack despite how amazing she is.

I glance over at Alaric, who is obviously using the pack link to send wolves to the eastern border to meet the vamps, and I notice the way his eyebrows are pinching together with worry.

"I've been meaning to ask you. How did your wolf react to the boys?" I need to distract him until Drake gets through the border or Darren and Phoebe complete their task, whichever comes first.

"He claimed them instantly. Why? How does your wolf feel about Kayne?"

"The same," I admit. "He claimed him the moment I looked into his eyes."

"Good. For the record, Lennox, I'm glad you're Skarlyt's mate. I know I was a little..." He pauses, searching for the word.

"Alpha-hole-ish?" I provide, and he raises an eyebrow but smiles.

"I was going to say skeptical, but your word works too. Anyway, I'm glad she found someone like you. She deserves to be happy."

"She does," I agree. "And I'll spend the rest of my days ensuring she stays that way."

"We just need to get through this, and then we can get started living the rest of our lives together. Let's head back to the house to see what they've come up with. They're not getting through the border any time soon so it should be safe."

We turn from the barrier and the mages jeering indistinctly on the other side. Alaric stops to talk to some of the wolves and witches who are standing watch. With the mages stuck outside, they are in no direct danger. Still, they look fierce and forbidding enough that I'd think twice if I was on the other side.

Chapter Twenty-Five

Lennox

As we make our way downstairs, I see Seb blink out of existence. What the fuck?

"Pretty cool, huh? He learned some new tricks while he was away. I can't wait until all this shit is over so he can teach me. Did you know that he can even transport another person? Imagine if we want to go on vacation somewhere. We wouldn't have to drive or fly. I could just teleport us there. How cool would that be?" Skar asks, coming up and wrapping her arms around me. That would be pretty awesome. Never having to worry about paying for plane tickets, waiting in line, or sitting in uncomfortable airplane seats. Don't even get me started on the hours wasted in flight.

"Yes, it's going to be awesome, but let's get through this first before we start planning, okay?" I say as I give her a kiss. It gets heated a lot quicker than I expected.

"Here they come, lovebirds," Darren interrupts us. "Don't want to ruin the mood, but it's time to check on Joe."

"Didn't you guys already go see Joe?" I ask, sounding more

impatient than I expect. Skarlyt and I are both breathing heavily by the time we pull apart.

"Phoebe refused to go without Alaric. When she gets her mind set on something, you don't try to change it," he responds as Alaric returns to our group with a very pleased Phoebe at his side.

"Let's go," Alaric says.

Darren leads the way back outside to a small shed on the other side of the house.

"So, what's the plan?" I ask as we walk.

"This," Skar says, holding up a small vial. "It's a truth potion. We're going to pour it down his throat and let him sing like a canary."

"Will it work?" I ask and immediately feel her hardened gaze on me.

She slaps my arm with a scoff. "Of course, it will."

"Ow. Remind me never to question the abilities of my mate again," I chuckle, earning a smile from Skarlyt. I pull her into my side once more. Now that the threat of Kirnon is dealt with, I no longer need to worry about having to constantly look over my shoulder. Then again, living in a pack with the only living phoenix shifter means we will constantly be in danger anyway. I knew this pack was too good to be true, but I'll still choose it over the Ironwood pack any day of the week.

Walking inside, I see a set of stairs leading down, and we begin to descend. This is crazy. It looks like a garden shed from the outside, but once you get down the stairs, it almost looks like a sterile hospital psych ward with solid doors lining the hallway. We end up at the last door and open it. I see the guy from the other night, Joe, inside, sitting on a cot.

"Finally come to kill me?" he asks with a small chuckle. Why he thinks that's funny, I have no idea. Whatever floats his boat, I guess.

"No. Actually, we have a few questions for you," Alaric says.

Joe spits toward us, "As if I would tell you anything."

"Good thing we came prepared for that," Alaric says, moving to roughly wrench his arms back as Darren steps forward to hold his head back, forcing his mouth open.

Joe was far from being an impressive specimen before, but now he is downright pitiful. He's no longer bound, but there are silver manacles around his wrists and ankles. His face is already sallow from the loss of power.

Skar hands me the potion. "Pour that down his throat." I look at her in shock. I expected that she would be the one to pour it down his throat, but I'm glad that she's letting me. Even with the drain on his powers, he could still have some juice left, and I don't want her to get hurt.

I walk up and prop his mouth open, pouring the potion down his throat before placing my hand over his mouth and nose so he can't spit it out. This way, he has no choice but to swallow it. Once his Adam's apple bobs, showing that he's ingested it, I step back along with Alaric and Darren.

"What the fuck was that?" he asks, spitting anything he can out of his mouth. He even tries to put his finger down his throat to make himself throw it up.

"That was just a little something to help loosen those lips of yours, and don't bother trying to throw it up. It's already in your system," Skar tells him. He looks at her with menace, clamping his mouth shut, as if that will work.

"First question. How many of you are there?" Alaric asks.

"More than you could possibly imagine, dog," he responds. Okay, so apparently this isn't his first rodeo, and he's found a way to answer with the truth without giving away any actual information.

"Why did you come here?" I ask, hoping that a little more specific question will get us a better answer.

"We came for the baby phoenix. We need her power." We

already knew that. I was hoping he would give me a little more information.

"Why?" Phoebe is the one who asks this time.

He stares at her with the promise of death in his eyes. I can tell he hates her with a passion. Alaric said that they have history. I guess he wasn't lying.

"Well, dear Phoebe. Once we lost you, our power reserve got cut in half. We've been so used to having two phoenixes to drain that the loss of one is too much. We need to replace you, and—since you've aligned with these dogs—your bouncing baby girl is our best bet." He says the last bit with a sneer.

"Wait, what do you mean, cut in half?" Phoebe asks, stepping closer to him. Alaric grabs her and pulls her into his side.

Joe starts laughing maniacally. "You didn't really think you were the only phoenix we have been draining, did you? Of course, you did. You always were a self-centered bitch."

"You have another phoenix?" Phoebe asks, and it's good she does because it forces him to answer in a more straightforward way.

"Yes, Phoebe dear. We have another phoenix in our care."

Phoebe begins to shift, unable to contain her anger. Bands of orange fire stream out from here at all angles, and, though none of us burn, the temperature in the cell noticeably rises.

"Where is she?" she screams.

They didn't exaggerate when they said that a phoenix's screech can make your eardrums bleed. I lift my hand to my ear to see if there is blood pouring out. I pull my hand away and look. Nope. No blood. Not yet anyway.

"Safe and far away from you, where she should be," Joe answers. Again, he's obviously telling the truth, but his answer is vague.

"Where is she?" Phoebe asks again, and there is murder in her voice and eyes. Each word is punctuated by stream of flames aimed toward Joe. He barely dodges them and lands back on his cot.

"Halifax," he says, the word escaping him. I am not sure if it's the truth potion or the fear of Phoebe that brings it out of him.

"What's her name?" It's Skar who asks this. I don't know why it's relevant, but maybe I'm missing something.

Joe's gaze shifts to her, and I can see an underlying hint of anxiety in his features as he answers. "Sophia." He grits the name out through clenched teeth, as if he's trying to fight the potion. Every single person in the room sucks in a breath.

Okay, I'm definitely missing something.

No one gets to ask anything else as Phoebe completes her shift in a whirl of orange and red and grabs onto Joe, throwing him against the wall and setting him ablaze. I can hear him screaming in pain for a long time before his screams finally die out, and only the smell of burned flesh remains.

"Okay, does someone want to tell me who Sophia is?" I ask the room.

"Sophia is Phoebe's twin sister," Skarlyt answers, and I watch as Phoebe shifts back, burying her face in Alaric's chest while sobs start wracking her body. In an attempt to give them a few minutes of privacy, I wrap my arm around Skarlyt and guide her out of the room.

I look over in Darren's direction. "We should probably go check to see if that worked or not."

He simply nods, looking stunned, and the three of us head up the stairs.

As we exit the shed, Drake walks up.

"Whatever you just did, it has them all teleporting away." His long, blonde hair is still streaming from the run he must have just completed to bring us the news.

Perfect. Maybe now we can have some peace for a while. Well, as much peace as we can while preparing for the next battle that is sure to come. "I'm going to link the pack, letting everyone know that it's safe to return home," Darren says, his eyes glossing over as I hear his message in my own head.

I turn to Skarlyt. "I know this is fast, but how do you feel about having our mating ceremony tomorrow? I don't want to wait. I just want to be declared your mate in front of Mother Moon and receive her blessing."

She doesn't answer, she just presses her lips to mine and jumps up, wrapping her legs around my waist. I'm going to take that as a yes.

I hear Drake scoff something about "mates" as he walks a few steps away with Darren, but I don't let it stop me from slipping my hand behind my mate's neck and my tongue into her mouth.

Alaric and Phoebe walk out of the shed, and that does grab our attention. Phoebe is wearing Alaric's shirt, tears still flowing freely out of her eyes. Skarlyt jumps down and rushes to her.

"Don't worry. We'll find her," she whispers.

"I hoped that her situation was better than mine. That she wasn't being used—" She lets off a little hiccup, and I walk closer, pulling my mate into my side as Alaric does the same. "How long has she been with them? Do they at least treat her well? I have so many questions that I need the answers to."

"I know, Pheebs. With Sebastyn's teleporting and all the new spells he's learned plus your phoenix fire, we will have her back in no time."

"You promise?" Phoebe asks, looking at my mate with hopeful eyes.

"I do."

I nuzzle my mate's neck. I don't agree with her promising to have Sophia here in no time. That's not a promise she should make, but now it's out there so I will do whatever it takes to ensure she keeps it.

"We will do anything to make sure she gets here safe. She's family. We don't give up on family," Darren adds.

"On a lighter note. Alaric, how do you feel about having a mating ceremony tomorrow?" Skarlyt asks, and Phoebe's tear-streaked face quickly turns toward excitement.

"Really?" she squeals.

Both Skarlyt and I nod and, just like that, my mate is taken from me and pulled toward the house by Phoebe. They're already discussing flowers, dresses, and everything else that goes with planning a mating ceremony, and I smile.

"Be prepared not to see your mate until bed tonight," Alaric laughs, and I growl, making him laugh even harder. "Hey, you're the one who decided to have a mating ceremony on a day's notice. Between your family and Constance, they'll be up planning until dawn. You will be lucky if Skarlyt actually gets to come to bed."

Shit. That's not what I wanted when I suggested it. I planned on reassuring us both that we are alive, over and over again, before waking up and cementing our bond tomorrow.

"I guess Kayne and I can at least get some sleep," I shrug, and Darren laughs in a way that tells me that is also unlikely. "So, what's the deal with Sophia? I've known Phoebe all her life and had no idea she has a sister."

The two of them look at one other.

Alaric sighs. "We found out just after our mating ceremony. It was actually Skarlyt who found a birth certificate for Phoebe in London. She kept digging and found a second birth certificate timed only seconds after for Sophia."

"Wait. So that means either Phoebe's parents abandoned a second child, which I find highly unlikely, or..."

"Phoebe was adopted. We're not sure what happened to her biological parents. All we do know is that they had twin girls and then died days later. How her mother, who was obviously a phoenix, was able to not only stay under the radar of the supernatural community but die without anyone knowing is still baffling."

"I thought the only way to kill a phoenix was if they turned their inner flame on themselves and went supernova," I say, baffled.

Alaric nods. "That's what we've been told too. Although our limited information on phoenixes could be wrong. Hell, we all thought phoenixes were extinct, and now there's two living in my house."

"This is just so crazy," I say, shaking my head. "But the more phoenixes we can find the better. Especially since the mages seem so interested."

"That was my thought as well. I'm hoping that the more we learn and find, the better I will be able to protect Aurora and any future phoenixes we have."

"I understand that too. If Kayne really is a hybrid, he's going to be sought after too. I haven't had a chance to talk to Skarlyt about it yet, but I'm wondering if we should try and conceal that information as much as possible."

Darren steps up beside me. "There are only a few people who know. Kirnon was going on about it, but everyone else thinks that it's impossible for a true hybrid child to exist. He's safe for now."

"That's good and will work for now, but long term we're definitely going to need to figure something out for both of them," Alaric adds.

"So, it's true. The child is a hybrid?" Drake asks, walking on the other side of Darren. Shit. I completely forgot he was with us. Vampires are quiet and creepy.

I stop, turning toward him with what I'm sure is a murderous look on my face. He holds his hands up. "I promise you have nothing to worry about from me or mine. I will keep this secret for you."

"Why?" I demand.

He lets out a breath. "Because I've come to realize what my father tried to teach me. That it's important to have powerful allies. And having the alpha of the Westwood pack and the future high priestess of the Coven of the Moon as enemies would be very bad." Not what I was expecting him to say but at least he is honest.

"If I find out you're lying..." I growl out.

"You won't. I won't make the mistake of taking on the pack or coven a second time. My entire coven is already pretty pissed at me for my actions the other night. I won't risk losing more of them."

I nod, not truly trusting his word but trusting in myself and knowing that I will take him out without a moment's hesitation if he threatens my family.

Chapter Twenty-Six

Skarlyt

"You can wear my dress or Charleigh's, and we can run out in the morning to get Lennox an outfit and the flowers and basically everything else we'll need while the guys set up here. We'll have time because you're having your ceremony at night, right?" Phoebe pauses for the first time since hearing that we want to have the mating ceremony tomorrow and looks at me. I open my mouth to respond, but she keeps going with a wave of her hand, "Of course you are. The weather tomorrow should be—"

"Pheebs?" I say, cutting her off.

"Yeah?"

"I think my mom's going to want to be in on the planning too, so maybe we should wait until we get inside." She stares at me a moment, seeming to be lost in her own head before she registers what I just said.

"Oh yeah. Come on. Charleigh, Rose, and Felicia will probably want to help too," she says, pulling me faster toward the house. I pick up speed, trying to keep up with her strides. What seems like only moments later, we're reunited with our family in the bunker.

"Skarlyt and Lennox are having their mating ceremony tomorrow!" Phoebe exclaims loudly as we walk up to them.

Everyone looks shocked, but no one is as shocked as my mother, who is holding Kayne in her arms.

"Yeah. We decided not to wait. We already claimed each other after all, so it's just the ceremony left." I tell her with a shrug.

"But we had all those plans for your ceremony. The vision board, the books, the invitations." She gets a sullen look on her face.

I step closer to her, putting my hand on her arm. "It's just a ceremony, Mom."

"It's not just a ceremony. It's the biggest day of your life other than when you take my place as high priestess."

I shake my head at her. "No, Mom. The biggest day of my life was when Kayne was born, and the day I met Lennox was a close second. The ceremony is really just a big party, and the goddess already blessed my mating with Lennox by giving us a true mate bond." She still looks sad, so I continue. "Besides, we can use some of the ideas for tomorrow, and whatever we don't use, we can save for Sebastyn's mating ceremony."

She nods, though tears still brim in her eyes. "Okay." With convincing my mom to throw away her ideas of me having this huge ceremony out of the way, the rest of us get to work.

I scoop up my baby boy and snuggle him quickly before I'm whisked away with the rest of the women in planning mode. I have just enough time to feed and burp him before Phoebe is taking him from my arms and passing him to Lennox without a word.

I look up at him as he cradles our baby boy. "You don't mind watching him for a bit while we plan, do you?"

"Of course not. Us boys will hang out for a bit and then head home. You can meet us there," he says, placing a soft kiss on my lips before striding out the patio doors where the rest of the men are hanging out. I watch him walk with a dreamy stare.

"Enough drooling. Time to plan," Charleigh interrupts my ogling of her brother, and I laugh.

"If I must," I joke.

About an hour later, we're all sitting around the kitchen table at Phoebe's. Charleigh and Felicia are both on their laptops with my mom and Lennox's mom, Rose, hovering over their shoulders, approving or dismissing the flowers and outfits that can be quickly obtained.

I hear a car parking and glance at the clock. Shit. It's already eleven o'clock. Who would be coming here at this time?

"That's probably Sebastyn and Sarah," Phoebe says, quickly getting up and rushing to the door.

I get up and follow her, stepping outside.

"Having fun, sweetheart?" Lennox asks from his seat on the porch, Kayne in his arms.

I walk over and sit down beside them. "I thought you two were going home to bed."

"We were going to, but Kayne didn't want to leave you."

I raise a brow. "Kayne or you?"

He smiles. "Both."

I bark out a laugh.

"Well, it shouldn't be too much longer. Let's greet Sebastyn and Phoebe's friend Sarah, and then we can go home." I tell him, bending down to place a soft kiss on his lips. "They are doing all the planning for me anyway."

I watch as Sebastyn gets out of the car and Phoebe embraces another woman. It's too dark to get a good look at her, so I stand on the top step and wait. As she comes into the light, I see her beautiful olive skin, green eyes, and long brown hair. Her clothes look baggy and worn, like she's had them for a long while, but she is still stunning.

"Sarah, this is Skarlyt, Lennox, and Kayne. Guys, this is Sarah," Phoebe says, making introductions.

The moment her green eyes meet mine, a spark goes through me. It makes me want...no *need*...to help her. I can't tell why, but I feel a connection to her. Maybe it's because we're both witches or maybe it's the Mother's divine intervention once more. I don't know, but I am going to help this woman.

She breaks eye contact, looking down at Kayne first and then up at Lennox. Rather than most other women's reactions to him—mouth dropping open at his hotness—her shoulders turn inwards and her eyes dart straight to the ground. I share a concerned look with Phoebe, who pleads with her eyes for me to say something. I don't understand. Phoebe wasn't this bad when she came here. What's different?

"Hey, Sarah," I say, stepping away from Lennox and closer to her. "Phoebe says you're a goddess with a sewing machine. Think you could help me with something?" Her eyes dart up to mine and seem to sparkle with excitement.

When she nods, I turn to Sebastyn. "Can you run home and get Mom's dress? You know—the one in the trunk?" His eyes darted over to Sarah quickly before nodding and teleporting away.

"Come on. Let's introduce you to the rest of the girls," I say, holding the door open and letting Phoebe guide her inside.

"Maybe you should wait out here," I tell Lennox, and he nods.

"She doesn't seem to be a fan of men. Not that I blame her. I met her dad a couple of times back home. He's a real piece of work. I had to step in when he and Charleigh went head-to-head a few times when she was a teenager. He worked at the grocery store at the time, and he always had a comment to whisper under his breath about how Charleigh and Felicia dressed or acted. Charleigh never had a problem standing up for herself, which he didn't like. It wasn't good. If he treated Sarah like that her entire life, it's going to take a lot to get her comfortable here." As he finishes speaking, I look inside the house to where Phoebe is introducing Sarah.

I give him another soft kiss.

"This one, right?" Sebastyn says, popping back in, holding my mom's mating dress.

"Yes!" I tell him and reach up on my toes to kiss his cheek. "Thank you."

I notice his lingering looks at the door where Sarah just walked in, and I raise an eyebrow.

"Something I should know?"

He shakes his head before pulling his eyes away to look at me.

"I'm not sure yet. There's just something about her..."

"I know what you mean," I tell him. "We'll make it right."

"You don't understand Skar. We drove for hours together. In her car. Alone. She hardly said anything to me. When I moved to change the radio station, she flinched like she was expecting me to hit her. Whatever happened to her was bad. Like, really bad," he says, concern lining his features.

I wrap my arms around his shoulders and pull him in for a hug. "We'll figure it out and help her. I promise." It's the second promise tonight I've made with no idea how to keep it, but I'm determined to. I have every intention of getting Sophia here and safe and helping Sarah learn that how she was treated was not okay. It may take me a while, but it will happen.

"My soul just *aches* at the thought of her being hurt," he admits in a whisper.

"Wait. Do you think she's your mate?" I question, stepping back to look in his eyes.

"I don't know, but I've never felt like this before. I just met her, and I know without a doubt there isn't anything I wouldn't do for her. I don't know about mate, but she's special."

My mouth drops open in shock, looking back toward the doorway. "Well then I better get to work."

I rush back inside holding the dress to show Sarah who quickly demands I put it on so she can get started on the alterations. We don't have to do too many, just a few minor ones, especially around my boobs. Since I'm breastfeeding, my normally large boobs are enormous now, and Sarah explained that we will need to take a bit of fabric from the bottom of the dress to sew into the sides.

Sarah is a little shy and timid at first, but once you get her talking, it's easy to see why Phoebe cared enough to bring her here. She's so helpful and seems to genuinely have a good heart.

I know she grew up a mage, but I don't think they've completely corrupted her soul. I'm making a mental note to look for a way to reverse the minor taint that's there. It might be as simple as inducting her into our coven to replace the tainted bonds with pure ones.

After saying goodnight to everyone with promises to return first thing in the morning, Lennox, Kayne, and I begin our trek home. What was supposed to be an afternoon and evening of fun, sexy times, and quality time with my little family turned into a whole thing, and I'm exhausted. I would love nothing more than to jump Lennox's bones the moment we walk in the door, but the truth is that I am too tired and fall asleep immediately after laying down.

Standing here in my mother's dress, studying Phoebe's mirror, I look at myself. Really look. The makeup has done an amazing job, but you can still see the slight bags under my eyes from lack of sleep last night. To say that it's been a stressful week is an understatement. I've been kidnapped, rescued, claimed my mate, learned new potions, bound the father of my child into his wolf form, helped defeat a bunch of deranged mages, and planned a mating ceremony. It's been pretty hectic. That's without considering the fact that I delivered a baby the week before.

The ceremony is set to start at dusk. Because Phoebe and Alaric's ceremony was so beautiful with the stars and moon reflecting off of the surface of the lake, I have a feeling it's going to be a new tradition.

I walk out the back deck of Phoebe's house to find Lennox. According to Phoebe, we aren't supposed to see each other today, but I don't believe in that superstitious human crap. We're already mated. This is just the ceremony to show the world. Besides, I have a surprise for him.

I find him down by the lake, skipping rocks with the boys and Josh.

"Not going to swim away on me, are you?" I ask him. He spins toward me, scooping me up in his arms without even pausing to look at me.

"Never," he replies.

"Boys, can I steal Lennox for a minute, please?"

The boys look at me and nod, turning back to see who can get more skips.

"Don't go too close to the water, though," I warn them and add a signal toward Josh to watch them. He's young, but he understands the international signal for "you are the official grown up now" and "don't let them mess up their fancy clothes."

"What's up, babe?" Lennox asks, his arms still wrapped around me as I lead him to the empty boat house by the dock.

"I have a mating present for you," I tell him as I grab my phone from my pocket. The look on his face is priceless. His eyebrows are pinched together in his "extremely worried" look.

"Are we supposed to get each other presents?" Oh, that's what he's worried about. I bark out a laugh.

"No, silly. I think it's a human thing—Phoebe said something about it. I just have one for you because I'm awesome, but I have to tell you something first..." I watch as various emotions flit across his face. Confusion and worry being the main ones. Finally, I get the courage to continue speaking. "It's about Kayne. He's a hybrid, meaning he will have access to both my magic and a wolf. Because of this, he will be in constant danger, and I need to know if you're still wanting to take on the role of his father."

I hold my breath as an enormous smile crosses his face. "Of course, I do. I already knew about him being a hybrid. Alaric told me the other night. Him being a hybrid doesn't matter to me. It just means we both get to train him, but I do think we should limit the amount of people that know."

I nod in agreement. "Good. Here," I reply and hand him my phone. I watch the emotions flit over his face again as he reads. Confusion, curiosity, and, finally, excitement cross his features.

"Really?" he asks.

"Yes, really. I filled out the form last night and paid for it to be rushed. They sent the confirmation email this morning. You are officially listed as Kayne's father on his birth certificate." He says nothing, just picks me up as I wrap my legs around his waist and kicks open the door to the boat house and walks me inside.

Once inside, he leans me back against the wall and begins kissing me with so much passion that I feel my panties getting wetter and wetter by the second. I start to grind myself up against his length, but he pulls back with a little growl. "I can't wait."

"Then don't. Take me, Lennox," I whisper to him and feel him already undoing his pants with one hand. Within seconds, he's pushing my panties aside and thrusting into me, extracting a moan from my mouth. Mother, he feels so good. I can't wait to spend the rest of my life with this man.

I use his shoulders as leverage and begin meeting him thrust for thrust. We are looking into each other's eyes as we orgasm. I can see the love he already has for me there. I can almost see our future playing out in our eyes. Us both old and gray, still with the same passion and heat for each other as we have today.

He leans forward and places a soft kiss on my lips. "I love you, Skarlyt Moon."

"I love you too, Lennox Johnson," I reply as he slowly slips out of me and places me on my feet.

"Skarlyt." I hear my mother calling my name.

Shit. She's probably looking for me to do my hair. I get a small wave of anxiety before I realize that I'm a grown ass woman, mated, and I have a child. I don't need to answer to anyone about where I am or what I'm doing.

Lennox, though, obviously doesn't realize it because he looks like a little kid who just got caught stealing out of the cookie jar. The look on his face is priceless, so I grab my phone and take a quick picture.

"I better go see her," I say to him, giving him one last quick kiss before heading out to see my mom. I was right, she wanted to help me get ready.

"Where were you?" she asks, and I raise my shoulders as I continue sauntering up to the house. From the knowing look on her face, I can tell she knows exactly where I was. I don't need to tell her.

We have a traditional mating ceremony with both Alaric and my mother presiding over it. Because Lennox is now part of the pack and I'm a member of the coven, we need to make vows of allegiance to both as well as to each other.

Alaric starts first.

"Do you, Skarlyt Moon, take Lennox Johnson as your bonded mate?"

"I do."

"And do you swear allegiance to the Westwood pack, and to me as your alpha?"

I smirk at him and pretend I need to think about it before finally saying, "I do." He raises his brow at me, silently berating me for pulling the prank.

Mom's turn.

"Do you, Lennox Johnson, take Skarlyt Moon as your bonded

mate?

"I do."

"And do you swear allegiance to the Coven of the Moon, and to me as your high priestess?"

There is no hesitation in Lennox's reply as he turns to look into my eyes. "I do."

"With that done, in front of Mother Moon and the witnesses here, I declare Skarlyt Moon and Lennox Johnson bonded mates. May she bless your union," Alaric finishes with a proud smile.

Now, to party.

Our night is fantastic. We are surrounded by our friends and family. Lennox and I dance the night away with Kayne sandwiched between us. I can't believe how complete I feel with these two in my arms.

Just a couple of months ago, I couldn't imagine ever being with another man, let alone a shifter. Now, I can't imagine my life without him in it.

Chapter Twenty-Seven

Lennox

*L*ennox, Alaric says through the pack link. It's both surreal and utterly annoying to hear an alpha's voice in my head. Surreal because there was a time, not so long ago, when I believed I would never have one again and annoying because it's interrupting what could be a very fun, very sexy afternoon with my gorgeous mate.

Yes? I respond, hoping that whatever he needs is not going to pull me away from my mate and my pup.

Can you grab Ashton and go meet our guests at the entrance to the pack?

Ugh. I sigh. Definitely not what I wanted to hear.

Sure, I grumble through the pack link. *I didn't know we were expecting company.*

I get no further response, so I turn and look at my gorgeous mate where she's currently dancing in the kitchen with Kayne on her hip. She's so beautiful. Even now, in her black leggings and flowy top and her hair still tangled from our afternoon activities while Kayne was napping.

"Skarlyt," I say, not wanting to interrupt the beautiful sight in front of me but knowing that I need to.

"Oh no you don't, mister. I know that look. It's the day after our mating ceremony. You're not leaving this house," she says, and I wince. That is what we agreed to. Both of us said that no matter what, we were going to lock ourselves in this cabin for the next four days and have our own little honeymoon. We both agreed to put off going away somewhere warm and tropical until Kayne is a little older and we can leave him with Constance. Neither of us are ready to leave him overnight—not after the past few days.

"Babe," I begin, but she holds up her hand to stop me.

"Lennox," she growls—like actually growls—like she's the wolf and not me. If she wasn't my mate and I wasn't positive that she wouldn't hurt me, I would be terrified. Hell, I am terrified anyway. No one can get revenge like my beautiful mate.

"Alaric needs me."

"Well, he can fuck right off." She walks toward the bedroom and grabs her phone off the nightstand. "In fact, I'm going to tell him right now."

I increase my speed and take the phone out of her hand. "Babe, you can't do that. It's pack business."

"Pack business, my ass." I hold the phone behind my back. She scoffs as she reaches for it, but it's not a full attempt since she is still holding Kayne in her arms.

She steps back and puts her free hand on her hips. "Well, what did he want anyway?"

"He asked me and Ashton to go meet some guests coming down the driveway, They must be caught outside the barrier."

"Oh," she pauses to think. "If they can't come through the barrier, I don't particularly want them here," she says, slipping on her shoes and grabbing her bag. Before I can protest, she holds up a hand to stop me. "Don't even—I am going to drop Kayne off with my mom, and I'll meet you."

I have little choice but to follow her out the door and head in

the opposite direction as she stomps toward the coven's head-
quarters.

Within minutes, Ashton is jogging up next to me, and I let out
a little sigh. I don't know who's waiting for us at the barrier, and I
don't know why they can't get through on their own. But with
Ashton next to me, the anxiety that I was feeling begins to subside
a little.

"Do you have any idea what we are doing out here?" I ask, and
he shakes his head but raises his head to scent the air. He tenses as
soon as he inhales.

"It's my father," he announces matter-of-factly, though his eyes
are wide and glazed.

We increase our pace and a curve in the driveway reveals
Christian, Matteo, Aryn, and Lucian standing in front of their
parked, black SUV across the border.

"Looks like he brought the whole crew," Ashton warns.

"Finally," Christian snarls under his breath

"What can we help you with, Christian?" Ashton growls. His
words are polite, but there's so much venom in his tone I can practically taste it. Not that I blame him. .

"I'm here to see your alpha." His comment matches Ashton's
tone in malice.

We could just leave him here. He can't get across the barrier, I
offer to Ashton through the pack link.

He looks like he's thinking it over but ultimately shakes his
head.

No. Alaric wanted us to bring him to him.

I step up to the barrier and reach my hand out to Christian
first. He looks down at my hand in disgust, seemingly not wanting
to touch me.

"Do you want to cross or not?" I ask with a level of snark that I
think my mate would be proud of.

Reluctantly, Christian places his hand in mine and I pull him across the border before repeating my action with Matteo. Rather than let go of my hand immediately, Matteo holds on and squeezes a little harder than necessary.

"Follow me," I say, leading the way with the Ironwood pack members following behind me and Ashton bringing up the rear.

We are halfway through our awkward, silent walk to the pack house when Skarlyt makes her appearance. She is beautiful, and my heart skips as she bounces on her toes to kiss my cheek, but she has absolute murder in her eyes, and she aims it at the men behind me.

"What's this?" Christian demands with an angry gesture toward Skarlyt. A flash of shock shows on Christian's face before he throws his hands up in the air as if he's exasperated with our antics.

"Interbreeding?" He spins to look back at his son. "Not only did you choose that alpha over me, but you chose a pack that allows interbreeding?"

The way he says the word *interbreeding* makes it seem like it's something dirty instead of something beautiful. I always knew that the Ironwood pack was backwards. But I didn't realize just how backwards until I came here.

"You will watch your tone when speaking about my mate," I growl, pushing Skarlyt behind me gently. I allow my dominance to rise to the surface.

Surprisingly, his eyes slip down to the ground in submission, and I pull my dominance back.

I keep Skarlyt close as we follow the group. Despite the excitement of the last two weeks, the Westwood pack has resumed activities as normal. Perhaps they are just trying to be polite, but none of the shifters we pass acknowledge our parade of strangers.

As we make our way through the pack land and the little village there, Aryn stops dead in his tracks. I've never had an issue with Aryn. In fact, I've often questioned why he follows Christian so blindly because, out of all of Christian's enforcers. bold Aryn and Lucian are the only two that have always been kind and loyal toward Ashton.

Although we were never close, Aryn and Lucian are close enough to my age that we went to school together. They were always friends, running around and causing a ruckus together, but something changed once they hit eighteen. They were suddenly no longer the carefree guys that I knew as children. It wasn't long before they threw in their lot with Christian and accepted roles as enforcers for him. They turned cold, but I still caught glimpses of the men that they had been when they were alone—without Christian or Matteo.

"What's going on over there?" Aryn whispers to Skarlyt and I when we catch up to where he's stopped. The two of us look around, trying to figure out what he means, until Christian's growl grabs our attention.

"Are you kidding me?" Christian shouts. "Not only does this pack allow intermating but they go against the goddess and allow this?" He continues complaining, but it is mostly to himself. Nobody bothers to answer, probably because we all know that he's going to have a laundry list of complaints about the way this pack is run, by the time he leaves. Ashton continues walking toward the pack house, Christian, Matteo, and Lucian follow closely, but Aryn stays rooted in the spot, still staring into the distance at a group of people standing next to the lake.

"You mean Paul and Stu?" Skarlyt asks, searching the group before turning to watch Aryn nod.

"They're true mates," Skarlyt states, raising an eyebrow to him, challenging him to say something about it.

"This isn't the Ironwood pack. Whether your true mate is the same species, different species, same sex, or even human, love is love. The people here are not so proud that they go against the goddess's will," I supply, feeling a little bad for Aryn who opens and closes his mouth like a fish. It's not his fault that he's been subjected to Christian's way of leading a pack for his entire life.

He nods and doesn't say anything else as he turns and jogs to catch up with his group. I exhale in relief. At least he wasn't an asshole about it like Christian. I watch with curiosity as he and Lucian whisper back and forth, but I don't think they'll cause any trouble.

"Huh," Skarlyt says to herself, tilting her head to the side in the adorable way she does when she's thinking.

"What?"

"I think..." she begins but closes her mouth, shaking her head. "Never mind."

By the time we make it into the house, Christian and his group are already speaking with Alaric in the kitchen.

"What did you do to the mages?" Christian yells. Alaric simply raises his eyebrow in question, looking at Skarlyt's appearance beside me.

She shrugs, and I roll my eyes. He smirks before turning his attention back to Christian.

"I'm not sure what you mean."

"What I mean," Christian punctuates each word with an anger that looks foolish next to Alaric's calm, "is that the mages in Morpeth are totally out of control, and I want to know why." Christian bangs one fist on the wooden tabletop, and Alaric smirks.

"So, you had them under control before, huh?" Alaric asks casually, but his smile turns dangerous.

"What—" Christian begins to complain, but Alaric cuts him off. He pushes back from the table with force, his chair grinding against the floor, and stands.

"They are 'out of control,' right?" Alaric looks like he knows the answer to the next question already. "So how were you keeping them 'under' control, Christian?"

Goddess knows I questioned this possibility myself. Morpeth had far too many unexplained disappearances, and recent events have revealed there were an inordinate number of mages in town as well. Still, the thought that Christian was trading shifters as fuel for the damn mages is disgusting. I hear a sharp intake of breath and look toward Aryn and Lucian. They are standing at the back of the room by the door—possibly protecting an exit? They glance at each other and search Christian's face for a sign. Their shock tells me one thing: they didn't know.

Even with only Alaric, Phoebe, Ashton, Skarlyt, and I representing the Westwood pack, Christian is quickly losing the support he brought with him.

"What kind of arrangement did you have with the mages?" Alaric commands. Gone is my carefree alpha. In his place is the one everyone expects. His dominance is so strong it floods the room, each of us fighting to keep our eyes off the floor. Many of us, Christian included, do not succeed.

Alaric realizes this and pulls back a little, giving us room to breathe so that Christian can answer. He opens his mouth to answer before closing it quickly, shaking his head.

"I asked what kind of arrangement you had with the mages?" Alaric growls deeply.

"We are..." Christian says, looking over to Matteo as if he's somehow going to save him. Alaric simply raises a brow at him and waits for his answer. "I do not—I do not expect you to understand. All I have done is protect my pack."

"You mean you provided them with shifters from your pack in exchange for protection, right?" Alaric says, and my eyes immediately shift to Christian. What kind of alpha would do that? I thought maybe he was turning a blind eye to the mages—not that he was willingly supplying them. My eyes once again find Aryn and Lucian by the door.

"How dare you!" Aryn screams. He is being held back by

Lucian, but the shorter man's face is already red, and he is beyond trying too hard to protect his alpha. Christian stands, spinning on the spot to face his enforcer nose-to-nose.

"How dare I? How dare you!" Lightning fast, Christian grabs Aryn up by the throat and pins him to the wall. "I gave you everything. Everything comes with a price."

"You gave me nothing," Aryn spits in his face, allowing his wolf to come to the surface. It takes a little longer than it did with me or Alaric but, after a few moments, Christian releases his throat and lowers his eyes to the ground. How fucking weak is this alpha?

"You ruin lives," Aryn says through clenched teeth, stepping closer to him. "You renounce the goddess, demand we throw away her gifts, mistreat your mate, renounce your own son. You're no alpha."

Christian tries and fails to raise his eyes.

"I challenge you for the title of alpha of the Ironwood pack." The words fly out of Aryn's mouth as if they surprise even him, and we all suck in a breath. My eyes instantly seek out Alaric's. His eyes flash with sadness so quickly I almost miss it before he turns back to Aryn and Christian.

"Aryn, let him answer," Ashton says, stepping up bravely and placing a hand on Aryn's shoulder. His gaze turns from Christian to Ashton, rage simmering beneath his eyes.

"Do you accept?" Alaric growls at Christian.

"No. I absolutely do not accept this weak wolf's attempt to overthrow me," Christian says loudly not realizing that all of us in this room just witnessed that he is the weak wolf—not Aryn.

"Then the pack is mine," Aryn growls in response.

Christian looks to Alaric for help, but he shrugs his shoulders. "It's within his rights. He is clearly the more dominant wolf. He issued you a challenge, and you refused. If a challenge is denied by an alpha, the pack is automatically forfeit to the challenger."

Christian glares daggers at him before turning his murderous gaze around the room, stopping at Aryn. "Fine, then, I accept. If you're willing to lose your life to make a point, it's your choice."

Alaric claps his hands to get everyone's attention.

"We will have the challenge—" he begins, but Aryn interrupts.

"Now."

Alaric looks to Ashton, who nods in agreement.

"Very well. Outside, gentleman."

Ashton, with his hand still on Aryn's shoulder, leads the way to the back porch with the rest of the group following behind. My mind is reeling at the events unfolding before my eyes. Like Ashton, I thought I had rid myself of Christian and the Ironwood pack, but now I get to watch history in the making.

Matteo and Christian whisper back and forth, clearly uneasy about the situation but unable to do anything about it. By the time Skarlyt and I make our way onto the grass, Aryn is already shifted, his large gray wolf pacing back and forth. Behind him, Lucian paces a similar track with more nervous energy instead of menace.

"The first to get his opponent to submit will be declared as the new alpha of the Ironwood pack," Alaric declares loudly, stressing that the goal is submission. Aryn releases a shockingly guttural growl, and only Matteo and Christian shake their heads in disagreement.

Christian begins to remove his clothes, scrunching his eyes up in concentration before an agonizingly slow shift overtakes him. We all suck in a breath, bewildered by the sight in front of us.

"What the fuck?" I whisper under my breath. Christian's wolf looks sick. He's so thin I can see the outline of every single rib.

"He looks—he looks like Kirnon," Skarlyt says from her place at my side. I nod my head and pull her in close. I look over at Ashton to see his response, but all I see is rage. After dealing with Kirnon, we now know that the main reason Christian's wolf would look like that is because he rejected his true mate.

"I don't think..." Alaric begins, but Aryn quickly jumps on top of Christian's smaller black wolf, pinning him to the ground. Drool slips through his sharp canine teeth onto Christian's snout. Within seconds, the smaller black wolf wines in submission.

Aryn rears back. His victory is assured, but his rage is so powerful I'm not sure he will stop his attack. I prepare myself to step in, though I am not sure that's permissible in a challenge like this.

Instead, my mate surprises me by stepping forward, her slender arms raised in a sign of peace.

"Skar," I whisper, reaching to pull her back.

"Just—let me—" she struggles to explain but assures me, "I know what to do, Lennox."

It only takes a few steps into the circle of challenge for her to get their attention. Aryn looks confused, but steps aside. Christian's head remains down—so submissive he cannot even meet her eyes.

"May I?" she asks Aryn, and he takes another step away. She turns to Christian, and I run to join her as she gets far too close for my comfort. "I think I can help you. If you let me, I think I can set you free."

I realize what she intends and turn to look back at Ashton. He nods, also recognizing her actions. In front of me, Skarlyt is reaching her hand out toward Christian's wolf. It takes everything I have not to pull her away.

"There's two of you in there," my beautiful, compassionate mate says sympathetically. "The man has done horrible things... but you are innocent. You have suffered at his hands more than anyone."

The wolf whines and lowers himself, flattening himself to the ground. Skarlyt bends, her hand sinking carefully into his thinning, black fur.

"Skar—" I warn, but she just shakes her head.

"I can't do it for you. But if you're willing to fight for control, I can help you close the door."

The wolf looks up at her pitifully, and I cannot recognize Christian at all in those eyes. Without further preamble, Skarlyt closes her eyes. I see her brows knit as she focuses her attention on some inner battle I cannot fathom. The wolf at her feet whines, and I prepare to pull my mate away at a moment's notice.

There's a scent that I now recognize as magic, and the wolf rises, shaking its head like its coming in out of a downpour. I step in front of Skarlyt as she rises and watch in wonder as Christian's wolf immediately recovers the way that Kirnon's did.

Behind me, Skarlyt laughs into a smile, and I see tears in her eyes.

He is still thin, but his bones no longer protrude painfully along his spine and hips. The matted clumps of black fur along his flank already look fuller.

Aryn shifts back, still watching Christian's wolf warily. "What was that?"

"I gave his wolf peace. It was not his fault that his human rejected the bond. But he will no longer be able to shift back and forth. Now, he can only be a wolf, but he can be free," Skarlyt explains.

I take a step forward, ready to defend my mate, but there is no need. Rather than anger, Aryn looks at her in awe.

"Thank you," he says, rising to his feet as he looks curiously at the wolf before him.

He wastes no more time on the defeated alpha. Aryn immediately turns, grabs Lucian by the collar of his shirt, and pulls him into a surprisingly heated kiss.

Despite my immediate surprise, everything falls into place. When they turned eighteen, they must've recognized each other as true mates and, because of the backwards way of life in the Ironwood pack, have been denying the bond ever since.

"I give you the new alpha pair of the Ironwood pack," Alaric beams as Aryn steps back from a breathless Lucian, both of them wearing grins from ear to ear.

I turn in time to watch Christian's wolf slowly make his way over to Ashton, lowering himself to the ground and rolling onto his back in a submissive position. Ashton drops down to his knees and places his hand on the neck of the wolf with tears in his eyes. Wanting to allow them this moment without an audience, I turn my gaze back to Aryn.

"As my first act, the Ironwood pack would appreciate the honor of becoming your ally," Aryn announces to the group that has gathered there. He has pulled on a pair of shorts, and his mate is tucked into his side.

Alaric smiles, coming down from his place on the porch to clap him on the back. "The Westwood pack accepts your allegiance and offers you ours in return."

I expect Matteo to complain or challenge Aryn himself, but he drops to a knee and bares his neck in submission instead. Even Matteo is smart enough to give up a losing fight.

Christian's wolf retreats into the woods, and I wonder if he and Kirnon will find each other—if they will recognize each other when they do.

Alaric invites Aryn and Lucian to stay for the evening and share a meal to celebrate, but my day has already gone too far off plan. With the future of the Ironwood pack determined, the rest of my evening is spent showing my beautiful mate just how happy I am to have come here to this pack, how happy I am to not only have found her but also a true home.

Since she left Kayne with Constance for the afternoon, we decide to make good use of the time before she returns him for bed.

And, boy, do we ever.

Epilogue

Darren

T he alpha house is full of activity and new faces. Aryn and Lucian, the new alpha pair of the Ironwood pack, are sharing a bottle of Faerie wine with Alaric. Phoebe, beside them, drinks a seltzer water, but her cheeks are just as rosy as if she was well and truly done in by the drink.

I'm trying to enjoy the celebration. The grill has been going all afternoon, and Ashton, looking more carefree than I've ever seen him, is making burgers to order. We have drinks and desserts. Phoebe even got her hands on what she's calling a "wedding cake" to celebrate the rash of recent matings and births. We are starting to get really good at throwing a party without much warning.

Instead, I am standing alone, watching everyone else celebrate while I nurse a now-warm bottle of beer. Ever since Joe admitted that Phoebe's sister, Sophia, is being kept hostage in Nova Scotia, I feel a powerful urge to rescue her. I can't get rest, and I can't focus on anything else Maybe it's because Phoebe is mated to my brother, or the fact that she and I have gotten so close since she came here. I can't help but feel that I need to go there. I can't explain it, but I need to be the one to find her.

"Hey, bro. What's up?" Sebastyn asks, startling me by slapping me on the back and coming to stand beside me. "You look...well... you look kind of pitiful."

"Have you ever gotten the feeling that you need to be somewhere or find somebody that you've never met before?" I ask, turning to face him.

"Actually..." he begins and shoots a quick glance toward the house and the party there. "Yeah, I have. Wait. Why?"

"You know how that Joe guy said that Phoebe's sister is being held captive by those mages in Nova Scotia?" I ask, and he nods. "Well, ever since he said her name, I can't get it out of my head. I feel this strong pull to go find her, like I need to be the one that's there." I shake my head. "I can't explain it properly. I just need to go, and every second I spend *not* headed in that direction just *hurts*," I finish. I think he's going to tell me I'm crazy, but he doesn't.

"Halifax, right? When do we leave?" he asks. I can't help it. I wrap him up in a brotherly hug. I know I can always count on him to have my back. I'm so grateful to Mother Moon for bringing him back safely to us right when I need him. I've missed my best friend.

"Tomorrow," I respond and step back. He smiles and nods at me.

Tomorrow, I start the search for Phoebe's missing sister and find out whatever she is to me. Whether it's Mother Moon's influence or my own, the overwhelming need to find her and keep her safe is the only thing on my mind.

We're probably going to run into some issues getting her away from those mages. Good thing we have an amazing group of supernaturals on our side.

I have a feeling we're going to need their help before this is all over.

* * *

Want more from the Westwood Pack?
Of course, you do!
Information on Book Three, Twin Flames, is here:
https://fdfairauthor.wixsite.com/website

About the Author

F.D. Fair is the author of the Westwood Pack Series. As an avid reader of Paranormal Romance Novels for the past 20 years, she turned her love of everything paranormal into steamy True Mate novels with a twist.

F.D. Fair lives and works in southern Ontario, Canada and

spends her time when she is not working or writing with the loves of her life—Her husband and 3 boys.

She is as weird as they come but is proud of it. Embracing her weirdness makes for some great stories.

Sign up for FD Fair's Newsletter:
https://dashboard.mailerlite.com/forms/76323/
5809623843156931o/share

Make sure to stalk her...

Instagram:
https://www.instagram.com/f.d.fairauthor

Facebook:
https://www.facebook.com/profile.php?id=100071688648516

Goodreads:
https://www.goodreads.com/author/show/21734156.F_D_Fair

Twitter:
https://twitter.com/FdFair

Bookbub:
https://www.bookbub.com/authors/f-d-fair

More from Foundations

Eilish Bohannon is the witch destined to lead the coven, but only if her older sister doesn't kill her first.

Set in Charleston, SC, the Bohannons lead a coven whose legendary powers date back to ancient Ireland. In each generation, one witch is destined to rise to High Priestess. Oldest sister, Seraphina, is certain the role is hers and will do anything to ensure Eilish doesn't interfere with her plans.

Even if it means getting rid of her baby sister for good.

If Eilish is to survive and claim her rightful role, she'll need the support of her middle sister, Anya, and a lot of help in the form of a vampire named Ian Cross…who was seemingly placed right in her path by the goddess Rhiannon. Their attraction to each other is immediate. Searing. And, ultimately, *forbidden*, since no coven will follow a Priestess who has bonded with his kind.

On their quest to find the answers needed to stop Seraphina, they consult with one of the oldest members of the coven, a crone named Henwen, who presents them with another problem – a Bohannon grimoire exists and has been purposefully hidden. Eilish and Anya will need to find the book if they have any chance of survival…

…as it holds the power of the Bohannon coven and can only be controlled by the witch destined to own it.

This dark and imaginative paranormal story by International Bestselling Author Emily Bex has romance as hot as a steamy Charleston summer with a pinch of Wiccan magic, a little mystery, and a lot of murder.

Foundations Book Publishing

Our mission is to exceed the expectations of our authors and the reading community with an uncompromising commitment to quality, individualism and personal pride. We measure our success one book at a time.

You can find more great works in multiple genres including Romance, Literary Fictions, Thrillers, Suspense, Young Adult, and more!

Visit us at FoundationsBooks.net

www.ingramcontent.com/pod-product-compliance
Lightning Source LLC
Chambersburg PA
CBHW050354260626
47156CB00003B/730